Hank sat at his desk, listening

He heard the rustle of Erica's dress dropping to the floor. Then he heard a splash. In the next room, on the other side of the closed kitchen door, Erica was in the tub. Hank swallowed hard.

If only he knew what she wanted. Erica *had* said that in her world, in 1989, bathing with a man wasn't considered outrageous. So what *was* it considered? Did she want him to...did she expect him to...?

There was only one way to find out. Hank pushed back his chair and rose. He forced himself to walk to the door, took a deep breath and knocked.

"Erica?"

"Yes?"

"Erica...I was wondering if you'd like me to scrub your back."

"I—I haven't got any clothes on, Hank."

"I know."

ABOUT THE AUTHOR

"I always set my books in places where I've lived or visited," says Toronto author Dawn Stewardson. "But this time it was impossible. I mean, you just can't get to 1862 Nevada—not unless you have a time machine!" Dawn compensated by doing a lot of research before she wrote *Blue Moon*, and the result is a wonderfully authentic story. "Mark Twain and his brother, Orion Clemens, actually did live in Nevada in 1862," she assures us. "The Paiute Indians were at war with the white settlers, and every incident in the story either did take place or might have...."

Books by Dawn Stewardson

HARLEQUIN SUPERROMANCE

HARLEQUIN INTRIGUE

Blue Moon

DAWN STEWARDSON

Harlequin Books

TORONTO • NEW YORK • LONDON
AMSTERDAM • PARIS • SYDNEY • HAMBURG
STOCKHOLM • ATHENS • TOKYO • MILAN

Published December 1989

First printing October 1989

ISBN 0-373-70383-X

To Brian Henry and Marsha Zinberg,
who encouraged the idea
for this book.

With special thanks
to my parents
and to Grace and Craig
for their help.

And to John, always.

CHAPTER ONE

"WHAT WE'RE STANDING IN, ladies and gentlemen, is called the ore chamber. It was the largest area excavated in an old mine. From this chamber, horse-drawn wagons carted the ore to a quartz mill for refining, and those wagons needed room to turn around.

"Now, look straight up and you'll see an example of what started it all in the Sierra Nevada. That purplish streak right above your heads is a gold vein."

A dozen people gazed upward. Several of them aimed cameras at the ore chamber's ceiling. Shutters clicked. Flashes exploded, barely visible against the brightness of the cavern's artificial light.

Erica looked up at the ragged stripe cutting through the rock, not bothering to take the video camera from her backpack. Gold, in its natural state, was as drab as most other rock. The vein was a little disappointing.

In fact, everything about Broken Hill Mine was disappointing. Stopping off for a tour here, instead of driving straight into Mountainview, hadn't been her best spur-of-the-moment idea.

She glanced at the Nevada guidebook once more. According to it, Broken Hill offered tourists "a trip into the genuine atmosphere of a typical, 1860s gold mine."

Some typical mine. Where was the dank, musty, smell? And where was the dirt? From the looks of

Broken Hill, a cleaning lady paid regular visits. The rock walls would undoubtedly pass a white-glove test with flying colors.

And where was the all-pervading darkness? Mines were notoriously pitch black—particularly mines that had been abandoned before the advent of electricity. But not this one. Spotlights illuminated every crevice so brightly that she was tempted to dig her sunglasses out of her backpack.

All in all, Broken Hill Mine had less "genuine atmosphere" than a Disneyland attraction. Erica closed her guidebook, telling herself to make the best of things.

"This vein," the guide said, continuing his spiel, "is what we call a quartz ledge or a lode. When early prospectors came across a ledge, they'd lay a claim, then take a sample to have assayed."

The guide pulled a small chunk of rock from his hip pocket. "Look at this. You can actually see a few specks of gold in it."

The others pressed closer to him. Erica glanced about the confines of the chamber, scanning it for a potential escape route.

Clearly, she wasn't going to get the foggiest sense of what Broken Hill had once been like if she stuck with the official tour. But most of the mine must still be in its original state. That was what she was here to see.

Her gaze came to rest on a tunnel across from where they were standing. A sign reading No Admittance hung from the rope stretching across its entrance.

"You can purchase ore samples like this one in several souvenir shops in Mountainview," the guide was saying. "They make dynamite paperweights."

Souvenir shops!" No, he'd said *several* souvenir shops. Erica shuddered. That didn't strike her as the

least bit promising. In fact, it made Mountainview
sound as potentially useful, for her purposes, as Broken Hill was turning out to be.

If that was the case, when she returned to Boston
she'd be spending her first few weeks researching the
Old West within the confines of some musty archives.

She absently flipped through her guidebook until
she located its note about Mountainview:

> The mining town has been restored to replicate
> the mid-1860s. Buildings are open for viewing
> from 9:00 a.m. to 5:00 p.m. daily.
> During the 1860s, nearby Broken Hill Mine
> became one of the most profitable gold produc-
> ers south of Virginia City. As the closest town,
> Mountainview flourished.

And it had undoubtedly flourished, Erica thought
fleetingly, without the aid of souvenir shops. Well,
shops notwithstanding, Mountainview was her destination for the night. Once she'd seen everything she
could in the mine, she'd hop back into the rental car
she'd picked up at the Reno airport and drive the last
couple of miles.

She glanced at her watch. With the help of time
zones, it was barely three-thirty. And her hotel room
in Mountainview was confirmed for a late arrival.

"Now, if you'll come along with me," the guide
said, interrupting Erica's thoughts, "we're going to see
a collection of the sort of tools that were used to ex-
cavate these very tunnels."

The rest of the tour group moved off. Erica hung
back, feigning interest in the gold vein. The others
rounded a turn in the main passage leading from the
chamber. Not a soul looked back.

Quickly, Erica crossed to the roped-off tunnel. The air at its entrance felt several degrees cooler and considerably damper. This was more like it! Officially off limits, perhaps, but far more like it.

And if she just ducked under the rope...

She tried to ignore the pang of guilt that warned she'd be trespassing. After all, a single length of rope couldn't be meant as a very serious barricade. It was likely only there to keep children from wandering down the tunnel. She'd simply take a quick look. She'd be in and out with no one even noticing.

Erica shrugged off the backpack that had served as her hand luggage on the plane. She stuffed the guidebook into it, took out her flashlight, then smoothed down the Velcro closer and snugged the pack over her shoulders once more.

Glancing quickly about the empty ore chamber, she lifted the rope and darted under it.

In the first few feet of the tunnel, where light straggled in from the ore chamber, a gray twilight prevailed. Beyond that was total darkness.

She clicked on the flashlight and took a few, tentative steps forward, smiling with satisfaction when little clouds of dust rose at her feet. This was *definitely* more like it. The cleaning lady obviously didn't do roped-off tunnels.

She shone her light across the rocky walls. They were rough and grimy—streaked here and there, with dark, rusty-looking stains. Every eight or ten feet, shoring timbers braced the walls and ceiling of the passageway.

The flashlight's beam bounced along before her as she stepped carefully over the rough surface. Its glare picked up a wet patch on the wall. A soundless drip trickled from a crack above the patch.

Erica paused, wondering if this lone venture was really a wise idea. What if...

What if what? a little voice teased inside her head. This tunnel had been here for the past hundred-odd years. It wasn't likely to choose today to cave in.

She pressed on. Atmosphere she'd wanted and atmosphere she was getting. But the silence was oppressive, broken only by the sound of her breathing and the quiet footfalls of her Reeboks.

"Good thing you're not claustrophobic," she whispered to herself.

The whisper seemed out of place, as if the stillness wasn't to be disturbed.

She continued along quietly, trying to imagine what the mine had been like when men were working it. Had they talked and joked? Or had their filthy work been done silently? That was something she'd need to establish for the documentary. Maybe she could locate a diary or two.

On the right, her light picked up an entrance to a narrower passage leading from the tunnel. She shone her beam into the dark shaft, noticing that a jagged vein, about half as wide as the one in the ore chamber, ran along its ceiling.

She hesitated, then walked on. There was no point asking for trouble. The main tunnel she was following had to be safer than a secondary excavation.

The air was becoming progressively colder. And it had begun smelling dankly stale. Erica shivered, deciding she'd had enough authenticity for the moment. She removed her backpack, pulled the video camera from inside and snapped its light unit into place.

She'd tape a little of the interior, then head back. She clicked on the power switch and began panning slowly along the wall. The soft whirr of the tape, usually not noticeable, sounded like a roar.

The image in her viewfinder was dull. Her taped record of Broken Hill was going to be far from top quality. She moved closer to one of the shorings, shot it in detail, then clicked the power off and quickly packed the camera away.

Something was making her nervous. No doubt it was merely her imagination.

She started back along the tunnel, annoyed at the anxious little lump that had formed in her throat. Why was it there? She glanced quickly over her shoulder. Only blackness. What had she expected? A boogy-man?

She began whistling into the silence…and then her breath froze in mid-whistle. There'd been a barely audible sound behind her. She stopped dead and whirled about, pointing her flashlight down the tunnel, her ears straining to hear, her eyes straining to see.

Nothing. Her imagination was into overload. And then she heard the noise again. It was closer this time. It sounded like…it couldn't be…but it sounded like pebbles falling.

A second passed…then another. She stared into the darkness until, just at the outer range of visibility, she saw a few small rocks break free from a shoring. They rattled to the floor amidst a shower of dirt.

Erica took a step backward, ordering her mind to stop racing. Something was wrong. Surely this shouldn't be happening.

The mine was still again. She breathed deeply for a few moments, feeling her heartbeat starting to slow back to its normal rhythm.

Then, with no further warning, all hell broke loose!

The shoring she was staring at began to quiver, it creaked loudly, then moaned as a hail of rocks tumbled from above it. They bounced wildly off the wall, hitting the floor with noisy force. And, beneath her, she felt trembling.

The reality of what was happening struck home. She was in the midst of a tremor!

Her adrenaline began pumping, and she turned wildly back the way she'd come. The flashlight smashed against the wall and went flying from her hand. Its light beam vanished. The surrounding blackness engulfed her. She heard another storm of rocks raining down, and her nose filled with dust.

She began running in the direction of the ore chamber, groping along the wall beside her as she ran. She stumbled through the darkness, moving as fast as she dared on the uneven floor. She had to escape from this tunnel!

The dust-thickened air was making her choke. The noise of falling rocks was becoming louder... or was that merely the pounding of her heart? She tried to run faster, unable to see a thing, trailing her hand blindly along the wall so she wouldn't smack into it. She was going to die in here!

No she wasn't. She couldn't possibly die in the depths of a Nevada mine tunnel. Especially not on the Fourth of July. What kind of proper Bostonian would accept a fate like that?

Suddenly a pale glow appeared in the darkness before her, reaching eerily out from the side of the tunnel. She hesitated, glancing toward its source. Light was shining faintly from an opening in the wall.

Erica focused on the light, realizing she'd made it back to the entrance of the secondary shaft. The vein along its ceiling was a snake-like shadow in the glow.

Earlier, that tunnel had been pitch black. So why, now, could she see a shimmering blue light in the distance? She stared at it, trying to make sense of what she saw.

The narrow shaft must lead out of the mine. The blue must be daylight! Mustn't it? That would make sense. But the light seemed strangely unreal.

A timber groaned ominously behind her, forcing a decision. She darted into the side shaft and began slipping and sliding down its steep incline.

The blue light flickered before her—a guiding light, shrouded by a thick veil of hazy air. It danced enticingly, growing incredibly bright as she neared it. Brighter and brighter...she'd be reaching the end of the tunnel, reaching daylight, any moment now.

And then a searing blow jolted her head. The light exploded, scorching her brain. And Erica felt her legs crumbling beneath her as the incredible brightness faded to black.

THERE WAS A JACKHAMMER POUNDING inside Erica's head. Foggy recollections of scrambling through a tunnel free-floated in her mind. But where was she now? What had happened? Was she dead?

No, she couldn't be. The awful throbbing in her head assured her she wasn't in heaven. And she'd never done anything bad enough to deserve being relegated to hell.

Tentatively, she moved her fingertips over the surface beneath her. A fresh surge of pain knifed behind her eyes, but her brain identified the object she was resting on. A couch...an extremely hard couch. But where?

Nevada! That was it. She'd left Boston this morning for Nevada. And now she was lying on a horribly uncomfortable couch, somewhere in the Sierra Nevada Mountains, with the worst headache of her life.

"Just lie quietly with your eyes closed. You're going to be fine."

She jumped at the sound of the deep male voice. Lightning split her temple, making her moan.

"Sorry," the voice said softly, "Didn't mean to startle you."

She heard the man coming closer, became acutely aware of his strong, male scent. It was unusual...yet vaguely familiar. Her mind struggled to identify the strange mixture of aromas. They were triggering a memory from her past—from long ago and far away.

A cool, masculine hand gently touched her forehead. Fabric brushed against her cheek—the man's jacket sleeve. Its weave was rough. She could smell the wool, too. Mostly, though, she could smell the man himself. Not an unpleasant smell...reassuring, in fact...and it definitely reminded her of something.

The memory clicked into place. Her grandfather. As a little girl, cuddled in her grandfather's lap, she'd smelled a similar confusion of scents. Gradually, her mind began to sort them out.

There was a faint aroma of male perspiration that had almost, but not entirely, been erased by soap...unperfumed soap.

And there was a musty smell of wool that had never known a dry-cleaner's chemical. And pipe tobacco. It had been years since she'd been with anyone who smoked a pipe.

And something else...she knew the final smell as well. Bay rum! How had she identified that? Had her grandfather used that old-fashioned scent? It's pungent aroma long predated modern after-shave—dated back, she was certain, for centuries.

Perhaps she'd died after all. Perhaps this man actually *was* her grandfather. Maybe he'd been apppointed as her guardian angel and was watching over her. Maybe everyone arrived in heaven with a splitting headache so that everything would seem wonderful when it disappeared.

Erica opened her eyes, curiosity defeating her better judgment. The effort caused marginally less pain than she'd expected.

The man with the wonderfully deep voice was sitting on a chair beside the couch, watching her. His face was a blur.

She tried to focus her vision. The effort hurt. But the man's image cleared. He wasn't her grandfather. He couldn't be anybody's grandfather.

His dark beard made judging his age a little difficult, but he wasn't more than thirty-something. Even with a throbbing head, she realized he was an absolutely gorgeous thirty-something. He had the blackest eyes she'd ever seen . . . a soft, deep black.

She wished he wasn't facing her straight on. She'd like to check his shoulder blades for wings. Heaven apparently wasn't something she could rule out just yet.

"Can you see clearly?"

She nodded. Bad move! Pain shot through her head.

"Good. That's an encouraging sign." The man smiled reassuringly. "I'm Dr. Lockhart. You were brought to my office from Broken Hill. Do you remember what happened to you?"

"Not exactly," she whispered.

"Well, don't worry. It'll gradually come back. Nothing appears to be broken, but you've got some serious bumps and bruises and a nasty gash above your hairline. I've cleaned it up but I reckon it's hurting something fierce. Am I right?''

"Right."

"Then I'm going to give you an injection that'll let you rest. When you wake up again, you'll feel much better."

Erica closed her eyes. A moment later she felt a cool swab brush her arm, then the tiny prick of a needle. She gave a silent little prayer of thanks for the wonders of modern medicine.

Everything else could wait until she woke up again and felt much better.

ERICA LAY, EYES STILL CLOSED, trying to remember. There'd been a tremor in the mine...she'd been running to escape...heading for daylight. Then something had happened. What?

There was a blank in her memory between running through the tunnel in that mine and waking up in a doctor's office with her head feeling as if she'd slammed it into a brick wall. But at least the pain had subsided while she'd slept.

What was the doctor's name? She couldn't remember that, either. But she definitely remembered his face.

She touched the couch beneath her. Rock hard. She was still in his office—wherever that was. Someone had covered her with a quilt. She was tempted to snuggle down under it and go back to sleep.

No. Better not. She opened her eyes. The room was so dim that she couldn't see much. She heard a door open and glanced toward the sound. The doctor was standing in the dark shadows.

He walked over and sat down in the chair beside the couch. "How do you feel?"

"Almost human, thanks." She pushed herself up into a sitting position, ignoring the momentary dizziness. "Is there anything seriously wrong with me?"

"Nothing permanent. That blow to your head has undoubtedly caused some degree of cerebritis—inflammation within the cranium."

"You're saying I have a concussion."

"Yes." The doctor nodded slowly. "I'm surprised you know that term. It's relatively new."

Erica eyed him closely, trying to decide if he was joking. She certainly hoped so because, if medicine was really that far behind the times in Nevada, he probably had a jar of leeches tucked away somewhere.

"You'll be fine," he continued. "You may be a little confused for the next few days and your memory could be a mite foggy. But that should be about it."

"Well, you're right about my memory. I've forgotten your name."

"It's Dr. Lockhart."

Erica nodded, relieved to find the motion didn't hurt.

"And you haven't told me your name, ma'am."

"It's Erica. Erica James."

"Erica . . . an unusual name."

"A little, I guess. Where am I? I mean, where's your office?"

"Mountainview."

"Oh. That's a relief. Mountainview's where I'm supposed to be. But I'm not supposed to be exactly here—not in your office, that is. What time is it?"

The doctor pulled out a gold pocket watch. "It's about nine o'clock."

How quaint. Seeing the watch on a chain reminded her of her grandfather again. And Lockhart was dressed in an old-fashioned outfit. But of course...the Fourth of July. He was likely on his way to an Independence Day costume party.

"Nine o'clock," she repeated. "That means it's midnight in Boston. The Fourth of July's over there. I hope I'm not spoiling your plans here, though."

"No. I haven't any special plans." Lockhart looked at her curiously. "What made you think of Boston?"

"That's where I'm from."

"You are?" He smiled warmly.

Erica recalled how handsome she'd thought he was. She'd been right.

"That's quite a coincidence," he went on. "I'm originally from Boston, too. I'd wondered about that...that thing you're wearing."

"My Boston University T-shirt?"

He nodded silently. "But what made you think of it being midnight in Boston?"

"I'm still on eastern time, I guess. I just flew here today."

"What did you say?"

"I just flew into Reno today. From Boston," she added at his puzzled look.

"Miss James, I don't want you to be concerned because your thoughts are confused. As I mentioned, it's to be expected. Tell me, do you have an active imagination?"

"I guess you could say that. Why?"

"Sometime's people's imaginations do strange things after a head wound. Maybe you'd explain to me what you mean by saying you *flew from Boston*. Would you be a bird or an angel?"

Erica laughed. "I'm afraid I can't claim to be an angel."

"I see. But you believe you flew...all the way from Boston...today. And you've been in Reno, as well."

A ripple of discomfort ran through Erica. Dr. Lockhart's sense of humor was on the weird side. And she couldn't see that it was the least bit appropriate for him to be teasing a patient he'd barely met, especially when she wasn't in the best of shape.

"This *is* still the Fourth of July, isn't it?" she asked, enunciating each word precisely. Except for not remembering details about what had happened in the mine, her mind was perfectly clear.

"Yes. This is the Fourth of July."

"Then I flew from Boston today. I left," she continued firmly, "at eight in the morning. We made a brief stop-over in San Francisco, then got into Reno a little before two."

Lockhart smiled a nervous-looking smile. "Fine. I see. Now, why don't I give you another injection and let you get a good night's rest?"

"You don't believe me!"

"Well...I think you're a mite confused. That's all."

"I'm not confused in the slightest! Where's my backpack? My itinerary and my return ticket are in it. You're welcome to look at them. My pack's here, isn't it?"

"Yes. It's here. I put it away safely." Lockhart sat in the chair, staring at her, making her feel more uncomfortable by the second.

She looked away, glancing about the dimly lit room, suddenly realizing there was something strange about it. No...there was a whole lot strange about it. Just for starters, the light was so dim because it was emanating from a single, old-fashioned oil lamp.

"Where am I?" she demanded.

"Do you remember asking me that before?"

"Of course I do! I'm just getting a little suspicious about your answer. Who are you?"

"I'm Dr. Henry Lockhart, the first and only physician in Mountainview, Territory of Nevada. And you're in my office."

Erica stared around the room again. Each object she focused on made her feel more anxious. What had that stupid guidebook said about Mountainview? *"The town has been restored to replicate the mid-1860s. Buildings are open for viewing from 9:00 a.m. to 5:00 p.m. daily."*

Oh, Lord! Some *doctor's office* she was in! She was in a *replica* of a doctor's office in a damned tourist town. And it was long after five o'clock.

So what did that make this character who was sitting beside her, all decked out as if he'd just walked off the set of a Western? Was he an actor? Did he play town doctor for the tourists?

Whoever he was, he wasn't a real doctor. So what on earth had he been doing to her? And he'd given her a shot of something. Heaven knows what else he'd done while she'd been asleep.

Erica tugged the quilt up around her neck. "Who are you?" she hissed.

"Calm down, ma'am."

"Don't *ma'am* me! And don't tell me to calm down! I want to know who you are and what you're doing in this building so late at night."

"I'm Dr. Henry Lockhart and this building is my house. This room is my office."

"You're not a real doctor!"

"I certainly am. Harvard medical school. My diploma's hanging on the wall—right over there."

Erica struggled up, shoving the quilt aside. She reeled dizzily. The man grabbed her arm.

"Don't touch me!" She jerked free and lurched across the room. She glanced over the diploma's Latin inscription, read Henry Lockhart's name, then the graduation date—1851.

She turned back to face the man. "Perhaps you'd explain to me how, if you're a real doctor who graduated in 1851, you've managed to stay alive until now? Until 1989?"

"Did you say, 1989? Ma'am, I really must advise you to lie down again. You're getting yourself overwrought. Lie down, and I'll prepare an ice cap for you. It might be wise to perform a little bloodletting as well."

"Bloodletting! Not on your life!" Erica glared at him, almost as angry as she was frightened, ordering herself to be calm.

"Look, mister, I realize this act is probably part of your job, but I'm in no condition to find it amusing. Can we please forget this Old West nonsense? I've got a room booked at the Mountainview Hotel—the hotel in the 1989 tourist town called Mountainview. Clear enough? Now, why don't you just give me my backpack and I'll be on my way."

"Miss James . . . Mountainview does not have a hotel. And this is not 1989. This is 1862. And I don't have any notion what a tourist town is, but Mountainview is a mining town."

Erica stared at the man, her mind racing. Maybe this was a dream . . . a nightmare. That had to be it. At least she hoped that was it because that explanation was far more logical, far more palatable, than any other she could think of.

But she'd never had a nightmare seem anywhere near as real as this.

"Where's your phone?" Oh, Lord, her voice was beginning to squeak. She ordered herself to calm down. "May I at least use your phone?"

"My what?"

She swallowed hard. If she could only spot her backpack, she'd grab it and make good her escape. But she wasn't going to escape very far without her credit cards.

"Look...Dr. Lockhart, or whoever you are...I just want to get out of your quaint little 1862 office and get back to the real 1989 world. I don't mean to be rude, but this game you're playing has gone far enough."

"Miss James, I assure you I'm not playing any game. And this *is* the real world. You're not well. Do you remember dreaming about being in the future? That's probably what happened—you had a vivid dream brought on by that head wound."

Oh, Lord! What was dream and what was reality?

"Please lie down again and try to relax."

"I'm not lying down until I get to the hotel! Now—"

"Look, Miss James, this hotel you think exists... 1989...being able to fly...none of that is real. As I said, there isn't a hotel. And I can't simply let you wander outside to see for yourself. The saloons are packed with miners celebrating Independence Day. Pretty soon they'll be spilling out onto the street."

"Pa?"

Erica wheeled around. Her head spun. She grabbed a table for support. In the doorway stood a thin, pale little boy dressed in a rumpled nightshirt.

He rubbed his dark eyes sleepily, smiled shyly at her, then turned to the man.

"Go back to bed, Billy. You can see I'm with a patient. I'll be up shortly."

Erica stared at the child, trying to make sense of his sudden appearance. He looked about eight years of age...and he closely resembled the man. Those enormous dark eyes were riveting. Could the child be an actor, too? Even if he was, what was he doing here at nine o'clock? If it really was nine o'clock.

She stepped over to a window and pushed aside the curtain. Outside, the night was like black velvet. Only a few faint lights flickered in the distance.

"Where are the streetlights?" Her words came out a whisper.

"You aren't in Boston, Miss James. In Mountainview the streets aren't lit by gaslight."

Erica gazed at the little boy once more, trying to control the panic that was threatening to overwhelm her. What this man was telling her wasn't possible! It couldn't be for real! It was all a horrible joke! She took a deep breath before speaking.

"Do you live here, Billy...in this building?"

"Yes, ma'am. This is my house. Mine and Pa's and Cheyenne's."

"Cheyenne is Billy's dog," the man said quietly.

"And your mother?"

"My mother's dead, ma'am. She died when I was five. When we still lived in Boston. That was...four years ago. Right, Pa?"

"Right, son. That was back in 1858."

Erica could feel herself trembling. She leaned heavily against the wall.

The child was watching her curiously. He didn't look the least bit like an actor. He looked like a tired little boy who should be in bed.

"Billy...what's the date today?"

"It's the Fourth of July, ma'am. Everyone knows that! We had a parade and everything."

"Yes, but the year, Billy. What year is it?"

The child looked anxiously at the man.

"It's all right, son. Miss James banged her head and she's just a little confused. Tell her what year it is."

Billy nodded and turned back to Erica with a smile. "It's 1862, ma'am. It's July fourth, 1862."

"That's fine, son. Now get back to bed. I'll come up in a few minutes."

Hank Lockhart waited until Billy turned to go before glancing back at the woman. She stood silently beside the window, still clutching the curtain, looking incredibly confused and upset.

He filled his pipe, gazing at her uncertainly as he fumbled with the tobacco. He was a general practitioner, not a specialist in disorders of the mind. In Mountainview, it was his knowledge of physical ailments and diseases, along with his skills at removing bullets and stitching up wounds, that were important.

But this young woman was clearly hallucinating and just as clearly verging on hysteria. And he wasn't at all sure what to do about either.

A woman who believed this was 1989? He simply didn't know what to make of that. In fact, he simply didn't know what to make of anything about her. Her appearance was foreign. How had she come to be at the Broken Hill Mine? And how had she come to be in this condition?

He wished he knew how much of her confusion was due to the cerebritis. Because, if that wasn't causing her delusions, she must be insane.

But if the blow she'd suffered had caused her hallucinations, they should subside on their own. A sane woman couldn't go on believing she was in 1989 indefinitely—not in the face of reality.

Maybe exposing her to reality was what he should try. He'd been thinking that, first thing tomorrow, he'd have to find her a secluded room in a house. She should stay bedfast for the next few days. But seeing the real world of Mountainview might be more important.

She turned and gazed at him. "Look, this is all very convincing—especially Billy—but I *know* the year is 1989."

"Miss James, I have an idea. I'll bunk in with Billy tonight. You can sleep in my room."

"I'm not staying here overnight!"

"Ma'am...there's nowhere else for you to stay. And best you sleep upstairs. The horsehair couch isn't comfortable and my office is likely to be a busy place later tonight. Miner's get rough when they celebrate.

"So you get a good night's sleep, and in the morning I'll take you for a walk. Maybe a look around town will help you think more clearly."

Erica peered through the window once more, into the black night. If she walked out that door, where was she going to go? What was she going to find?

Each time she moved, a dizzying throb inside her head reminded her she was in no shape for hiking. She'd be doing well if she could make her way across the room. In her present condition, she could forget challenging the dark unknown beyond this house.

Wherever she was right now, whatever was going on, at least she and this man were one on one. Lord knows how many strange men were lurking outside.

And surely this fellow wasn't intending to attack her during the night, not with a child in the house.

Of course, she wouldn't take a chance on sleeping. She wouldn't close her eyes for an instant. But she couldn't see that she had much choice about going along with this situation until tomorrow. In the bright light of day, she'd undoubtedly be able to make sense of things.

She let the curtain drop, momentarily steadying herself against the wall. "All right...Dr. Lockhart. Thank you. I'll be grateful for a bed tonight."

"Good!" He beamed at her. "Good."

"May I use your bathroom for a minute?"

"My what?"

Oh, no. What should she call it? Erica scrambled vainly for a word. "You know...I need to..."

"Oh. The outhouse. I'll show you the way."

Outhouse! Why did that take her aback? How could anything have fazed her at this point?

"First thing in the morning," the man said, ushering her from the office, "before we take that walk, I'll go to the dry-goods store and get a dress for you to wear."

"No. Thanks, but really, I couldn't possibly let you do that."

The man shook his head. "You've got to have a proper dress, ma'am. You can't go out looking so strange. If you pin your hair up...put a hat on...and have a dress to cover those peculiar shoes... Come morning we'll fix you up."

Come morning. Erica closed her eyes. If, come morning, this didn't turn out to be a terrible dream, what on earth was she going to do?

CHAPTER TWO

HANK CLOSED HIS OFFICE DOOR behind Erica James. She seemed subdued, without a trace of last night's hysteria. He was certain taking her for a walk had been a sound idea, that she'd responded to the reality of her surroundings.

She hadn't asked many questions. And most of those she'd asked hadn't made much sense. But once she'd stopped talking, stopped saying strange things, she had clearly started concentrating on the town—examining the buildings and staring at each passing person.

Yes, a walk had been the right therapy. If he ever decided to go back East, he might think about specializing in disorders of the mind. There didn't seem to be any trick to dealing with mental confusion. All it required was a little common sense.

He watched her quietly, waiting for her to speak. She merely removed her hat and slumped down on the couch, staring into space.

Finally, his curiosity got the better of him. "Well, Miss James, what are you thinking? Did that seem like 1862 out there?"

She nodded slowly, brushing at the dress he'd bought, apparently uncomfortable wearing it. "Yes . . . I'm afraid it did. Last night I was so certain it couldn't be, that it wasn't possible. But all those buildings and all those people. How large is Mountainview?''

"Hard to say. New miners are arriving every day. I'd guess two thousand—maybe even twenty-two or twenty-three hundred.''

"That many. And those were real buildings...not facades. And the way the countryside stretches out of sight with no highways, only that dirt trail. And the smells and the main street—nothing but rutted mud. And all the animals. And the saloons—I counted seven of them. And not a tourist. Not one single tourist.''

Erica James gazed at him, shaking her head. "Yes, Dr. Lockhart. As incredible as it seems to me, I do believe this is 1862.''

"Good. Then you're well on your way to recovery. I—''

"Wait. Please. I need to check something, have to reassure myself of something. You said you've got my backpack?''

"Yes. Sorry, I should have given it to you earlier.'' Hank retrieved the unusual-looking red pack from his cupboard and handed it to her.

She ran her fingers over it in a nervous gesture, then placed it on the couch beside her. "I gather you haven't looked inside this.''

"Of course not.''

Without warning, she began tearing the fabric. His office filled with the sound of it ripping.

"Stop! You'll ruin it!''

"I'm simply opening it. That's just the velcro...'' She glanced at him and shrugged. "Velcro replaces zippers.''

Her gaze flickered momentarily to the buttons on his trousers. "And, uh, zippers replace buttons.''

He swallowed uncomfortably, resisting the impulse to cover himself with his hands.

"I'll try to explain this all in a minute," she murmured, quickly turning her attention back to the pack.

Hank eyed her anxiously, feeling his confidence about her rapid recovery draining away. *Velcro? Zippers?* The tendency she had to dream up strange words was a bad sign. She must have created an entire world inside her head—complete with its own, unique language.

She opened the pack and peered at the contents. "Everything's here," she whispered. "I knew I couldn't have dreamed the future.

"Dr. Lockhart, I wonder if you'd mind sitting down, if we could talk for a minute?"

"Of course." Hank settled into the chair beside her.

"And would you mind terribly if I call you Henry? And would you call me Erica? I'd feel less like a stranger."

"Well, I . . . well it isn't . . ." *Oh, blazes!* Inappropriate as the idea was, he'd better agree. It wouldn't do to upset her again.

"I reckon, as long as we're alone, you can call me Hank. Nobody in Mountainview calls me Henry."

She smiled a nervous-looking smile. "Thank you. Hank . . . I don't suppose the name H.G. Wells means anything to you, does it? Or his book, *The Time Machine*?"

He shook his head.

"No . . . I was pretty sure that was after your time."

"What do you mean, *after my time?*"

"Hank, I know this is going to sound completely absurd to you, but please listen for a minute. I really am from 1989. That's the year I actually live in. I'm from the future."

"I—" He tried to interrupt her fantasy.

"There's a concept called time travel," she rushed on, "that I've never paid any attention to, never believed was possible. But I should have because I've done it. I've traveled through time."

"Look, Miss James—"

"No, please. I realize you're thinking that isn't possible. That's exactly what I thought last night when you kept insisting this was 1862. I didn't sleep all night—just lay awake trying to make sense of things. And I couldn't.

"But after all I've seen this morning, there's only one possibility. Hank, as totally unbelievable as it seems to both of us, I have actually traveled through time.

"That's inconceivable."

"I agree. It's inconceivable. But, unless we're both trapped inside a marathon dream, it's a fact. This may be 1862, but yesterday I was in 1989—physically in 1989—not in my imagination. Something happened to me inside Broken Hill Mine. Something happened, and I ended up here, in your time."

Hank coughed nervously, hoping his face wasn't revealing how totally insane he knew this woman was. So much for their walk having helped her. So much for his thoughts about specializing in disorders of the mind.

"Miss James...I mean, Erica...do you have family somewhere? In Boston, perhaps? We could telegraph them and put you on a stage for the East. I think..."

His words trailed off as the woman pulled a squarish contraption from her pack. It was unlike anything he'd ever seen before. He couldn't begin to describe it.

"Hank, it was all the things I saw outside this morning that convinced me I'm in 1862. Let me show you some things from my world...from the future."

She held the squarish object out to him. "This is called a camera. After I've shown you everything in my pack, I'll use this camera to take a moving picture of you and record your voice. Then, when I'm finished, we can watch your picture through this little viewfinder here and listen to what you said.

"Now this," she went on, pulling out a book, "is a guide to Nevada published in 1989. I imagine you'll be interested in reading about what the state is like in my time."

She threw the book onto the couch, reached back into her pack and began pulling more objects from it.

"These are sunglasses. Voilà!" She perched the dark glasses on her nose for a moment, then tossed them aside.

"And this is called a battery charger. It helps keep my camera working. And this box of cassettes is my extra video tape. And this is my return ticket to Boston. See the date? I'm supposed to fly back in a week, on July 11, 1989, in something called an airplane that carries three hundred people and goes from coast to coast in about six hours. And this funny looking thing here is..."

HANK STARED AT THE PILE of objects on his office couch, absently lighting his pipe again. It must have gone out five times in the past two hours.

He reached for the camera and watched his image in the tiny screen once more. He didn't think the voice accompanying the picture sounded much like his...although the words were exactly those he'd spoken. But looking at the picture was like looking in a mirror.

He'd seen daguerrotypes, of course. But pictures that moved and talked—that looked so lifelike? Only a futurist would even dream of such a thing.

A futurist. The future. He glanced back at Erica James, trying to decide if the impossible was actually possible. The woman had shown and demonstrated and explained each of her strange belongings over and over. And she'd told him what little she knew about time travel.

"So somehow," he said, once more reviewing her explanation aloud, "more than one year...more than one century...exists at the same time?"

"It's too amazing a concept to comprehend clearly, isn't it?" Erica replied quietly.

He nodded. Amazing and almost unbelievable. Almost...but not quite. Erica James was from the future. What else could conceivably account for those belongings she had? It was possible her dark glasses were merely the latest fashion in Boston. But what about the rest of her possessions?

He hadn't been away from the East for that long! Not long enough for all of those things to have been invented. They were incredible.

And the future she'd described was incredible, as well. There were machines...*cars*...that was the word, instead of horses. And people flew. They'd even gone to the moon. If they could do that, was there any doubt they could come to 1862?

And they had boxes in their homes that showed moving pictures. That was what she'd come to Nevada to do, to research the Territory—the State, to her, he amended—before making a moving picture about a western mining town. A *documentary,* she called it, to be shown in those boxes.

He glanced at her once more. She was just a little bit of a thing—looked like a pretty child. But she taught at Boston University; taught courses in what she called *Film,* using amazing cameras like the one she had with her.

Yet she was a woman. In 1989, not only were women accepted as *students* at major universities, they were allowed to *teach* at them.

And, while women were off teaching at university or managing banks or designing buildings or doing a hundred different things they didn't do today, other people cared for their children.

And women could reliably plan when they had those children! And how many!

From everything she'd said, it appeared the twentieth century had turned life completely upside down.

He glanced at the guidebook once more, fascinated by what would become of Mountainview and Broken Hill in future years.

And Boston. She'd told him six hundred thousand people lived in that tiny Massachusetts Bay area in 1989. How did they all fit in? Today, space was already scarce there, with a population less than a quarter that number.

And there were *fifty* states! Of course, he'd expected Nevada would become a state, but Hawaii? She must have been joshing about that!

"Well, Hank? You convinced me I'm in 1862. Have I convinced you where I arrived here from?"

"Yes . . . incredible as it seems, I believe you have."

She smiled a relieved-looking smile at him. "Thank you for not telling me I'm crazy. And, while I'm at it, I don't think I thanked you properly for this dress and hat. I'd certainly have stood out as an alien if I'd gone walking in jeans and a T-shirt.''

Hank merely nodded, only half listening. This woman had the most engaging smile he'd ever seen. Her teeth were pearly white and incredibly even. And her lips were full and luscious. And her body! He was mighty tempted to suggest she change back into that thing she called a T-shirt!

And her deep blue eyes were enormous. And her skin was so smooth...and that gorgeous long hair. How could brown hair, even light brown hair, have so many golden streaks running through it? Even pinned up, the way he'd had her fix it to be less conspicuous....

He forced his eyes away from her. Looking at Erica James was causing him to have reactions he'd almost forgotten about.

She was a beautiful woman. There was no question about that. But dwelling on the fact didn't make much sense under the circumstances. Because, whether he chose to call Erica James an alien or a time traveler, she definitely wasn't part of his world.

And, for all he knew, she'd vanish in a puff of smoke at any moment. It was simply that he hadn't seen a beautiful white woman for a long, long time.

Aside from Indians, there weren't many women between St. Joseph, Missouri, and San Francisco. And there couldn't be many anywhere who looked and smelled as good as this one did—couldn't be many in 1862, at least.

He glanced at the little pile of strange objects once more, then at her. ''What happens next?''

''Why...why I go back, of course.''

''How?''

"Well . . . I don't know exactly how. I told you, I never paid any attention to the idea of time travel, thought it was simply fiction."

"Erica, I don't mean to alarm you, but if you don't know how to go about getting back, how do you expect to manage it?"

"I . . . I guess I'll have to start by figuring out how. But I got here, didn't I? If it was possible to get here, then it has to be possible to get back. That's only logical, isn't it?"

"I don't know what's logical at all. A couple of hours ago I'd never heard of this phenomenon you call time travel. Now you're asking me to comment on the logic of its operation. I'm afraid my opinion wouldn't be worth a plug of cheap chewing tobacco."

"Well, there has to be a way back. If I got to 1862 through a tunnel in the Broken Hill Mine, then the same tunnel must lead back to 1989. That strikes me as a perfectly reasonable assumption, don't you think?"

Hank puffed on his pipe and looked doubtful.

"And I'm certain that tunnel in Broken Hill is the way I got here. The last thing I remember is stumbling down it, heading for daylight. That must be when I banged my head.

"Which reminds me—you didn't really explain how I got from there to here."

"A couple of prospectors found you lying unconscious outside a tunnel. They were on their way to Mountainview for supplies, so they brought you along to my office."

"Didn't they think it was pretty strange finding me there—what with my 1989 clothes and all?"

"I reckon they did. But people come from all over when there's gold to be had. Some look stranger than others. And miners don't ask a lot of questions. They figure a man's business is his own. The townsfolk, though . . . that's going to be a mite different.''

"What do you mean?"

"I mean, Gus, at the dry-goods store, was real curious about me buying those ladies' duds. And now that you've been out walking, now that my neighbors have had a gander at you, they'll sure be wanting to know who you are and where you came from."

"That's none of their business."

Hank chuckled. "They'll certainly figure it is. A young woman suddenly appears in the home of Mountainview's widowed physician? The townsfolk will be busting with curiosity. And they won't be shy about asking questions."

Erica shook her head firmly. "I won't be here long enough for us to worry about questions. All I need to do is get to Broken Hill. Once I locate that tunnel, I'm certain I'll be gone."

Hank stroked his beard thoughtfully. "Look, I don't know that you should assume making the trip back is going to be easy."

"Why not? I'll recognize the shaft. It has a gold vein snaking long its ceiling. Surely, once I'm inside it . . ."

"Maybe. But maybe not. What bothers me about this time travel is that, if it's so simple, why haven't I heard about anyone else ever coming here from 1989? Or from another other year? How old are you?"

"Thirty-one."

Thirty-one? She barely looked twenty. Life must be soft in the future.

"So you're thirty-one and I'm thirty-five. That means between us we've accumulated sixty-six years of living, spanning two centuries. And neither one of us ever met or heard of an actual person who's traveled through time.

"If it's a common occurrence, why haven't we? If it happens frequently, why would you have believed the concept was simply fiction?"

"I . . . I don't know. Maybe it isn't common at all. But that isn't the point. The point is if there's a way here, there's a way back. There has to be!"

Hank nodded slowly. The longer they talked about this, the more upset Erica was getting. She clearly didn't want to even consider the possibility—or the likelihood—that she'd never find her way back to the future.

He didn't have to be a specialist of the mind to know forcing her to face that would only upset her further. The best thing he could do would be go along with her, let the reality of her situation sink in gradually. The longer she spent in 1862, the more she'd come to accept the idea her stay might be permanent.

"All right, Erica. I'll take you out to Broken Hill. I'll head over to the livery stable right now and have my horse and buggy hitched up. But don't get your hopes too high. You might not be able to find your way back right off. I've got a notion you could be staying in 1862 for a while."

He rose to leave, thinking he had far less appealing notions.

"WHOA!" HANK REINED BARLEYCORN to a halt and looped the reins over the buggy's rail. "Here we are."

Erica stared at the opening in the side of the rocky cliff. It appeared barely large enough to allow a man access. She glanced across the buggy. "This isn't Broken Hill."

"Sure is."

"It can't be! Yesterday it was an enormous mine, not a little hole in the wall."

Hank shrugged, shooting her a wry-looking grin. "Well yesterday in 1989, Broken Hill may have been enormous, but yesterday in 1862, I expect the mine looked just as it does now.

"According to the guidebook of yours, Erica, Broken Hill became a profitable gold producer *during the 1860s*. Well, the *during* must not have happened yet—that's all.

"Let's go." He swung easily out of the buggy, walked around in front of the bay mare and offered Erica his hand.

Clutching her long dress and the ridiculous petticoats beneath it into a bunch in front of her, she gave her free hand to Hank and carefully negotiated her way to the ground. She reached back into the buggy for her pack.

"Just a minute." Hank grabbed a small blanket from under the seat. "Give me that. I'll cover it up and keep it out of sight until we locate your shaft."

"But I'll need to get at my camera. I want to film the inside of the mine before I go back."

Hank shook his head. "As I just finished reminding you, today is 1862. No camera. And no red *nylon* pack." He smiled a self-satisfied-looking smile as he enunciated the new word.

"And let me do the talking. Normal women don't talk half as much as you do." He wheeled around and started off toward the tunnel entrance, her blanket-wrapped pack bundled under one arm.

"I'm a perfectly normal woman!" Erica hurried after him and silently cursed her outfit.

At least the good doctor hadn't decided to buy her "normal" shoes. From the looks of the thin-soled slippers and laced bootees the women she'd seen this morning had been wearing, her Reeboks were a million times more practical.

Even in them, she was having trouble keeping up over the rough terrain. And her short legs weren't helping. She ran a couple of steps, wishing she were taller.

Hank Lockhart certainly walked rapidly. Without those cowboy boots he was wearing, he wouldn't be more than about five foot ten or eleven, but he took long strides.

Erica stared at his back. It looked every bit as good as his front. He had extremely broad shoulders under his black suit jacket. And she liked the way his dark hair curled over the collar of his shirt and blended into his beard.

If Hank lived in her world, he'd be considered damned sexy looking. She wondered what women thought of his looks in his own world. The fact he'd stayed a widower for the past four years didn't say much for women of the 1860s.

She squinted against the bright sunlight, wishing he'd let her wear her sunglasses. Surely they could have passed them off as the latest thing from back East. But she'd gotten the distinct impression he thought she was soft, and she wasn't about to make any fuss that would reinforce that idea.

If he could march along under this scorching sun wearing a three-piece wool suit and a high-collared white shirt, she could manage without her sunglasses.

And she'd keep smiling under these layers of clothes. After all, she'd only be here for a while longer, only until they located that mine shaft. She forced a nagging doubt to the back of her mind again. Of course she'd only be here for a while longer.

Hank paused, waiting for her at the mine's entrance. Intermittent sounds of metal striking a hard surface were coming from inside.

She peered in. "Are you sure this is the main tunnel? It isn't very wide."

"It's wide enough. Come on."

Erica followed him into the blessedly cool darkness and promptly sneezed. Every bit of the dust and dirt and dankness she'd expected to find in Broken Hill yesterday was here today—and then some.

After only a few steps, the daylight vanished behind them. She stopped dead. This was too much like the blackness she remembered.

"You'll be all right." Hank found her hand and drew her forward. "Listen to those sounds of digging and scraping. There's someone working not far from here."

Hank's hand holding hers was mildly reassuring. She swallowed nervously and started along with him.

They walked fifteen or twenty yards through the pitch black tunnel, the noises getting louder with each step. Then, ahead, she saw a glimmer of light.

"Hello! It's Hank Lockhart, here!"

The noises ceased. "Hello, Doc!" a disembodied voice cried.

Doc? Erica almost laughed aloud at the image that popped into her mind. Snow White and the Seven Dwarfs! The last thing Hank reminded her of was a dwarf. The prince, maybe, but definitely not one of the dwarfs.

The glimmer of light began moving toward them, gradually becoming brighter. She made out a battered oil lantern . . . then the man holding it in front of himself. She doubted she'd seen a filthier man in her life. He stepped closer. She added *smelly* to her mental description of him. He must not have bathed since the 1850s.

"Doc! What brings you out here?" The young man peered past Hank at her. "Howdy, ma'am." He grinned broadly.

In the dimness she could make out only three teeth, but perhaps that was just an illusion—a trick of the poor light.

"This is Miss James, from . . . back East. This is Buck Dursely."

"Pleasure, ma'am."

He raised his lantern to get a better look at her, and in the light, she saw that three teeth was indeed the grand total.

"Nice to meet you, Mr. Dursely."

"Miss James is a teacher in Boston, Buck. She'll be heading back soon and telling her students all about Nevada. She'd be mighty interested in looking around Broken Hill if you wouldn't mind obliging us."

"'Course not!" Buck handed his lantern to Hank. "Just wait till I fetch a extra lamp."

Dursely vanished into the darkness, reappearing a few moments later with an even more battered lantern. "What'd you want to do, ma'am? Just mosey along?"

"Yes. Moseying sounds fine. Maybe we could mosey in the direction of the ore chamber?"

Buck laughed heartily. "Ore chamber? We ain't nowhere near needin' an ore chamber at Broken Hill, ma'am."

"Oh . . . well, have you excavated any side tunnels?" Erica held her breath, waiting for his answer.

Buck nodded, and she began to breathe once again.

"Fact is, we have. Struck a promisin' vein and followed it clear back out to daylight."

Her shaft! That had to be her shaft! She couldn't speak for the flood of relief sweeping her. She merely stood, beaming at Buck, knowing she must be looking like an idiot.

Buck didn't seem to care. He gave her a broad, three-toothed grin in return. "Want to see it, ma'am?"

At her nod, he started off. "A good thing we hit that vein. We was gettin' mighty down about our prospects at Broken Hill...was thinkin' of movin' on to California."

"Don't do that, Buck," Hank advised him. "I've got a feeling Broken Hill's going to turn out to be richer than you imagine. Wouldn't even surprise me if it became one of the most profitable gold producers south of Virginia City."

Erica shot Hank a wry glance in the dimness.

He merely grinned at her.

"Sure hope you're right, Doc! Sure hope you're right. Tunnel's just along here, ma'am."

Buck stopped walking and swung his lantern to the side of the tunnel, illuminating a smaller one.

Erica stared at the ceiling...at the dark, jagged vein running along it. "This is it," she whispered.

"Right you are, ma'am," Buck agreed. "That there's a gold vein. My partner's workin' it while I keep on in the main tunnel. But Lefty's gone visitin' in Aurora till tomorrow."

"If you wouldn't mind," Hank offered, "maybe Miss James and I could just poke around in this tunnel for a bit."

Buck looked at them doubtfully. "Ain't exactly dressed for it, are you?"

Hank shrugged. "Well . . . now that we're here . . ."

Sure, sure. Whatever you want, Doc. Just be careful. Tunnel's a mite steep. I'll be gettin' back to work."

"Thanks, Buck. I'll bring the lantern along when we're done."

Buck nodded and headed down the tunnel.

"You sure this is the one, Erica?"

"Absolutely! I recognize the way that veins snakes along."

"So . . . what do you do now?"

"Well, I guess I head down it. That's what I did yesterday. I guess I head down it and end up back in 1989." She could hear the uncertainty in her voice and looked anxiously at Hank, hoping he'd say something to reassure her.

He merely passed her backpack to her. "I'll wait here. Wouldn't want to chance finding myself time traveling."

She shrugged the pack over her shoulders.

Hank handed her the lantern. "Take this. If you can't see, you're liable to fall and bang your head again."

"But Buck's expecting it back."

"Take it along—to remember me by when you're home. I'll see Buck gets a new one."

Erica shot Hank the best smile she could manage, gathered her skirt up a little and started cautiously down the sharp incline, holding the lantern before her.

It was deathly quiet in the tunnel. She recalled the rumbling roars that had chased her yesterday. In its own way, this silence was just as terrifying.

Carefully, she navigated the first few yards, then looked back. Hank was barely visible in the darkness.

"Good luck, Erica," he called quietly.

She took a deep breath and turned away. Some-where ahead of her was the blue light of day. Some-where ahead of her was the year she belonged in.

CHAPTER THREE

ERICA SAT ON THE COUCH in Hank's office, barely managing to fight off the urge to cry. Hank stood quietly by the window, watching her. He'd said almost nothing since they'd left Broken Hill. To be more specific, he'd said almost nothing since she'd come back out of the tunnel.

He'd been standing in the darkness of the main tunnel, waiting for her, even though she'd stayed inside until the light of her lantern became a weak flicker.

She'd walked from the tunnel to the hole that opened into daylight, then back again. With the lantern's dim light, she'd examined the walls on both sides, searching for anything that looked unusual, any clue to the way back to her world. There'd been nothing but rough, grimy, solid rock.

Even the blue, guiding light hadn't seemed the same. Yesterday, it had been a magical, shimmering glow. Today, it had been pure and simple daylight.

What had gone wrong? Why hadn't the tunnel led her back to 1989? She glanced across at Hank and voiced her questions.

He shrugged slowly. "I don't know, Erica. Like I said before, I didn't figure the trip back would be as easy as you did. But I just don't know."

"What am I going to do?" Her voice was trembling. She bit her lip, praying Hank would have an idea.

He ran his fingers through his dark hair, walked slowly over to the couch and sat down on the chair beside her. "Are you sure this time travel works two ways? Are you certain there's not just a hole in time that people sometimes fall through and there's no way back?"

"Oh, Hank, I'm not certain of anything!" She swallowed over the lump in her throat. Hank wasn't saying what she wanted to hear at all. "But I have to believe it works both ways because I can't stay here! I can't possibly! This isn't where I belong. And I don't want to be here, not even a little bit. Everything's so...so..."

She caught herself in time. Telling Hank Lockhart that 1862 was primitive and filthy and smelly wasn't going to endear her to him in the least.

"Hank, everything's so different from what I know. And this whole situation is scaring the hell out of me. I can't stay in the century before the one I was born in! I have to go back...Or is it go forward? Whichever it is, there must be a way! If there isn't, I'll never see my parents again...or my friends."

"Erica, try to calm down. What you said earlier made sense. Since it was possible for you to get here, it's logical there's a way to get back."

She nodded eagerly, wanting to believe him more than she'd ever wanted anything in her life. "You really think so? You aren't just saying that?"

"No. It makes sense there's a way...just could take us a mite of time to figure out what it is."

Yes, there had to be a way back. She simply wouldn't believe there wasn't.

"Then that's what we have to do, Hank, figure out what it is." And they'd be able to do that. She had to cling to her belief they could.

"Right. Now, what about in 1989? People will realize you've disappeared. Will someone be trying to get you back? Maybe that's how the return trip works—from the other end."

"There's nobody who'll miss me for at least a week, not until I'm expected back in Boston. And, even then, people might just assume I'm working on something at home. It's summer. I don't have to show up at the University for weeks. And my parents are in Europe until August."

"You don't have a husband expecting you back?"

"No. No husband."

Hank eyed her curiously.

"I'm divorced."

"Divorced. That's not very common now. Is it then?"

Erica shrugged, feeling marginally guilty. "Fairly common. Must be the longer life expectancy. The prospect of spending fifty or sixty years with one man is pretty scary." She silently congratulated herself on still being able to joke.

"Fifty or sixty years? What in blazes is the life expectancy in 1989?"

"About seventy-five years, I think."

"Really! It's barely forty-five now!"

"See?" Erica managed a weak smile. "There's another reason I have to get back. I'll live longer."

"Right. You have to get back. We'll find the way. But at the moment you're here and we have to decide what to do about you."

She stared at Hank for a moment before realizing what he must be implying. "Oh, of course! I'm sorry. I realize I can't stay here...in your house, I mean...can't have you bunking in Billy's bed. And I've already taken up half your day. And you probably have patients to see...and where's Billy been? Who's been looking after him?"

"Billy can pretty much look after himself. If he needs anything when I'm not around, we have a neighbor, Mrs. McCully, who's always home. One of her sons is Billy's friend. In fact, they went off fishing, first thing this morning."

"And as far as my days go, they aren't real busy. I have the occasional patient come by—usually with a toothache or some such ailment. But most of my doctoring's done at night. After dark, when the saloons get active, I see the results of some of the activity."

"Well, at any rate, I'm sorry to have been such a bother to you, Hank. I'll just..." Erica ran out of words. She'd just what?

There was no hotel in Mountainview. And, even if there was, she had no money—at least no money anybody in this century was going to accept as legal tender. And, from what Hank had told her, there weren't any jobs for women in 1862.

Well, maybe that wasn't quite true, but prostitution wasn't something she'd ever considered as a career choice.

"Hank, I'm feeling a little lost in the idea department. Just what are my options until we find the way back? I'm afraid I need somebody to tell me where I can go and what I can do. Hank, I'm afraid I need a friend."

Damn! Her tears were starting to spill over. She simply couldn't hold them back any longer. She swallowed hard, rubbed her hands across her eyes and glanced at Hank, trying not to sniff.

He was looking at her with an extremely uncomfortable expression. "I don't rightly see there's anywhere else you can go."

"But I can't stay here! You just said so."

"No, I didn't. You're the one who said that. I said I don't rightly see there's anywhere else you can go. The only other possible place—aside from a miner's tent—is a room in someone else's house. And, I don't mean to brag, but most folks in Mountainview aren't near as liberal as I am.

"I mean, most folks around here wouldn't be accepting of a woman from the future. To be blunt, they'd call your strange belongings magic and call you mad as a hatter."

"But, Hank, I have no money. I can't just freeload off you for however long I'm here."

"Can you cook and clean?"

"Of course."

"Well then, in exchange for your board, you can act as my housekeeper. I sure could use one. Haven't had one since I left Boston."

Erica tried to smile. At least he was willing to let her be useful. But cooking and cleaning were at the top of her list of ten most hated things.

"What about your neighbors, Hank? What about their questions? Wouldn't that be a problem? Oh, rats! I'm not very good at thinking in 1862 terms, but isn't the town doctor supposed to be an example of virtue or something?"

"Tarnation, Erica! You're the most argumentative woman I've ever met. Will you just be quiet and do as

I say? You'll stay here. There's no other real option. If we boarded you out, you'd go saying too much and, the next thing I knew, you'd be getting burned as a witch.''

"Hank! They don't do things like that in Nevada. Not in 1862. Do they?"

"I'm not sure. We haven't had many witches up to now."

Erica smiled at his wry humor. The smile hardly felt forced at all. At least, until she got out of 1862, she could stay with Hank Lockhart. At least she had a friend.

"Now," Hank muttered, "we do have to figure out what to tell people about you. We need a believable explanation of who you are and how you got here."

"A cover story."

"A what?"

Erica shrugged. "It means a story you tell people to cover up the truth—your believable explanation."

"All right...a cover story." Hank grinned. "What'll it be?"

"What's wrong with just saying I'm a teacher from Boston? It's even true. And Buck Dursley bought it. Believed it," she translated, seeing Hank's blank expression.

He shook his head. "I told you, miners don't ask many questions. But the townsfolk will want to know how you got here from Boston. They know you didn't arrive by stage...and we can hardly tell them you flew. And, even if we come up with an answer as to how you got here, there's still the problem of explaining why you're staying in my house. An unmarried man...a woman. Any woman, let alone a beautiful one. It just isn't seemly.

"We need a damned fine reason for you being here or we're both going to be tarred and feathered."

Erica glanced away from Hank, pretending to be thinking up a reason for her staying in his house instead of about the fact he thought she was beautiful.

That pleased her and made her anxious at the same time. The attraction she felt for him was mutual...which would be all well and good if Hank hadn't died several decades before she'd been born. Every time she thought about that aspect of the situation, an upsetting little chill ran through her.

She looked back at him, wishing she could get things straight in her mind. One of them wasn't real. They couldn't both be alive at the same time, because they were from different centuries. And, if they couldn't both be alive, then one of them wasn't real...was some sort of illusion. But here they were, together, both apparently alive.

"How about," Hank said slowly, "we say you're my patient. We say I have to keep you here while I treat you...and we say your concussion made you forget the past? That way, you can't tell anyone where you're from or how you got here because you don't remember."

"Amnesia! Great idea!"

"What?"

"What do you mean *what*? It was your idea."

"The word!" Hank snapped. "I don't know that word."

"Amnesia?"

"Yes."

"Oh. Sorry. That's what it's called now...I mean then. People who forget the past have amnesia."

Hank shook his head. "Doesn't even sound like an English word!"

"Well, we don't have to use it. We probably shouldn't if it hasn't been created yet. But your idea's good, Hank. If anyone asks me anything, anything at all, I can just say I don't remember."

"Reckon you could manage to say that little?"

"If I put my mind to it . . . I *reckon* I could."

A door slammed in the back of the house.

"Pa! Pa! I've got fish!"

Hank quickly stood up and headed for the inner door of his office. "Just let me see to Billy, before he comes rushing in here with those fish."

Erica sat quietly after Hank closed the door behind himself, suspecting she should follow him and offer to clean the fish. That was undoubtedly part of her job as housekeeper.

But she'd never cleaned a fish in her life. And the idea of trying to do it was revolting. Fish came in clean little fillets, inside cardboard packages, in the frozen foods department.

Not here they don't! a little voice muttered inside her head.

She picked up a magazine—*The Monthly Abstract of Medical Science*— from the table beside Hank's couch and glanced at the contents page. "On the use of Chloral in the Treatment of Pulmonary Consumption," by Dr. Z. Schtscherbinenkoff... "A Typhoid Epidemic, Apparently Arising from Infected Milk," by Dr. Alexander Ogston.

A typhoid epidemic! She closed the journal and put it back down, wishing she could banish the upsetting feeling that she was going to learn far more about life in 1862 than she'd ever wanted to.

A sudden knocking on the outside office door jolted her from her thoughts. A patient! One of Hank's infrequent daytime patients had arrived.

She hesitated for a moment, then rose. She'd simply let the person in. She didn't have to answer any questions. She couldn't. She didn't remember anything.

Erica crossed the room and pulled the door open. Before her eyes was a broad expanse of tan skin. She was gazing at a naked, hairless male chest. Its owner smelled like a bear.

She looked up. An enmormous Indian, his face devoid of expression, stared down at her for a moment. Then he silently pushed past her and stood, muscular arms crossed, glaring daggers at her from the center of Hank's office.

Oh, Lord! She really was going to learn far more about life in 1862 than she'd ever wanted to!

The Indian stood motionless, staring at Erica, his coal-black eyes unblinking.

Her hand moved involuntarily to her hair. She told herself not to be ridiculous. Indians out to scalp people didn't come pounding on doors in broad daylight. At least, she didn't think they did.

Of course, until sixty seconds ago, she wouldn't have thought a naked Indian brave would be standing in Hank's office.

She let her gaze sneak low enough to establish the man wasn't entirely naked. A *loincloth*—that's what they were called. He was wearing a buckskin loincloth. It hung from a rawhide thong around his waist, covering his essentials...more or less. He had incredibly muscular thighs. She quickly glanced back up.

The brave's hair was at least as long as her own. Two dark braids reached well past his shoulders. He'd be a fantastic video study—a long, straight nose, high cheekbones, large eyes. She wished her camera was within reach. Maybe she could...

"Sequinta!"

Erica wheeled around at the sound of Hank's voice. He was smiling at the Indian, heading across the office to greet him.

"I'm honored you've come to my home, Sequinta."

The Indian nodded almost imperceptibly at Hank. Then his gaze flickered to Erica for a fraction of a second.

Hank turned to her immediately. "Would you excuse us please, Miss James?"

"I . . . I wondered . . ." She paused. Hank was glaring at her. "Of course . . . Dr. Lockhart." She backed quickly out of the office, pulling the door soundly closed.

What on earth was going on? What did the Indian want? Whatever it was, Hank clearly believed it was none of her business.

She glanced about the kitchen, at the command center of her new position as housekeeper. She'd certainly be facing a challenge. There was no running water, no electricity. There wasn't anything that even looked like an icebox and, given that she'd never even mastered a gas bar-b-cue, she'd undoubtedly be courting disaster with the wood-burning stove.

At least there wouldn't be much cleaning to do. Hank's home was a far cry from what she'd have pictured the town doctor as living in. There was only his office and the kitchen on the main floor and two small bedrooms upstairs. Not a lot to clean.

On the other hand there was no vacuum, and she knew without looking there wasn't going to be a bottle of anything remotely resembling Glass Plus in the cupboards.

The murmur of Hank's voice drew her attention back to his office. Then Sequinta began speaking...in reasonably good English. She was awfully curious about what that Indian was doing here. Maybe if she stood quietly right by the door, they'd talk loudly enough that—

"Ma'am?"

The reedy little voice sent Erica a foot into the air.

"Sorry ma'am."

She turned to face Hank's son. "It's okay, Billy. I wondered where you'd gone."

"I was putting my fish in the cold cellar." His words ended in a deep cough.

"You all right?"

"Yes, ma'am."

She gazed at the child for a moment, recalling how skinny and pale she'd thought he was last night. Then, with her peripheral vision, she caught a motion to Billy's left. She glanced over and focused on an enormous dog.

It was sitting a few feet away from the child, drooling onto the wooden floor and watching her with a wicked-looking glint in its yellow eyes. She stared at it nervously, wondering if its teeth were always visible.

She knew even less about dogs than she did about little boys. The only canine she was even on a first name basis with was Franklin, a Jack Russell terrier who lived in the apartment across the hall from her own. But Franklin, in his entirety, was smaller than the head of this animal that was eyeing her.

She recalled Franklin's master saying Jack Russells had been bred to kill rats. This creature watching her looked as if it had been bred to kill crocodiles.

Billy glanced down at the ashy-gray monster, then back at Erica. "His name's Cheyenne."

"Yes. Yes, of course. I remember you mentioning him last night."

The little boy peered at her intently. His eyes were every bit as soft a black as Hank's.

"My pa just told me you don't remember anything. He said you'll be staying here awhile because you don't remember anything."

"Right. Yes. Your father's right. I don't remember anything much up until last night. But I do remember hearing about Cheyenne. What kind of a dog is he?"

"Pa says he's mostly wolf."

Erica felt herself stepping backward and stopped, remembering Hank's wry sense of humor. She grinned at the child. "Do you think he's really mostly wolf, though?"

"Guess so. Other dogs bark. Cheyenne howls."

"Oh." This time she didn't stop herself from stepping back. Based on what she could see, Cheyenne might well have the biggest teeth in Nevada. She stared at the animal, aware her behind was pressing firmly against the office door.

A wolf. The size was about right . . . and so was the coarse, gray coat. Throw in those large, triangular ears and bushy tail, and he certainly fit the bill.

"Have you had Cheyenne for long, Billy?" She bit her tongue before the next question, the one about how many people the animal had eaten, could pop out. Why was she thinking of Little Red Riding Hood?

"Since he was a puppy. Pa got him from some Indians."

"From Indians. So that's why his name's Cheyenne."

Billy gazed at her blankly.

"You got him from Cheyenne Indians?"

"No. We got him from the Paiutes. They're the only tribe of Indians that live around here. But Cheyenne's a better name for a dog."

"Oh." Terrific! Just terrific! Overnight, she'd gone from being a university instructor to a straight woman for a nine-year-old.

"How did your father happen to get him from the Paiutes?"

Billy shrugged. "He's a doctor. He saved some of their lives."

And for saving their lives they'd foisted this beast on him? She wondered, fleetingly, what they'd have given Hank if he'd killed some of them. A grizzly bear?

The door suddenly opened behind her. She stumbled back, banging into Hank's chest.

He grabbed her arms and straightened her up. "Been making friends with Billy and Cheyenne?"

"Absolutely!"

"Good. I have to go out—may not be back till late." He glanced at Billy. "Anyone comes by, son, find out what the problem is. If it's serious, tell them I'll be along as soon as I can."

Erica looked through the doorway. The Indian hadn't left. "Where are you going, Hank?"

"Out."

"With him?"

"Yes."

"Why?"

Hank shot her a sidelong glance that made her feel extremely nosey.

"The local band's had a problem with a couple of settlers. Sequinta was sent to fetch me. The chief wants me to try to help out."

"You're going there? To their village?"

"Camp," Hank corrected.

"I can come along, can't I?"

A surprised-looking expression crossed Hank's face. He shook his head.

"Hank—"

"Billy, take Cheyenne outside. He looks thirsty."

Hank waited until his son had left before speaking again.

"Erica, Billy's going to think it's mighty strange that you're calling me Hank."

"Oh...I'm sorry...I thought you just meant I should be formal in front of outsiders."

"Well...it's not proper. Billy knows men and women don't... I'll have to think of some way to explain why you were using my Christian name. Guess that'll wait till I get back, though."

"But I *can* come along, can't I?"

"No, Erica. I already told you. You can't come."

"Why not?"

Hank glared at her. "The Paiutes sent for me. Not for me and you. I don't know how things work in your world but, here, women don't get involved in men's business."

"But, Hank, most women here aren't from the future, are they? Seems to me that makes a big difference. From my point of view, I'm in the middle of history."

"From my point of view, you're mighty uppity!"

"I don't mean to be! It's just that if you let me go with you, I can see firsthand what an Indian camp is like. Hank, think what that will mean when I go back. I can include material about Indians in my documentary. I hadn't given that a lot of thought, but it'll reflect history more accurately."

"Tarnation, Erica! I'm not history! I'm me and this is now. I don't like being called history. I don't like it a bit. You can't come." He turned on his heel.

"Hank, maybe I could help."

He hesitated, glancing back. "How could you possibly help?"

"I'm not sure exactly how, but maybe I could. After all, I know what happened in history... I mean, I know how what's happening now, in 1862, turns out. It's like who won the Civil War and Lincoln being assassinated and all those other events I've been telling you about. I know things about Indians, too."

"What things?"

"Uhh..." What things? Good question. All she really knew was how badly she wanted to go to that camp. Indian history wasn't her strong suit, but a first-hand look at the Paiutes would do a fair bit to change that.

"Well, Hank, I know about some of the issues between the Indians and whites. I know some of the types of incidents that got the two sides really upset... how problems might have been handled better. I'm not sure exactly how I could help, but something I know might turn out to be useful."

Hank looked at her doubtfully. "Well... possibly it would. But Sequinta wouldn't like you coming along. None of the band members would like it."

"What if you gave them a good reason for my being there? Maybe you could tell them I'm a writer or something."

"Another 'cover story'?" Hank almost smiled. "You know, they might even believe that. I write a little—just as a hobby—and Chief Numaga knows I do... and he's met my friend, Sam. Sam's a professional writer."

"There we are then." Erica smiled pleadingly.

"I don't know..."

"Oh, Hank! It seems to me that while I'm here I should see and learn all I can. And, if there's anything I can tell you...anything I know that could help you...there very possibly might be, you know."

"Well, I reckon there might be at that. All right. Sequinta's going to figure I'm a danged fool, but come on. The Indians already think white people have mighty strange ways. Just don't ask me to let you bring that camera along."

"No. Of course not."

"And make sure," he hissed, ushering her through the doorway, "you keep those ridiculous blue shoes hidden and let me do all the talking."

ERICA GLANCED GUILTILY across the buggy at Hank. He was definitely having second thoughts about bringing her with him. Well, no. He must be up to fourth or fifth thoughts by now. He'd clearly had second thoughts the moment he'd told Sequinta she was coming.

The Indian had given her a cold glare, muttered a few words to Hank and stalked out of the office. He and his pony had been at the end of Main Street before she and Hank made it across to the livery stable.

She racked her brain, searching for an innocuous remark to break the strained silence. "I was surprised an Indian would come into town wearing only a loincloth."

"A what?"

"A loincloth. That thing Sequinta had on."

Hank shot her a derisive look. "It's called a breechcloth. I thought you knew about Indians."

"Well...*loincloth* is the word in 1989."

"Well, it's not the word now . . . in the *real* world."

"Oh. At any rate, I was surprised," she mumbled.

"Why? It's at least ninety degrees in this damnable sun." Hank wiped his neck. "I'm wearing a wool suit. You're wearing a dark dress. And Sequinta's wearing a breechcloth. Seems to me, if there's anything surprising, it's that white folk are so foolish."

Hank lapsed into silence once more.

Erica gazed at the surrounding land. The route to Broken Hill had been reasonably green, but this was a virtual desert—a small wasteland beneath the towering Sierra Nevada. Sagebrush was the only visible vegetation, and the dazzling sunlight, reflecting off the sandy soil, made her long for her sunglasses.

Barleycorn's hoofs clip-clopped rhythmically along the trail, each step adding to the cloud of yellow dust hovering in the air around the buggy.

Erica shifted uncomfortably on the bench seat, trying not to breathe very deeply and wondering why it had never occurred to her during any of the Westerns she'd seen that buggies would be so bone-rattling.

She counted two hundred clip-clops before trying another topic of conversation. "I was also surprised that Sequinta spoke English."

"You shouldn't have been. A goodly number of Paiutes do. When white settlers began coming here over twenty years ago the Indians made an effort to be friendly."

Erica counted to two hundred again, wishing Hank was a little more forthcoming with information.

"Billy told me you'd saved some of the Paiutes' lives."

Hank nodded.

"How?"

"A yellow-fever epidemic hit the tribe. Their shaman wasn't having much success treating it. Fortunately, I managed to do a little better."

"And that's why they trust you? Ask you to help out with problems?"

"I reckon it is. The epidemic broke out the first summer Billy and I were in Mountainview. I got to know the band members pretty well. And two of the children who survived their illness were Chief Numaga's daughters."

"So you're a local hero."

Hank chuckled. "To some. Their shaman, White Cloud, has never been fond of me. She seems to resent my medical knowledge."

"She? Shamans can be women?"

"Erica...are you sure you know anything about Indians?"

"I...I don't know everything. I know what shamans are. But I thought medicine men were always...men."

"Well, female shamans aren't very common. I guess they didn't get mentioned in all the *history* books."

They trotted along, in silence, a little further.

"What's the problem the chief wants your help with, Hank?" Oh, Lord! She wished she could call back the question. She was sounding more like an inquisitor every time she opened her mouth.

Hank looked over at her curiously. "Erica, are all women in 1989 like you? Do they all talk so much? Ask men so many questions?"

"They don't usually have to. The men generally volunteer more information than you do."

"To women?"

"Well…yes, to women. Things changed, Hank. It's like I was telling you before—women and men are much more equal in the future."

Hank nodded slowly, flicking the buggy whip lightly against Barleycorn's flank. "Chief Numaga's problem," he offered tentatively, "is that a couple of settlers who've been coming to the camp to trade have been bringing whiskey along and getting Indians drunk before they make their deals."

"That's awful!"

"It's a pretty common trick. And not just with Indians. A lot of miners have traded away fortunes in gold and silver, even lost their claims, after somebody got them drunk."

"But, as far as Numaga's problem goes, a group of Paiutes went to the settlers' cabin and poured all the remaining whiskey out of the barrels they found there. The settlers complained, and four Paiutes ended up in the Aurora jail."

"And the chief expects you to get them out?"

"Not me personally. But the Indian agent hasn't been any help, so I reckon Numaga wants me to talk to the territorial secretary."

"You know him?"

"Yes. Fellow by the name of Orion Clemens. His brother's a friend of mine—the fellow I mentioned who's a writer—my friend, Sam."

Sam Clemens? Erica stared across at Hank. "Sam Clemens? You have a friend named Sam Clemens?"

Hank nodded.

"Sam Clemens, as in Mark Twain?"

"Who?"

"Mark Twain."

"Don't know anyone by that name."

"Hank, this Sam, this writer, where's he originally from?"

"Grew up along the Mississippi, as I recall."

Good grief! Hank Lockhart was friends with Mark Twain...apparently before the man even began using his famous pseudonym.

"Hank, do you think maybe, while I'm here, I could meet your friend Sam?"

"I suppose. As a matter of fact, it might be a good idea to talk to Sam about what happened to you. I wouldn't want to tell most people, but Sam's a clever man. He just might come up with a thought about getting you back."

Erica felt a faint glimmer of hope at that idea. Their trip to the mine had left her awfully discouraged. But surely someone knew something that would help her. "Have you had any other ideas, Hank? Is there anyone else who might know something?"

"Well, I thought I'd send a telegraph to Harvard. The librarians there will do research for alumni. I expect they'll be able to turn something up."

Hank smiled at her. "It's just a matter of time, Erica. I'm sure we'll be able to get you home safely."

The glimmer of hope burst into a tiny flame. Maybe Hank was merely practicing his bedside manner on her, but it was working. She felt much better.

"Starting with Sam's a good idea though," Hank went on. "We should maybe pay him a visit. He's over in Aurora right now. It's not far."

"He doesn't live in Mountainview?"

"No. Most of the time, he's off in a tent, prospecting. He truly believes he's going to strike it rich. But whenever he runs out of money, he spends a little time in Aurora—writing articles for the *Esmeralda Star* during the day and telling stories in the saloons at night. Sam's quite the storyteller.''

"Yes... quite the storyteller,'' Erica repeated quietly. A visit with Mark Twain! That would almost be worth the trauma of finding herself in the past.

She tried to remember the Mark Twain stories she'd read. Had there been any about time travel? Because, if he'd written about it that meant...

It meant what? Trying to fit together things that happened in two different centuries was awfully confusing. If Twain had written about time travel, then he must have known something about it. Or would he only have known what she and Hank were going to tell him?

She couldn't make sense of her train of thought. It was like the chicken and egg question.

"And Sam's brother is the territorial secretary of Nevada,'' she murmured, trying to get at least some facts straight in her head.

"Right. I've gotten to know Orion pretty well—what with all the Indian trouble we've had over the past couple of years.''

"All the Indian trouble you've had over the past couple of years?'' The words squeaked a little on their way out. Erica hoped Hank hadn't noticed.

He nodded. "The Paiute war with the whites. It's been pretty bad.''

"The Paiutes have been at war with the whites?'' This time the squeak was more pronounced.

Hank glanced across the buggy. This time he'd obviously noticed.

"Erica, the more you talk, the more I'm thinking you don't know anything at all about Indians. We've had serious problems since the winter of 59, 60. A lot of people have been killed—both whites and Indians.

Weren't you aware there's an Indian war going on in the Territory?''

"What do you mean *there's an Indian war going on in the Territory*?'' Oh, Lord! Even the squeak was becoming difficult to get out. "You don't mean it's going on now, do you? As in today? As on July 5, 1862?''

"Well...yes. I can't rightly swear about today. There aren't daily Indian attacks. But the hostilities are pretty constant.''

"And you're taking me to a Paiute camp? Despite these pretty constant hostilities?''

Hank reigned Barleycorn to a halt and glared across at Erica. "Miss James, it was not my idea to take you to a Paiute camp. It was, in fact, against my better judgment. It was, you may recall, at your insistence.''

"Well you might have been a little more informative! I wanted to see an Indian camp, but I certainly didn't have a war camp in mind!''

"Been more informative? Been more informative to the little lady from 1989 who knows all about *history*? Who told me she knew all about Indians? Who sweet-talked me into bringing her along by telling me she could be of some help?

"How in blazes was I supposed to know you were hornswoggling me, Erica? That you didn't know about the Indian war? You don't know a danged thing about Indians, do you?''

"I do too know a danged thing about Indians! I know a whole lot of danged things about Indians. I just didn't happen to know the Paiutes were in the midst of a war with the whites in 1862. I admit it. Over the past hundred and twenty-seven years, there's been the odd thing happen that I don't know about.''

Hank clicked the reins. The mare started forward once more.

"If I don't get to the camp soon," Hank said between clenched teeth, "Numaga will be insulted. Otherwise, I'd turn around and take you back to Mountainview.

"But just to set your mind at ease—before you become completely hysterical—most of the hostilities have been north of here, around Pyramid Lake. Numaga's kept his band out of the war up to now."

"I had no intention of becoming completely hysterical. I'm not the least bit worried."

"Good." Hank shot her a quick sidelong glance. "Then why don't you take your hands off your hair? If someone decides they want your scalp, holding on to it won't help."

CHAPTER FOUR

"THAT SMOKE UP AHEAD is coming from the camp."

Erica breathed a sigh of relief that Hank was speaking to her again. His tone even sounded civil.

"Hank...I'm sorry about getting upset earlier. You just took me by surprise, telling me about the Indian war."

"Well, I can't expect you to know every last thing that happened before 1989. But I sure never thought anyone'd show up someplace there was a war going on and not know about it."

"I didn't intend to show up here! Dammit, Hank, I didn't ask to be dragged backwards into an adventure! It simply happened."

"I wish you wouldn't do that, Erica."

"Do what?"

"Cuss. Ladies shouldn't cuss. I've heard you do it several times. It's not seemly."

Erica gritted her teeth, reminding herself this was a different world. The sooner she got out of it the better. But she needed Hank on her side, needed his help to get her out.

She looked ahead, anticipating her first glimpse of the Paiute camp. While she was stuck in 1862, she'd darn well make the best of it.

On either side of the trail, vegetation was rapidly replacing desert. Birds twittered in the stand of trees they were passing.

"Those are piñon pines," Hank offered. "Their nuts are one of the Paiutes' main foods."

They passed a small herd of grazing ponies, the trail curved, and the camp suddenly materialized before them.

"I thought there'd be teepees!" Erica swore silently at herself as the words slipped out. Hank was right. Apparently, she didn't know a danged thing about Indians.

He merely shrugged. "The Paiutes build these for the summers. They're called *Karnee*s."

Erica smiled a quick thanks that he hadn't criticized her latest display of ignorance, then turned her attention to the nearest of the twenty-or-so *Karnee*s.

It was a circular, hutlike structure—a branch frame covered by brush and tall grass. A rack, constructed of long branches, stood beside it, hung with hunks of drying meat.

She looked around, trying to take in the overwhelming mixture of strange sights and smells, desperately wishing Hank had let her bring her camera.

Children, mostly naked, seemed to be everywhere. Several small boys were wrestling on the perimeter of the site. Near them, a group of girls played with a ball. Behind the circle of *Karnee*s, other children were splashing in a muddy stream.

Chickens wandered freely among the shelters. Dogs lay here and there, singly and in furry heaps of two or three.

Women, wearing hide dresses, worked about the camp. Surprisingly, after Sequinta's long braids, the women's hair was cut short.

"That's Chief Numaga," Hank murmured, nodding toward the far side of the camp. "The one wearing that heavy, bear-claw necklace."

Erica gazed across at the four men sitting outside the largest *Karnee*. They were bare-chested, but wore leggings rather than breechcloths.

Several children noticed the buggy and dashed over to it, pointing and giggling. The dogs joined in, barking, making Barleycorn dance skittishly.

Hank reined the bay to a halt.

Erica glanced over at him. "What happens now?"

"Don't quite know. I've never arrived with a woman in tow before. Normally, the chief would come over to greet me himself. But Sequinta will have warned Numaga you're with me."

"Warned Numaga? Hank, I'm hardly the bubonic plague come calling."

Hank shrugged. "But you *are* a woman. I suspect you'll have to be presented to Numaga. I doubt it's proper for him to come to you."

"And then? Once I've been presented?"

"Then you'll probably be turned over to the women—I reckon to Ashtaw, Numaga's wife."

"The women! I don't want to be turned over to the women! I want to hear about that problem with the whiskey."

"Erica..." Hank muttered wearily.

"Oh, rats! And *rats* isn't a cuss word, Hank. But, if I have to be with the women, will you at least ask Numaga if I can meet the shaman? Or, since she's a shaman, doesn't she count as a woman?"

"I'm not sure. But White Cloud resents me, Erica. She isn't likely to be friendly to someone I've brought here. And, next to Numaga, she's the most powerful person in camp. In some respects, she's even more powerful. If she doesn't want to talk to you, she won't."

"But she might not object. She might be as curious about me as I am about her. You'll ask if I can meet her?"

"I'll see. If I haven't already insulted Numaga by bringing you here, I'll see. If it seems appropriate, I'll ask."

"Thank you, Hank."

HANK HAD GUESSED CORRECTLY about Indian protocol. The chief hadn't come to the buggy himself. Rather, Sequinta had been assigned to escort the visitors to the largest *Karnee*. Numaga had greeted them there.

Hank had deferentially presented Erica to the chief. Then, almost immediately, Ashtaw had been summoned to take Erica on a tour of the camp.

But at least Hank had asked if she could meet the Shaman. And at least Numaga had agreed.

The camp, however, proved fascinating in itself. They'd barely started off when they passed a trio of old men making arrows. One chipped away at arrowheads with a knifelike tool. The other two straightened shafts by rubbing them back and forth through holes in stones.

Ashtaw led the way to the *Karnee* nearest Numaga's. The young woman outside it gave Erica a long, pointed stick, then skewered a piece of dried meat onto it.

Erica glanced questioningly at Numaga's wife.

"For your journey home," the Indian murmured.

Erica nodded politely to the young woman, trying to indicate her gratitude.

Ashtaw smiled, apparently approving, then proceeded to take Erica from home to home. Most of the women were busy working—filleting fish and hanging the strips to dry, grinding bowls full of grains and berries, weaving baskets or scraping rabbit skins. None of them spoke English, but each greeted Erica with shy smiles and a gift of food.

At one *Karnee*, a nursing mother quickly put her infant into a cradleboard before acknowledging her guests. Erica smiled down at the little boy. The cradleboard was lined with thick rabbit fur; the baby gurgled contentedly inside it.

Ashtaw gently touched Erica's arm, drawing her attention from the child. "You will meet the Shaman now."

Erica followed the chief's wife across the central area where pots hung over low-burning fires. Thin streams of smoke curled upward and faint smells of simmering food mingled with the stronger animal smells of the camp.

Ahead of them, on the far side of the circle, stood an arbor constructed of four long poles and a brush ceiling.

In its shade, sitting on a buffalo robe, was one of the oldest-looking women Erica had ever seen. Her dress, in contrast to the plain hide dresses the other women wore, was heavily decorated with beadwork.

"That is White Cloud," Ashtaw murmured.

The shaman stared straight ahead, not acknowledging the approaching women. She sat motionless, looking like a female Buddha. Both her body and wrinkled face were almost perfectly round, and her nose, though short, was extremely broad. But her mouth was a thin, tight line.

White Cloud's hair was her one attractive feature. It wasn't cut short but hung, like a veil of pure silver, almost to her waist.

As Erica and Ashtaw reached the arbor, the old woman slowly turned her head to look at them.

The shaman eyed Erica with the same expressionless look Sequinta had displayed in Hank's office. But there was something more in White Cloud's gaze, something eerie.

A tiny shiver seized Erica as those piercing, coalblack eyes appraised her. She felt as if...it wasn't possible, of course...but she felt as if her very soul was under scrutiny.

"White Cloud," Ashtaw said softly, "this is the woman the doctor has brought."

The old Indian didn't speak.

Erica's sixth sense was screaming at her to be careful about what she said. No lie would get past White Cloud, no cover story would be believed for an instant. Suddenly, she regretted ever hearing of the shaman.

"I'm pleased to meet you," she managed, wishing her voice sounded less ragged.

White Cloud stared at Erica's face for an eternity. Then her eyes slowly swept Erica's body—down to the ground and back up.

Finally, she spoke. "Where have you come from?"

"From the East—from Boston."

"How did you reach my land?"

"I . . . I just came."

"Why?"

"Ah . . . I'm interested in the West."

"You came one sunrise ago."

Erica's mind raced. "Yesterday. Yes. I arrived yesterday."

"And you will leave..." White Cloud's words trailed off.

Erica was uncertain if the old woman had been asking a question or making a statement.

The shaman said nothing further, but her penetrating gaze didn't waver.

Erica shrugged nervously. "I don't know exactly when I'll leave."

The corners of White Cloud's mouth appeared to twitch momentarily. Erica wasn't entirely sure they had. The woman was making her immensely uncomfortable.

"I believe that you do not know."

Erica stared at the shaman's face. The old woman wasn't talking about not knowing a departure date. She was talking about not knowing something else. What?

White Cloud's gaze flickered to the ground then back up so rapidly that, if Erica had blinked, she'd have missed the eye movement entirely.

But she hadn't.

She looked down. The hem of her dress was caught up a little; her Reeboks were clearly visible.

Her heart began racing; she glanced back up.

White Cloud was smiling a tiny, cruel-looking smile. White Cloud knew!

"BUT WHITE CLOUD CAN HELP ME, Hank! I'm sure she could explain what happened yesterday, how I got here. With any luck at all, she knows how to get me home."

Erica could feel herself becoming more upset by the moment. She glanced back as the trail curved away from the Paiute camp; the circle of *Karnees* disappearing behind a dense stand of bush. She turned and glared at Hank once more.

Her frustration had to be coming across loud and clear. Yet he merely stared straight ahead, occasionally flicking Barleycorn's flanks with the reins.

"You could at least have asked her about time travel, Hank. I was so taken aback when I realized she knew I was from the future that I didn't know what to say. I figured you would, though...thought I'd be better off leaving things up to you.

"I thought I'd be better off," she repeated pointedly to Hank's silent profile. "I certainly didn't expect you to hustle me back to Mountainview without even talking to her. I might have already been in 1989 again if you'd asked for her help."

"If I had asked for White Cloud's help," Hank muttered from between clenched teeth, "you'd be precisely where you are. The only difference would be that we'd have given a vindictive shaman the pleasure of gloating.

"Erica, White Cloud is an incredibly malevolent old woman, and she resents me. She blames me for subverting her influence with Numaga, and she'd like nothing better than an opportunity to get revenge. If I'd told her we needed her help, she'd have danced with glee. And the last thing in the world she'd ever do, even if she could, is help us."

"We wouldn't have been asking her to help *us*, Hank. It's only *me* who needs help."

"But you're with me. In her mind that would make helping you tantamount to helping me. And she simply wouldn't do it. In fact, if she does know anything useful, she'd likely have lied about it. She'd probably make things worse for you if she could."

"Worse? Worse? Hank, my life has gotten a hundred and twenty-seven years off course! I have no idea how to get back to where I belong, no money, no clothes and barely the vaguest sense of how your world works. The only way things could be much worse would be if I didn't have you!''

Erica paused, the truth of her own words sinking in. ''Which means,'' she continued slowly, ''that I shouldn't be sitting here railing at you for not talking to White Cloud. I apologize, Hank. It's just that I'm used to being able to cope with my problems. But I obviously can't cope with this one. At least, not on my own. And I do appreciate your help. Without it . . .''

Her voice trailed off. Without his help she couldn't even imagine what she'd do. ''I guess I just have to trust your judgment, Hank.''

He shot her an embarrassed-looking smile. ''That's all right. I'm perfectly trustworthy. Look, if worst comes to worst, we'll talk to White Cloud. But you have no idea how evil that woman is. Even if she did agree to help, I'd be danged suspicious about what she might try.

''And anyways, Erica, things probably aren't near as bad as we've been thinking they are. Maybe this time travel is fairly common after all. If White Cloud knows about it, other people must as well. It's just a matter of finding someone else who does . . . someone I wouldn't worry about trying to send you into the sixty century or someplace. And, as I told you, my friend Sam's a good bet.''

Erica tried to convince herself Hank was right. He simply had to be right! White Cloud couldn't possibly be the only person in 1862 who knew about time travel.

Mark Twain . . . she had to start thinking of him as Sam . . . but Mark Twain or the librarians at Harvard or someone Hank hadn't even thought of yet would be able to tell her how to get back to 1989. Someone other than White Cloud had to know the secret. And, in the meantime, Hank was a person who could be relied on.

He reached over and patted Erica's hand.

The gesture made her feel immensely better. She had a friend. She smiled across at him, suddenly wishing he was more than that. The wish, she realized immediately, was dangerous as hell!

Her thinking was still muddled about how the two of them could possibly even be here together, when she'd been born in 1958 and he'd been born in... Good grief! A rapid calculation told her he'd been born in 1827.

But however they'd happened to come together, these circumstances surely wouldn't continue indefinitely. And there was no way she intended to get mixed up in a relationship that was going to come to an abrupt halt when she went back to her own time.

If only Hank wasn't so damned attractive. He looked too good to be real. *And that,* a tiny voice whispered in her ear, *is because he isn't actually real.*

Erica shook her head wearily. Given that she'd barely managed to pass Logic 101, how could she expect to puzzle this out?

But it was obvious that once she got home, Hank wouldn't be the least bit real. Even if he lived to be a hundred, he'd be dead long before she was born. Only, here and now, he was very alive...and very appealing.

She gazed out across the barren land that stretched toward Mountainview, focusing on the scenery, not wanting to watch Hank.

They'd left the oasis surrounding the Paiute camp behind and were in near-desert once again. Gnarled clumps of sagebrush clung to the sand like ancient, miniature oak trees, like the artwork of a bonsai gardener.

But there undoubtedly weren't any gardeners in the vicinity. All there were, she thought, forcing her mind back to the situation she'd landed in, were characters from 1862 Nevada—a cast of Indians and whites who didn't get along with one another.

She glanced across the buggy at Hank. "What about Chief Numaga's problem? What did he have to say?"

"It's pretty much as I expected. He wants me to contact Orion Clemens about getting those braves released from the Aurora jail."

"And will you?"

"I'll do what I can. Orion's up in the territorial capital, though. It's a long trip to Carson City. I can't be spending four or five days traveling up there and back. So, hopefully, just sending a message will do the trick."

"How long will it take to get a message to him? How soon will you hear back?"

Hank shrugged. "Depends how busy the telegraph offices are. And how busy he is."

"The office in Mountainview will be closed by now but, first thing in the morning, I'll send messages to both Orion and to a friend at Harvard—ask him to see about your problem, send us anything they can turn up there. Getting my friend to drop into the library, instead of telegraphing the library direct, will probably speed up the results."

The *results*. She snuck another glance at Hank, wondering if he really believed they'd manage to get her home or if he was simply humoring her.

What was there liable to be in Harvard's library? Harvard's *1862* library? There certainly wasn't going to be an instruction book for time traveling. If such a book existed, trips through the centuries would be commonplace.

But maybe there was something...some clue that would head them in the right direction.

"Hank, assuming they turn up a book or some articles that mention time travel, how long will it take for the material to get here?"

"Well, they'd have to send it by stagecoach from St. Joseph, Missouri. That trip's about three weeks. Plus, there's the time it'd take to get from Boston to St. Jo."

Erica closed her eyes, fervently wishing telephones had been invented earlier.

"Don't look so worried, Erica," Hank said softly. "We probably won't have to wait for that. I've got a lot of faith in my friend Sam's knowledge. He knows about the strangest things."

Erica nodded slowly, wishing she had as much faith as Hank did—or as much as he was pretending to have.

"Unless something comes up in Mountainview tomorrow, we'll head over to Aurora—see what Sam has to say. And nothing's likely to come up. People here don't get sick much during the summer.

"In winter, someone's always coming down with a bad case of the croup. And I sometimes see a dozen or more miners in a day with serious frostbite. Tents aren't the best places to live when the weather's below freezing.

"This time of year, though, my practice is pretty quiet—except for the occasional shootings and knifings in the saloons, of course."

Erica flashed a questioning look at Hank, hoping she'd find he was grinning at her, hoping that last bit had been a joke. He wasn't even looking at her, and he wasn't smiling. Apparently, he'd been serious.

Terrific! Frostbite, the croup, shootings and knifings. Lord, how she wanted to get out of here.

She gazed ahead, over Barleycorn's broad back. The sun was a red beach ball, hanging low on the dusky horizon before them. She was going to get home to 1989. She had to keep believing that, had to keep telling herself White Cloud couldn't be the only person who knew about time travel.

Yes. With Hank's help she'd get home. But there was no doubt she'd be spending at least one more night in 1862.

BILLY MOPPED AT THE LAST of his eggs with a biscuit.

Erica watched him with relief. Either he hadn't noticed how dreadful breakfast was or, for a nine-year-old, he was incredibly tactful. The eggs had been passable, but the biscuits she'd baked in Hank's woodburning stove resembled a cross between muffins and rocks.

Of course, the little boy had been talking a blue streak ever since he'd gotten up, so he probably hadn't tasted a thing.

Just as well. Erica surreptitiously picked at the bottom of her own biscuit. She hadn't quite succeeded in scraping all of the burned bits off it.

Despite the thorough instructions Hank had given her before leaving for the telegraph office, breakfast hadn't come anywhere near qualifying as a culinary triumph.

Under the table, Cheyenne was pressing his flank against her knees, panting noisily and staring up at her as if he hadn't eaten in a week.

Erica hesitated, leery of losing her hand, then gingerly slipped the biscuit onto her lap. It vanished instantly.

Cheyenne licked his lips and grinned at her, his yellow eyes begging for more. Apparently her baking qualified as a triumph in his opinion. She raised her opinion of the dog half a notch.

"'Course the summers are best," Billy said, resuming his chatter, "cuz there's no school! I hate school! And Miss Appleby is the most horrible teacher in the whole world! She's mean as a wolverine! She keeps a wood switch at her desk, and whenever anyone's bad..." Bill made an evil face.

Erica laughed across the kitchen table at his grimace. From what she'd observed, little boys didn't appear to have changed much over the past century.

"In the summers I mostly go fishing with my friend Johnnie McCully. Or we swim in the river or we explore the mountains or sometimes we help prospectors look for gold." Billy stopped talking long enough to search through his pants pocket.

He stretched his clenched fist out to Erica for an instant, then flashed it open to display his treasure.

She stared at the irregular little lump sitting on the child's palm. "Is that...?" She paused, not wanting to seem stupid. It looked genuine, but it must be fool's gold.

"It's real gold, ma'am!" Billy beamed proudly. "I was helpin' Three-finger Jack pocket-mine last summer, and we hit pay dirt."

"Pocket-mine?"

"Yeah. You know. Sometimes you can find gold that's collected in one little spot in the hills. You know. Instead of being just a few grains here and there in the dirt it's...

"Well, anyway, there was so much it took him two days to get it all dug out, and he gave me this nugget for bringing him luck."

"My pa says miners are a real super...super..."

"Superstitious?"

"Yeah. My pa says miners are a real superstitious lot and that's why Three-finger Jack gave it to me."

A flicker of curiosity about Three-finger Jack's name flitted through Erica's thoughts. She glanced down at Cheyenne, then forced aside the suspicion that popped into her mind. A man could lose a finger hundreds of different ways.

"My pa says—"

"What does your pa say?" Hank's voice interrupted.

Erica jumped, her glance flashing to the doorway between the kitchen and Hank's office.

Hank grinned across at her. "Two telegrams are on the wire."

He tossed a large, lumpy parcel, wrapped in brown paper, onto the dry sink. "Now, tell me what you're claiming I say, son."

"I was showing Miss James my gold nugget. I was telling her Three-finger Jack was superstitious and that's why he gave it to me—cuz miners are a superstitious lot."

"Well, that's true enough," Hank agreed, glancing from Billy back to Erica.

"Every miner who strikes it rich figures somebody did or said something that brought the luck. And they fear the luck's likely to disappear again. That's why they reward the lucky person—in hopes of keeping the luck around. And the better the luck, the bigger the reward."

"And what happened to Three-finger Jack after he'd struck it rich? After he rewarded Billy? Did his luck disappear?"

"I reckon that depends on how you look at things. I wouldn't say his luck disappeared as much as he was plum foolish. He paid off his debts, then went on a shopping spree. As I recall, within a week he'd gone through over four thousand dollars and was back to buying groceries on credit and wandering about the hills searching for another pocket of gold."

"Maybe I should try to find him, Pa. Maybe Johnnie and me should go searching for him today. Maybe I'd bring him luck again."

"Perhaps you would, Billy. But what I want you to do right now is take your bedroll over to Mrs. McCully's. I stopped by there a few minutes ago and she's expecting you. Miss James and I are going to Aurora and we might be late getting back."

"Can't I go with you, Pa? Are you going to see Sam? Can't I go?"

"No, not today. Anyway, I thought you'd just decided to go looking for Three-finger Jack."

"I'd rather see Sam."

"Well, maybe next time. What about fetching that bedroll now?"

"Yes, sir." Billy obediently pushed back his chair and hurried across the kitchen.

"I wouldn't mind at all if he came with us," Erica murmured as Billy raced up the stairs at the far end of the room. "I enjoy having him around."

Hank shook his head. "As I said, we might be late getting back. Aurora's seven miles through the mountains—at least a couple of hours each way. And Sam's tall tales tend to excite Billy. I don't like him getting overtired."

"I hadn't realized little boys were delicate," Erica teased.

Hank merely gazed at her, his expression telling her the comment hadn't amused him.

She scrambled to change the subject. "You're lucky to have Mrs. McCully nearby."

"Sure am. Don't know what I'd do without her. Billy loves being at her place. And she has seven children of her own, so one more around doesn't make much difference. In fact, now and then, emergencies come up that keep me away for several days at a time, but that doesn't seem to bother her at all."

Erica laughed. "In 1989, wonderful day-care like that would cost you a fortune."

"Well, Mrs. McCully and I have an agreement. She looks after Billy as if he was one of her own sons, and I don't charge her family for my doctoring. And besides tending the children through various illnesses, I'll bet I've patched up her husband, Bert, a dozen times. He's the barkeep at the Dry Gulch Saloon—seems to have a talent for getting trapped in the middle of barroom brawls."

"You know, Hank, until I arrived here, it never even occurred to me that tending bar could be a hazardous occupation."

"Well, in a mining town, almost any occupation can be hazardous."

Billy pounded back down the stairs and paused at the bottom, clutching a roll of bedding. His dark eyes were dancing exactly the way Hank's did at times.

Hank grinned over at him. "Good luck finding Three-finger Jack, son."

"Come on, Cheyenne!" Billy called, dashing over to the door. He shouted goodbye a second before it slammed behind them.

"Does he ever walk?" Erica asked with a grin.

"Now and then. Walking, instead of running full steam ahead, is the first sign I notice when he isn't feeling well."

"By the way, that parcel's for you." Hank gestured in the direction of the dry sink. "I figured you wouldn't want to keep on going around in the same dress."

"Oh, Hank! You shouldn't have! But thank you. I *was* starting to feel a little dowdy." Not to mention awfully grimy, she added silently. Washing with a basin of cold water and a rag had left her longing for a hot shower.

At least she'd packed a change of underwear in her hand luggage. Years ago an airline had lost her suitcase—and had taught her the wisdom of carrying essentials with her in her hand luggage.

She'd just keep on rinsing out her lingerie...and surely she'd be back home before her deodorant ran out.

Strangely, Hank smelling faintly of perspiration simply struck her as manly. Or maybe it was the scent of his bay rum she liked. She was growing inordinately fond of that scent.

But regardless of which it was she found appealing, Hank was an exception. Most of the people she'd gotten close to over the past couple of days simply stank! She certainly didn't relish the thought of joining their ranks.

"Aren't you going to open this?" Hank passed her the package.

"Of course. It feels like Christmas in July." Erica laid the parcel on the kitchen table, untied the string and folded back the brown paper.

"Oh, Hank! It's absolutely beautiful!" She pulled the dress from its wrapping and held it up against herself. Tiny blue flowers dotted the fine white cotton. The dress had a stand-up collar and long, puffed sleeves. Its bodice was gathered into a million narrow pleats, and its skirt was a series of flounces, each reaching a few inches farther to the floor than the one above it.

"Do you like it, Erica?"

"Like it? I love it! It just might be the most beautiful dress I've ever had!"

Hank grinned, clearly pleased with himself. "I thought the blue of those flowers would match your eyes."

Erica glanced up, surprised he'd noticed the color of her eyes.

"And it does," he added quietly. "It matches perfectly."

Hank stood gazing down at her with a look that told her he'd noticed a whole lot more than the color of her eyes.

She swallowed hard, suddenly aware how awful she must look.

"Hank...are we in a hurry to leave for Aurora?"

"Not really. As likely as not, Sam'll be off after a story till suppertime. Why?"

"Well I wondered if...if it isn't too much trouble...if I could have a bath before we left? Before I put on this new dress?"

"A bath? You don't look the least bit dirty, Erica."

"Well, I feel dirty. I guess that's because I'm used to taking a shower every morning."

"Every morning?"

"One of the joys of having running water."

"But every day?"

"Most people do, Hank."

"Really? Most people here only bathe about once a month."

"Oh." Erica tried not to look appalled.

"But people don't bathe every day in winter, do they?"

"Yes. All year long."

"Well I'll be! And it doesn't make them sick? They don't catch a lot of colds?"

Erica shook her head, feeling absurdly guilty about wanting to be clean.

"Look, Hank, on second thought, forget I asked about a bath. It isn't important. I wasn't thinking of how much effort a bath must be when you have to carry water in from the well."

"No. No, that's all right. No trouble at all. The tub's just out back in the shed. I'll fetch it and get some water. We can heat up a few buckets full. Won't take more than an hour or so to get things ready for you."

Erica moaned silently. She definitely wasn't going to win an award in the perfect-houseguest category.

CHAPTER FIVE

BILLY STOOD SCUFFING THE TOE of his boot in the dust, staring into the darkness of Broken Hill, wishing Johnnie was with him.

"He shouldn't have thrown those eggs he was collecting at his sisters," he muttered to Cheyenne. "He knows his mother makes him stay home and weed the garden for doing that."

Cheyenne sat down and began scratching his side with a hind leg, raising a cloud of yellow dust with each thump.

Billy gazed back into the tunnel, hoping to hear a sound from inside. Buck or Lefty might be able to tell him where Three-finger Jack was prospecting.

He rubbed his gold nugget in his pocket for luck, trying to decide if he wanted to brave the blackness without Johnnie. Pocket-mining was a whole lot better than shaft mining. Walking around the hills with Three-finger Jack was more fun than digging in a dark old tunnel. But, if he couldn't find Jack...

A sharp clang echoed along the tunnel.

"One of them's in there, Cheyenne." Billy leaned into the opening. "Buck? Lefty? It's me. Billy. Billy Lockhart."

"'Lo, Billy," a greeting drifted back. "Be there in a minute."

The dog stopped scratching; his ears perked up.

"It's only Buck, Cheyenne."

A moment later the man appeared, rubbing his eyes against the sunlight, smudging a large patch of black across the dusty gray of his face. He glanced around.

"You alone, Billy?"

"Yup. Just me and Cheyenne. Johnnie has to weed the garden. Mrs. McCully won't let me help him. She says Cheyenne steps on her vegetables."

"Thought your pa might be with you," Buck offered. "And that lady, maybe."

"Miss James?"

"Yeah, Miss James." Buck grinned. "They were here yesterday. She sure is purty."

Billy mentally pictured Miss James. She was real nice. And she smelled real good. But he hadn't thought about purty. He imagined Mrs. McCully's face...then his teacher, Miss Appleby. He grimaced at the thought of her.

"I guess," he agreed. "I guess Miss James is purty, all right."

"Sure is, Billy. 'Bout the purttiest thing I ever seen. Lefty's goin' to be might sorry he was away and didn't see her."

Billy shrugged. "I was lookin' for Three-finger Jack, Buck. Do you know where he is? I brought him luck, you know. Thought maybe I could bring him luck again."

"'Fraid I ain't seen Jack. But what about me? I could sure use some luck. We struck a promisin' vein a while back, but there ain't no sign of any mother lode yet."

"Well...I don't know if I'm lucky for all miners or just for pocket miners. Jack said he'd never have found that gold if I hadn't been with him. But I don't know if my being here's lucky for you or not, Buck."

"Hope it is, Billy. I do hope it is. Your pa was tellin' me he had a good feelin' about Broken Hill. Maybe you comin' here's goin' to help things along."

"You really think so, Buck? I could stay awhile if you really think so. I could try to find Jack tomorrow."

"Tell you what, Billy. I was just about to get my fire goin' and heat up some beans for lunch." Buck gestured past a stand of brush at the charred remains of previous fires. "Why don't you and me eat together?"

"Okay! And I could look at that promising vein if you want me to, Buck. Maybe that would be a lucky thing to do."

"Maybe it would," Buck agreed, starting off.

Cheyenne suddenly scrambled to his feet, growling.

Buck paused, glancing down at the dog.

Billy eyed Cheyenne anxiously. "Something's wrong, Buck."

The man looked around. "Don't see nothin'."

Cheyenne stared in the direction of the fire pit and continued to growl.

Billy looked closely, seeing nothing unusual. He took a step forward.

Cheyenne barked sharply, moving quickly in front of the boy.

"Well, I'll be..." Buck whispered.

Billy glanced at the man in time to see him draw his gun from his belt.

Slowly, Buck raised the gun, pointing it toward the firepit. Billy's gaze moved along the length of the short barrel, past the brush, his eyes searching for what Buck was aiming at.

An earshattering crack split the silence.

A long shape jerked into the air for an instant, then dropped back to the ground.

A snake!

Billy swallowed hard, suddenly finding breathing difficult. "A rattler?" he asked, barely managing to squeak the question out.

"Looks like." Buck strode over to the body and stared down at it for a moment. "Yup, a sidewinder." He grinned back at Billy. "Guess we got some fresh meat to fry up with our beans."

Billy tried not to make a face. "I . . . Miss James cooked a real big breakfast. I don't think I could eat more than some of the beans for lunch."

Buck stuck his gun back into his belt and pulled his knife from it's sheath. He bent down, reaching for the snake. "Well, Billy, one thing's plum certain. You ain't just lucky for Three-finger Jack. I might be dead if you hadn't come by, so you must be lucky for me, too—either you or that danged dog."

"We're partners. Me and Cheyenne are partners, so I guess we're both lucky."

Buck grinned. "Well, Billy, what with havin' you and your pa and that dog on my side, I can't see me not havin' good luck with this mine. And, if I do, I'll sure remember who brung it."

HANK SAT AT HIS OFFICE DESK, fidgeting with his pipe, wishing he was already on his way to Aurora instead of still here, trying to ignore the sounds of Erica bathing in the kitchen.

Each muffled splash focused his attention on the door between them.

Erica James was in the next room—naked. He forced his eyes away from the door, back onto the latest issue of *The American Journal of the Medical Sciences*.

"Advances in the Treatment of Diseases of the Skin" was the title of the first article.

Hank's gaze wandered to the door again. He didn't give a continental about the treatment of diseases of the skin. The only skin he had any interest in belonged to Erica James. It was the smoothest, whitest skin he'd ever seen. And, at the moment, it was all wet and slick—probably flushed pink from the water's heat. He'd surely like to...

He stared back down at the article. "One of the most common..." The words began to blur. He puffed on his pipe, then cussed quietly. The danged thing had gone out.

What in thunder was the matter with him? He was a physician—a physician who'd been married. It wasn't as if he'd never seen a naked woman.

So why wouldn't this burning itch of desire leave him be? Why was merely thinking about Erica causing these reactions he hadn't felt in years? He stroked his beard thoughtfully.

Biology. Yes, that's it, he thought, answering his own question. It was pure and simple biology. Only, if it was just biology, why was he enjoying Erica's company so much? Why was he catching himself smiling so often? Why was he feeling so damned worried about her, wanting to protect her, feeling...

What he was feeling sure wasn't proper! At least it wasn't proper in 1862. But might it be in 1989? Would Erica think it improper or not?

From what she'd told him, everything was very different in her world—including courting behavior.

Courting! Now, why in blazes had that occurred to him? What sort of stupid dunderhead would even think about courting Erica James under the circumstances they were in? She didn't belong here. And she wanted to get back to where she did belong just as quick as she could.

And she should. She didn't fit into his world. She was much too talkative, asked far too many questions, had way too many opinions for a woman and was argumentative as hell! All her fussing would drive him crazy if she stayed here much longer.

Besides, he was obliged to help her get back. He'd as much as promised her he would, and he was a man of his word. And anyway, only a lunatic would entertain the type of thoughts that were creeping around in his brain.

But . . . what if it turned out she couldn't get back? What then? He felt another smile spreading across his face and ordered it away.

A noisy splash emanated from the kitchen, followed by quieter, dripping sounds. Erica must be getting out of the tub.

Silence reigned. She must be standing, naked. He could almost visualize her drying herself with that brand-new towel he'd dug from the back of his closet.

The itch he knew couldn't be scratched away was becoming more insistent by the second. If he weren't a gentleman . . .

Hank gazed at his journal article, seeing nothing but an image of Erica before his eyes. After an eternity, there was a tap on his office door; he heard it opening.

He turned in his chair.

Erica stood framed in the doorway, wearing the white dress. She looked like an angel.

"Well?" She smiled a shy smile.

She'd washed her hair. It hung to her shoulders in a dark golden riot of damp curls.

"Well...the dress looks...very nice. You look..." Words failed him. Didn't she realize a woman shouldn't be seen with her hair down loose? Not outside a bedroom, at least! She looked provocative as hell. It was damnable lucky he was sitting at his desk—that she couldn't see how she was affecting him!

She fluffed the bottom of her hair lazily with one hand; he almost groaned.

"I haven't forgotten you told me it wasn't *seemly* to leave my hair down, Hank, but it has to dry. Would it be all right if I left it like this for a little while? I'll pin it up before we reach Aurora."

"Well . . . well could you just pin it up until we get out of town? I reckon, after that, you could let it down again."

"Sure. I'll be ready in a couple of minutes." Erica turned and disappeared back into the kitchen.

Hank listened to her footsteps fade up the stairs, trying to fathom how he was going to spend the next couple of hours sitting in his buggy, beside Erica, without doing something no gentleman would ever do.

"THAT'S AURORA in the distance," Hank said. "You should start pinning your hair up."

Erica gazed ahead at the town that was nestled in a valley among the mountains and offered a tiny prayer of thanks they were nearing their destination. This ride had been longer than yesterday's excursion to the Paiute camp and, between the two trips, her backside had undoubtedly been transformed into one enormous bruise.

The buggy jolted over a particularly deep rut, making her think once more about how smooth pavement was. Even the old cobblestone streets in Boston were a dream compared to this rock-strewn trail.

With the last of her hairpins, she secured a strand of hair that was straying down her neck. Then she plopped the floppy white hat Hank had bought firmly onto her head and looked over at him.

"Well? Do I pass inspection?"

He frowned. "You look too pretty. There aren't many more women in Aurora than there are in Mountainview and you're going to stand out like a lantern at midnight. I just hope we don't run into trouble. Some drunken miner's liable to take a notion to kidnap you."

"Do you have a bag with you?" Erica teased. "Maybe you'd like me to put it over my head!"

Hank didn't laugh. "It isn't only your head, Erica. It's all of you."

"Oh." She assumed that was a compliment.

Barleycorn clip-clopped along, carrying them slowly into town. The outskirts were an encampment of small tents. Farther along, Erica could see more permanent structures. The buildings gradually loomed larger and more numerous before them.

"Aurora looks quite a bit bigger than Mountainview, Hank."

"It is—close to five thousand people."

"And where does Sam live?"

"He stays at the hotel. He comes and goes but, when he's in town, he doesn't fancy a tent. Hotel's just along Winnemucca Street here."

Once they'd passed the rows of tents, the street was lined with tiny cabins—some made of wood, some of brick. These were followed by a series of small, roughly constructed shops fronted by a boardwalk like the one on Main Street in Mountainview.

In fact, Winnemucca Street was very much like Mountainview's Main Street. Most of the buildings were wood, painted white, but a few were simply wooden frames covered by tightly stretched canvas.

They passed a couple of general stores, two meat markets, a wonderful-smelling bakery, several blacksmith shops and three stables...none of which smelled the least wonderful.

Saloons were everywhere—The Last Chance, The Merchant's Exchange, The Real Del Monte.

"I thought there were a lot of saloons in Mountainview, Hank. But here, they seem to be every second building."

"Last count I heard was twenty-five."

"For a population of five thousand? A saloon for every two hundred people? Is drinking all people do in Aurora?"

"Drinking and gambling. Roulette, poker, faro, monte, blackjack—miners have all kinds of ways of losing their gold and silver."

Erica stared back at the street. Winnemucca was a mass of humanity, dogs and horses. There had to be a hundred men for each woman or child. And almost every one of the men looked disreputable. And almost every one of them was openly leering at her. She glanced nervously across at Hank.

"The sooner we locate Sam, the better," he muttered. "There's the Shamrock up ahead."

The Shamrock Hotel had once been painted white, but only the odd remnant of paint still clung to its weathered exterior. It was one of the few two-story buildings on Winnemucca. That didn't strike Erica as a plus, not when the structure was threatening to tip into the street at any moment.

In comparison, even the seediest of 1989 hotels would look like the Taj Mahal.

Hank reined Barleycorn to a halt in front of the Shamrock. "You'd better come inside with me, Erica."

"Are you kidding? I wouldn't stay out here alone on a bet!" She brushed at the dust on her white dress, succeeding only in smudging it.

Hank swung out of the buggy, secured the reins to a railing, then helped her down. She clung tightly to his arm, pretending she was oblivious to the crowd of men eyeing her.

As in Mountainview, almost every one of them was bearded. But Hank, it seemed, was the only man in Nevada who knew beards should be neatly trimmed.

He led her through the Shamrock's doorway. The street sounds of loud, rough male voices and spurs jingling on the wood of the boardwalk faded behind them, replaced by low mururs of men intent on poker games.

A rapid glance told Erica the hotel's lobby was as ugly as its exterior. And the hot air, hanging thickly with smoke, stank of stale beer. An air conditioner, she thought fleetingly, would be a god-send.

Several card tables sat in the left front corner of the barnlike space. Behind them was a long, wooden bar. Apparently, the hotel served drinks, too—which meant that twenty-five saloons weren't enough to satisfy Aurora's thirst for liquor.

The right front corner boasted a few dilapidated, lumpily stuffed chairs. A scarred check-in desk stood near the back. Beyond it, a rickety-looking staircase ran up to the second floor.

Erica sensed the poker players pausing at their games as she and Hank passed the tables. She kept her eyes aimed straight ahead at the check-in desk.

Behind it perched a little weasel-like man whose gaze had focused on her breasts the moment she'd walked through the doorway.

"Room, sir?" the clerk asked Hank when they reached him. His eyes didn't waver from Erica.

She released Hank's arm and crossed her own over her chest.

"No. No room. I'm just looking for Sam Clemens."

The weasel's gaze drifted to Hank. "Sam's gone. Left for the hills a couple o' days ago."

Hank swore under his breath. "Know when he'll be back?"

"Couldn't say. A month maybe. Maybe two. He'll be back when his money runs out—like always."

"Know where he went?"

"He's a day or so up the Carson River, I reckon. Said he was goin' to take the trail up to Honey Lake Smith's and prospect near there for a spell."

"Thanks." Hank reached for Erica's arm once more. "Let's go."

"Let's go where?"

"Back to Mountainview, of course."

"What do you mean, *of course*? We have to go after Sam. The man said he's only a day away. We have to talk with him, see if he knows anything."

Hank dragged her from the desk, presumably out of the clerk's range of hearing. From the way the little man was staring after them, Erica imagined he could lip-read.

"Look, Erica, the fellow said a day *or so*. And regardless of whether it's one or several, we can't go traipsing off into the wildnerness. At least you can't. And I sure in hell can't leave you here alone. We have no choice but to go back home.''

"Why can't I go traipsing off into the wildnerness? I traipsed to an Indian camp. I traipsed here. What's one more traipse? Hank, we just *have* to talk to Sam! You said you had faith in him knowing something about time travel. We can't wait months for him to come back here.''

"Erica, it's far too late in the day to head anywhere except back home. And if you think I'd take you to a mining camp—out where you'd be the only woman for miles around—you're plum loco!''

"Hank, you brought me here! And I may not be the only woman for miles in Aurora but, from what I saw as we came along Winnemucca, I certainly may be the only one who isn't a prostitute!''

"Shhh!'' Hank hissed. "Ladies don't use that word!''

"Oh... Oh rats! What am I supposed to call them? *Women of the night?* When they were standing out there in broad daylight?''

"Soiled doves,'' Hank muttered under his breath.

"What?''

"Soiled doves. That's the polite term.''

Erica made an effort not to roll her eyes. "Fine! Then I may be the only woman in Aurora who isn't a soiled dove! But my point is you thought it was okay to bring me here. How much worse could a mining camp be than this town is?''

"About a thousand times! Honey Lake Smith's is nothing more than a stopping off place for the overland stages. That's where their stables are. The only people who stay at the inn are stage drivers and the occasional miner who's struck pay dirt.''

"An inn? Honey Lake Smith's is an inn? Then what's the problem, Hank? We'd have a place to stay."

"Stay at Honey Lake Smith's? You don't know what in blazes you're talking about, Erica! Calling Honey Lake Smith's an *inn* is a joke! It's barely a shack with a few strips of canvas rigged up for walls. Erica, you can go from one room to another just by stretching the canvas a little farther apart at the seams."

"And Smith himself has a crooked reputation as long as your arm. His inn is definitely not a place for a woman! I'd have to walk around with my gun cocked."

"You've got a gun?"

Hank pulled a pistol from his jacket pocket. "Of course I've got a gun. Everyone has a gun. Hell, Daniel Hilbert, at the bank, is the only man in Mountainview who doesn't carry a gun. And the miners refer to him as *Miss* Hilbert!"

Erica stared at the evil-looking little weapon, forcing back her repulsion.

"Fine," she said, ignoring Hank's outburst. "We'd have an inn to stay at and a gun for protection. Hank, I simply have *got* to talk to Sam. I have to get back to 1989, and if it means going to Honey Lake Smith's, I'm going to have to go there."

"Absolutely not!"

"Hank . . ." Erica quickly bit her lip, but a tear of frustration made good its escape.

"Tarnation, Erica! The idea's insane!"

"Hank, it's my only chance! I can't sit around Mountainview just hoping there's something in the library at Harvard, waiting while it spends a month en route from Massachusetts to Nevada!"

"There's probably nothing in the library anyway. There's probably not a danged thing! At least talking to Sam will be doing something positive."

"Please, Hank? You wouldn't let me talk to White Cloud about my problem. Please don't keep me from talking to Sam, as well!"

Hank wheeled back to the desk. "Two rooms," he snarled at the weasel. "We'll need two rooms for tonight."

"WELL?" HANK DEMANDED from the hotel-room doorway.

Erica stepped a little farther into the room, glad her back was to him. Hiding her feelings wasn't her strong suit.

Of the two rooms the weasel had assigned them, this was the better one. But that certainly wasn't saying much.

The only thing it had going for it was color-coordination. She just wished she could believe the gray was an intentional color, not dirt.

"Well...the room will be fine, Hank. It's only for one night."

"When you see Honey Lake Smith's," he snapped, "you'll wish you were back here. At least these walls are wood. And there's a real bed, not a makeshift cot."

Erica took a deep breath, then turned. "Hank, I'm not half as soft as you seem to think I am. So what if the Shamrock isn't a palace? So what if Honey Lake Smith's is worse? I can cope with it. I have to. Otherwise, I'm going to end up in 1862 forever.

"And...and, Hank, I appreciate everything you're doing for me. I realize you don't want to be away from Mountainview for very long, that you've got Billy and your patients to think about. I'm very grateful you're giving me this time. I know I couldn't get home without your help."

"Well," Hank mumbled, "it's like I told you. I'm not all that busy in the summer. And Billy will be fine with Mrs. McCully."

"Look, Erica, why don't you wash off the trail dust and rest up for a mite? I have to see about stabling Barleycorn. And I think I'll pay a visit to the jail. While we're here, I'd like to check on those braves of Numaga's—make sure they aren't being treated like coyotes."

"I'd..." Erica paused. Much as she was curious about the jail, she liked Hank's idea better.

She felt stiff, tired and dirty. And the prospect of having to run the gauntlet of Aurora locals again was a definite turnoff. Maybe she could see the jail another time.

"Yes. Yes, I think I will have a little rest, Hank. You won't be long, though?"

"No. I won't be long." He stepped out into the hallway. "We'll get some dinner once I'm back. In the meantime, be sure you lock this door. Aurora's a lot rougher town than Mountainview."

Hank nodded to her, then turned in the direction of the stairs.

A lot rougher town, Erica mused. Rougher than the town where Hank patched up the results of knifings, shootings and barroom brawls. Wonderful.

She pushed the bolt securely into place and turned back to survey her room once more... her dim, dingy room.

She walked over to the window. A large dust bunny—a gray, color-coordinated dust bunny—lazed its way across the wooden floor, disturbed by the tiny breeze her long dress stirred.

Hank had paid the weasel extra for a room with a view. But the window glass was so filthy that the street, only one storey below, looked as if it were suffocating in smog.

Smog, Erica reminded herself absently, didn't exist yet.

She focused on the lumpy bed, suspecting it had things living in it, wondering how large they might be. Maybe she should just curl up in the chair for a few minutes.

She ran her gaze over it. It's covering looked at least as dirty as the blankets. Gingerly, she sat down and tried to make herself comfortable. It was impossible . . . but she was so tired.

She wiggled this way and that, trying to fall asleep, for what seemed an eternity. It must have been at least half an hour. Finally, she gave up. But, if she couldn't sleep, she could at least make herself a little more presentable.

Wearily, she rose, turned to the battered dresser and poured water from the chipped, enamel pitcher into the washbowl. She wet her hands, picked up the sliver of what purported to be soap and rubbed it until a tiny speck of lather appeared.

She glanced into the foggy mirror—no doubt an amenity found only in the Shamrock's deluxe rooms— and wondered if she'd ever again look anything like an Ivory Girl.

At the moment she'd give a whole lot for a bar of soap that was anywhere close to ninety-nine percent pure. Hell, she'd give a whole lot for a bar of soap that wasn't ninety-nine percent fat.

Her wet hands were halfway to her face when someone knocked on the door. Quickly, she fumbled with the ragged towel, then crossed the room.

"Yes?" She checked the bolt, pushing it a fraction tighter into place.

"Miss James?"

"Yes?" she curiously answered the woman.

"Lou the deskclerk sent me up."

Erica stared at the lock, wondering if the Shamrock possibly had maid service. She couldn't imagine it did. "What do you want?"

"Got a message for ya, Miss James."

A message? She didn't know anyone here. Unless Hank had thought of something on his way out and given the weasel a message for her.

Of course. That had to be it. Erica slipped the bolt back and pulled the door open.

Two women shoved roughly past her into the hotel room. The stench of whiskey wafted along with them.

"Close the door," one of them snarled to the other, eyeing Erica as she spoke.

"Look—" Erica began to protest.

The older woman threw up a hand, cutting her off. "We ain't gonna hurt ya none! Just wanna talk to ya a minute—set things straight before ya get any more uppity ideas than what ya already got."

Erica looked from one woman to the other, uncertain if she was more surprised or more appalled by their sudden appearance in her room.

Hank might call them *soiled doves* but, when it came to these two, *dirty buzzards* would be a more accurate euphemism.

The older appeared to be about forty...a haggard forty. Her low-cut red dress brought to mind a sausage casing, and her hair was a peculiar, brassy color that made Erica certain peroxide had been invented long before Miss Clairol had arrived on the scene with toners.

The younger woman's age was more difficult to judge since the makeup covering her bumpy complexion might have been applied with a palette knife. Her dark hair and shiny black dress gave her an uncanny resemblance to a giant beetle.

Erica tried to decide which of them smelled of liquor. She couldn't tell. Probably it was both.

For lack of a better idea, she shot them a tentative smile. "Well, you obviously know I'm Miss James. And you're..."

"I'm Spanish Dora," the Beetle snapped. "And this here's Mollie Willis. But this ain't no social call."

Erica held her breath and drew back a little, trying to avoid Spanish Dora's halitosis without being obvious about it.

"We just come," Dora continued, "to make sure you was takin' the Concord out o' Aurora tomorrow, that you ain't got no notion 'bout stayin'... *Miss James.*"

"The Concord?" Erica asked, deciding she'd be wise to ignore the sarcasm dripping from Dora's voice.

"The overland stage," Mollie snarled, exposing extremely discolored front teeth. "Ya plannin' on bein' on it? Ya better be—either on it or in yar fella's fancy buggy, 'cuz the Shamrock's ours. Dora's and mine. We don't need no help. An' we don't need no more women settin' up business in Aurora."

"I—I—" Erica paused, realizing she was so flabbergasted her mouth wasn't working properly. She swallowed and tried again. "Miss Willis, what did the desk clerk tell you about me?"

"Just yar name. An' that ya ain't married to that fella yar travelin' with. Lou didn't have to tell us nothin' else. We ain't dumb. We put things together."

"Things?" Erica managed.

"Yeah, things. Like yar fella gets ya the best room in the Shamrock. A room of yar own. He ain't payin' all that money so's ya can sleep in it!" Mollie guffawed loudly.

"Then," Spanish Dora added, "he takes his fancy buggy and hightails it straight over to the jail—cozy's up to the sheriff in case you run into any problems."

"And we all know how Sheriff Rawlsy is 'bout women. Bet he's gonna be here any minute for a visit with you—a real friendly visit." Dora eyed the bed meaningfully.

Erica exhaled a long, controlled breath. In the twentieth century she'd never, not even on her worst days, been mistaken for a prostitute.

"Miss Dora, Miss Willis, I assure you I have no intention of setting up business in Aurora. Or of entertaining your Sheriff Rawlsy—or of entertaining anyone else. There's been some confusion here. As far as I'm concerned you're welcome to the Shamrock. In fact, you're welcome to the entire town. Believe me!"

The doves looked at her dubiously.

"Really. The fellow I'm traveling with is...my brother. He simply had a little business to look after at the jail. But we'll be on our way in the morning. We'll definitely be leaving Aurora first thing."

"That the truth?" Dora demanded.

"Absolutely."

"Well...well, it's just that we saw you and then Lou said...but I reckon...I reckon maybe we had no cause

to come stormin' in here like a couple o' Washoe
Zephyrs.''

Erica forced a smile. Much as she'd like to know
what Lou said and what a Washoe Zephyr was, asking would only prolong this conversation.

"No harm done. But, if you wouldn't mind, I was
just about to have a nap when you arrived."

"'Course, 'course," Mollie mumbled, taking a step
back.

"You'll be gone then? In the mornin'?" Spanish
Dora asked.

Erica nodded. "I'll be gone in the morning." *If
there was anyplace else to go tonight,* she added silently, *I'd be gone sooner.*

She politely accompanied the doves to the door and
opened it.

Her heart stopped.

Standing before her was a large man—bearded,
dirty and swaying slightly from side to side.

He grinned down at her. "Why you's every inch as
purty as Lou said you was."

Erica stared at the man for an instant, wishing her
hands were firmly around that little weasel Lou's neck.

"Wrong room, Tex!" Spanish Dora snarled, shoving Erica aside and smacking her palms against the
man's chest. She pushed firmly, sending him weaving
backward.

The far wall halted his motion; he stood gazing at
them uncertainly.

Dora stomped out of Erica's room, grabbed Tex by
one arm and began propelling him down the hall.

Mollie rushed wordlessly after her friend.

Erica hesitated a split second, then followed the others into the hall. This was more entertaining than live theater!

The doves hustled their six feet of male flesh along between them, the bottom ruffles of their dresses flouncing rhythmically aginst the dirty wooden floor.

They stopped near the end of the hall, propped Tex up against the wall while Dora unlocked a door, then tipped him into the room. A second later, the door slammed shut.

Erica stood stark still as the bang echoed down the hall, anticipating the dull thud of Tex hitting the floor. She felt a twinge of disappointment when there was no further sound. It would have made a perfect ending to the performance.

She turned to go back into her own room. The noise of heavy footsteps began thumping up the stairs.

She murmured a tiny prayer that they didn't belong to another drunk and waited, poised to shut her door the moment she saw who was coming, wondering when peepholes had been invented.

A man rounded the top of the stairs.

Hank! She sighed with relief.

"Erica! What in tarnation are you doing standing in the hall?"

"Just . . . just soaking up a little local color."

He glared at her. "That's plum foolish! I told you to keep the door locked."

"I did but..." She paused. Hank might not find the story of her little adventure amusing. And she certainly didn't want to say anything that would get him thinking her presence could cause them trouble at Honey Lake Smith's.

"Hank, what's a Washoe Zephyr?"

He looked at her curiously. "It's a hot, dry wind—pretty common during Nevada summers. Leaves a fine, white dust over everything. Why?"

"I just heard the term someplace. What does the word *Washoe* mean?"

"Washoe's an Indian tribe." Hank grinned at her. "I guess that'd be another one of those danged things you don't know about Indians."

Erica made a face at him. "Speaking of Indians, how are Numaga's braves."

"Well," Hank said, pleased that she was interested, "they're more than a mite happier than they were earlier. Turned out the sheriff was none too pleased about being stuck with them in the first place.

"In fact, he was only holding them because the fellows whose whiskey they dumped were insisting on it. But nobody's spoken up about the Indians' side of the story."

"And you did?"

"Sure did. I took Sheriff Rawlsy over to the Last Chance and we had a few drinks and a little parley about the situation. Decent fellow, Sheriff Rawlsy."

Erica muttered something under her breath.

"What?"

"Nothing. Nothing at all. So you had your little parly. And what happened?"

"And Rawlsy decided the settlers would have to be content with being reimbursed for the cost of the whiskey. The braves are on the way back to their camp."

"Hank, that's wonderful! So you don't need Orion Clemens's help after all. Chief Numaga will be thrilled with you!"

Hank stared at Erica's expression. She was proud of him. He could see that written all over her face. She was proud of him, and he was suddenly feeling like a little boy who'd just been given a gold star.

"Well," he went on, hoping his voice sounded normal, "Numaga isn't going to be thrilled that I promised he'd pay the settlers for the whiskey. He's not going to think that's right."

"But you think it is?"

Hank shrugged, barely able to think of anything other than how beautiful Erica looked...and how proud she was of him. "I'm a physician, not a judge. All I know is it was expedient justice."

"And, with us heading up to Honey Lake Smith's, it seemed like a good idea to get those Indians out of jail before we left—any way I could. Lord knows how long it'll take us to track down Sam."

"Hank...I really don't mean to be turning your life upside down. If there was any other way—"

Suddenly, Erica reached up and kissed him lightly on the cheek, just above the start of his beard.

When she drew away, his skin was on fire.

"Thank you, Hank," she whispered. "I don't know what I'd do without you."

It was all Hank could manage not to wrap his arms around Erica right there in the hallway—seemly or not.

"Well," he mumbled, "you don't have to worry about what you'd do without me 'cuz I'm right here."

He forced himself to take a step back, away from her hypnotic scent, her intoxicating nearness.

"I—I just have to go to my room for a minute, clean up a little. Then we'll head over to the Cancan Restaurant and have dinner."

Hank walked to his room in a daze. Not only was Erica proud of him, but she didn't know what she'd do without him. That was downright sensational!

The only problem was, he'd started wondering what he'd do without her. And he *was* going to have to do without her if they ever learned how to get her home.

CHAPTER SIX

"YOU MUST BE TUCKERED OUT," Hank offered. "As I recall, Honey Lake Smith's isn't much farther."

"No. No, I'm fine—good for hours yet."

Ha! a little voice snorted inside Erica's head.

She gazed over at Hank, wondering how easily he picked up on lies. They'd been bouncing along this wretched trail all day. She'd probably never walk again. And she'd developed a headache that was beginning to reach her toes.

Hank caught her watching him and grinned. "You're good for hours yet, are you? I think that qualifies as what Billy calls a whopper."

Erica laughed. The sound reverberated painfully inside her head; she stifled a moan.

She'd give a million dollars for an aspirin. But her aspirins, along with the rest of her meager collection of 1989 treasures, were back in Mountainview. All she'd tucked into the pocket of her dress, before they'd left for Aurora yesterday, were a comb and hairpins.

Her possessions were back in Mountainview and she was in the middle of nowhere, being towed along an ungodly trail, with Barleycorn looking in desperate need of a rest.

She was beginning to question her sanity. How could traipsing off after Sam Clemens have ever seemed like a fine plan? Her brain must have been in neutral when she'd convinced Hank to agree to this trip.

But it had shifted into gear today and was giving her a loud, clear message. No woman in her right mind, armed with only the tail of a plastic comb for protection, would face the unsavory lot Hank claimed frequented Honey Lake Smith's.

Thank heavens Hank had a gun. Yesterday, she'd been horrified to learn he carried one. Today, she wished he had an entire arsenal stowed in the buggy.

Unless he'd been exaggeratig, they were likely to meet the dregs of humanity at the inn. What were his exact words? *The orneriest bunch of skunks you'll find in Nevada.*

Terrific! Absolutely terrific!

Well...maybe he'd been exaggerating. He'd only been to Smith's once. And that was a couple of years ago. Maybe things had improved.

And maybe pigs can fly, that annoying little voice inside her head muttered.

She began speaking to cut it off. "Do you think Sam will be at the inn when we reach it?"

"If we're lucky. But don't forget I expected him to be at the Shamrock."

"And if we're not lucky? Then what?"

Hank looked at her and shrugged. "Then you and I stay at Smith's overnight—which means I sit up with my gun drawn—and we head back to Mountainview first thing tomorrow."

"But—"

"Look, Erica, don't be argumentative. Enough is enough. If Sam's staying at the inn or camped nearby, fine. We'll talk with him. But he may be prospecting a fair piece away. If that's the case, we give up and see him when he comes back to civilization."

"But that could be months from now!"

"Dammit, Erica! I don't care if it's Christmas before he turns up! I'm not marching off into the wilderness, searching for him! Who do you think I am? Daniel Boone? Lord knows why I ever agreed to bring you up here in the first place, but if Sam's not easy to locate, we're turning back. If we started into the mountains trying to find him, I'd get us lost for sure."

Lost! Erica stared at the dense stand of pine trees they were passing. Overhead, the storm clouds that had been gathering were gradually closing in, restricting visibility.

She hadn't thought of the possibility, but of course they could get lost if they strayed from the trail.

They were in the unmapped wilds of the 1862 Sierra Nevada, not in the middle of the 1989 Yellowstone National Park. There was no crew of forest rangers to rescue idiots who wandered off.

Hank was right. They couldn't go tromping into the wilderness. Being stuck in the wrong century was awful enough. Getting lost and starving to death or being eaten by a grizzly rated far higher on the awfulness scale.

Stuck in the wrong century. The phrase repeated itself in her mind. What if she really was stuck here? Permanently? What if they couldn't locate Sam? Or what if they did but he didn't know anything about time travel?

Her worries were beginning to multiply. She ordered them to stop. If Sam couldn't help, they'd simply find someone who could. White Cloud's knowledge couldn't be unique.

Except…much as Erica hated to face the fact, there was no guarantee of that. But Hank had promised that, if worse came to worst, he'd talk to the shaman.

Hopefully, though, worse wouldn't come to worst. Hopefully, they wouldn't have to rely on a vindictive old woman's whim.

She glanced surreptitiously at Hank, wondering what he thought about this crazy mess, what he thought about her.

Actually, though, she had a pretty fair idea of what he thought about her. He'd dropped a lot of clues— the way he kept looking at her as if he'd never seen a woman before, the way he was trying so hard to be patient, making such an effort to help her.

And yesterday in the hotel, when she'd given him that innocent peck on the cheek, his reaction had been obvious.

She bit her lip, wishing for the hundredth time she hadn't been impulsive. She'd felt so grateful for all his help and so pleased he'd solved Numaga's problem that kissing him had seemed a natural thing to do.

But from the startled expression that had appeared on Hank's face, she knew it wasn't a natural thing to do in 1862.

Hank definitely hadn't thought the tiny kiss *seemly*. They'd been halfway through dinner last night before he'd relaxed and stopped behaving as if he was suddenly uncertain how to act around her.

Maybe she should have brought the issue into the open, said something about why she'd kissed him, explained it had meant nothing.

Except, she admitted reluctantly, it hadn't meant nothing. She wasn't given to insincere gestures of affection. That kiss might have been impulsive but she wouldn't have kissed Hank at all unless she liked him. And she did like him . . . a whole lot.

And somehow, that damned little peck on the cheek had made Hank a hundred percent real to her.

She still hadn't figured out the logic of time travel. But the instant her lips had brushed Hank's skin, the niggling sense that the two of them couldn't possibly be real at the same time had vanished.

She only wished she could decide if its vanishing was good or bad. Hank was definitely real. And she was definitely fond of him, was rapidly becoming much more than fond.

And Hank's feelings for her seemed to be progressing in the same direction and every bit as fast. So what was she going to do about the inevitable situation that they were heading toward?

ERICA STOOD STARING at Honey Lake Smith's in disbelief.

Hank had warned her that calling the overland stage depot an inn was a joke. But it was a quantum leap beyond joke. A tiny group of words skipped through her mind—*absurd, farcical, comic, ridiculous.*

In 1989, Honey Lake Smith's wouldn't meet the standards for a cow shed!

It was the shape of a giant shoe box, about twenty feet in length, constructed of rough, weathered planks. As far as she could see, not a single one of them abutted its neighbor without major gaps between them.

The "inn" stood at a rakish angle, which perhaps explained why the roof looked as if it was about to slide off the building.

No. On second thought, if not for the crooked metal chimney, poking through at its midpoint, the roof probably would have slid off long ago.

There were no windows, and the door consisted of a length of canvas that didn't quite reach the ground. Erica gazed under the bottom of the mud-spattered fabric. Among its other features, Honey Lake Smith's boasted a dirt floor.

"Ready to make your grand entrance?" Hank asked.

"Ready as I'll ever be."

"Just keep in mind some of these polecats won't have seen a woman in months."

Erica smiled nervously. "You're sure you don't have a bag I could put over my head?"

"I told you yesterday, Erica, it isn't your head they'll be most interested in. You stick right to me."

"Like glue. You can count on it." She grabbed Hank's arm.

He squeezed her hand reassuringly. "Take a deep breath for courage and we'll brave them."

Hank pulled back the canvas.

Erica took a deep breath.

Mistake! Big mistake! Honey Lake Smith's stank so strongly that she almost gagged. Animal smells, urine, human perspiration, whiskey, beer and undoubtedly a hundred other odors she couldn't immediately identify were fighting for atmospheric control.

She stepped inside with Hank, holding her breath.

The interior of the building looked like a set from an early Clint Eastwood western. All that was missing were klieg lights and a director's chair.

Half-a-dozen neanderthal-like men lounged about the dim room. If they'd been talking, they'd stopped.

Likely, Erica thought, her glaze flickering anxiously over the motley crew, none of them was able to talk and stare at the same time.

She wondered if staring also precluded using their weapons. Every one of them had at least one gun and a large knife prominently displayed.

Surely none of these men could be Samuel Clemens. But there were a couple of shadowy figures in the corner she couldn't see clearly.

One of the men she could see clearly began to suggestively fondle his knife.

Hank released the canvas. The room darkened, its only light source the gaps in the walls.

Erica clutched Hank's left arm more tightly. His right hand had disappeared into his jacket pocket—the pocket that held his gun.

She waited for her eyes to adjust to the gloom, focusing on a bedraggled-looking stuffed parrot set incongruously amongst the liquor bottles and kegs at one end of the bar.

"Is Sam here?" she whispered to Hank.

"No."

Her heart sank. Another inch or two and it would be in the pit of her stomach.

"That's Smith behind the bar," Hank muttered under his breath, starting across the floor, half dragging her along.

Her feet seemed to have turned to lead. She concentrated on forcing them to move, conscious of lustful stares burning into her body.

Success! They reached the bar unscathed.

"I'm looking for Sam Clemens," Hank announced to Smith.

His voice, Erica noted with amazement, sounded perfectly normal.

"Ain't here."

Hank shrugged with a nonchalance he couldn't possibly be feeling.

"I see he ain't here right now. Thought he might be staying here, though."

"Nope." The beefy barkeep wiped the back of his hand across his mouth, eyeing Erica as if he'd like to devour her.

"Might be along later," he offered, glancing back at Hank. "Came by last night. Tent ain't far from here."

"Do you know exactly where it is?" Hank asked.

Smith merely shook his head, his hungry eyes drifting back to Erica.

Her heart made it all the way to the pit of her stomach.

The room was deathly silent. She suddenly felt as if they were in the middle of a video drama and someone had just pressed the Pause button.

She stood stark still, hoping that after someone pressed Play, she and Hank wouldn't end up dead in Honey Lake Smith's. What an ignominious place to die!

But given the looks of this bunch of characters, there was a distinct possibility they'd walked into a death-or-dishonor—or both—situation.

With a screech, the *stuffed* parrot turned its head toward Erica.

She leapt a foot into the air.

The bird gave her a disdainful look and strutted a few inches along the bar.

"I know where Clemens's tent is," a voice muttered.

Hank and Erica turned.

The speaker stepped toward them...the man who'd been fondling his knife.

He was about thirty. He sported a scraggly beard, and even in the dim light, Erica could make out how steely cold his blue eyes were.

There was something extremely unnerving about the man. In 1989 Boston she wouldn't have been surprised to see his photograph blazed across the front page of the *Herald* as a rape or murder suspect.

"Mind giving me directions to find Sam?" Hank asked.

The man's icy eyes focused on Erica, making her shiver.

"I ain't real good at directions. Might take you there though . . . might."

The man stroked the handle of the gun that was tucked into his waistband, then gazed back at Hank.

"Name's Cready. John Cready." His lips curled into an unfriendly looking smile. He had very few teeth.

Erica looked away, an image of Buck Dursely flickering through her mind; Buck Dursely with his three teeth. Buck Dursely, who she hoped would keep working the Broken Hill Mine and would be the one to strike it rich there. If he did, he'd be able to afford a good set of false teeth.

She glanced back at Cready. Lacking teeth was the only apparent resemblance between him and Buck.

Buck Dursely had been an open, friendly fellow. Cready gave her the creeps. Bad as being inside Honey Lake Smith's was, the last place in the world she wanted to go from here was anyplace with John Cready.

Hank nodded, acknowledging the other man's self-introduction. "I'm Hank Lockhart."

Cready looked pointedly back at Erica.

"And this is Miss James."

"James?" the man repeated curiously, staring her up and down. "Know a James. I rode with Will Quantrill up till a couple o' months back. Know a James who rides with that gang.

"Guess that wouldn't be no kin o' yours though, would he? Frank? Frank James from Missouri?"

Erica's thoughts raced. Frank James from Missouri. Older brother of Jesse James! That had to be who Cready was referring to. Frank James and William Quantrill—as in Quantrill's Raiders.

She'd once read a book about the James boys, had been interested in the outlaws because of their surname. She desperately tried to remember details.

Some of the pieces she wanted fell into place. During the early years of the Civil War, while Jesse was just beginning to earn his infamous reputation, Frank James had ridden with Quantrill's Raiders, one of the roughest, toughest, gangs of criminals in the Confederacy.

She frantically scoured the recesses of her memory. What else did she recall about Frank?

He and James were the only two of the James children who'd turned to crime. Jesse ended up being the more notorious, but Frank had been someone no sane man would have knowingly crossed.

Erica silently screwed up her courage. She and Hank had to get safely out of Honey Lake Smith's. Coming here just might have been the worst idea of her life.

But if they trailed off after John Cready with the cards stacked as they were, she doubted he'd take them to Sam Clemens. And she had a horrible feeling they might not escape alive from wherever he did take them.

She smiled sweetly at Cready, trying to ignore the way her body was shaking, hoping he wouldn't notice. "Did Frank ever tell you about his family?"

"Na. Frank don't talk much."

Na! What a beautiful word! Her smile stopped hurting her face.

"No, Frank never did talk much. Not even when we were children. Frank's my brother."

Erica felt Hank's body stiffen beside her. She turned and managed an almost genuine smile for him. "Isn't that nice? Mr. Cready's a friend of my brother Frank."

John Cready took a step back. His hand strayed casually away from his gun. "Frank's sister. Son-of-a-bitch! If that don't beat all."

"As a matter of fact," Erica confided, "I'm hoping to see Frank soon—and my little brother, Jesse, too. Do you know Jesse?"

"Na. Na, ain't met young Jesse. But we been hearin' a lot about him."

"Yes." Erica shook her head ruefully. "He's been getting into a mite of trouble. It's just his youth, though. He's actually a good boy. He's the baby of the family, you know—mama's favorite.

"Well, anyway, I had a message from brother Frank not long ago. He and Jesse are planning on paying me a visit . . . any day now."

"That so?" Cready shoved his hands into his pockets and shuffled his feet.

"Well . . . I reckon I better take you on over to Clemens's tent right away, then. You'll be wanting to get back to where you come from. Wouldn't want your bothers to be lookin' for you and not findin' you."

Cready paused, glancing around at the rest of the men in the room. "This here's the James boys' sister," he informed them unnecessarily. Every single man had been obviously listening to the conversation.

"You all heard tell of Frank and Jesse," he added. "They sure wouldn't want their sister runnin' into any trouble up here."

Cready started for the door, then hesitated, glancing at Hank. "Want a slug of whiskey before we go?"

"No. It's my dry time of day," Hank said, managing to keep his tone casual. He turned back to Smith. "Mind having someone see to my horse?"

"Reckon I could."

"Thanks." Hank nodded farewell to the thugs in Honey Lake Smith's. Then he and Erica followed Cready out.

Fresh air had never felt so good! He'd been a madman to come up here himself, let along bring Erica along. For all he'd been trying to help her, it was a wonder this little trip hadn't gotten them both killed.

That collection of skunks at the inn today were a far worse-looking bunch than he'd encountered the first time he'd been here. Lord knows what might have happened if Erica hadn't come up with her cock-and-bull story!

He'd felt his heart stop beating when she'd started in on it, but deuced if she hadn't brazened her way through. She had even more gumption than he'd been giving her credit for.

He glanced at Cready, walking several paces ahead of them, then down at Erica. She was clutching his arm tightly. He could feel she was still trembling a little.

"So the James boys ended up in history books, did they?" he asked quietly.

Erica nodded. "Jesse's the one who became really famous. He took to robbing banks and trains and was eventually shot to death by one of his own gang members—for reward money. I think brother Frank made it to a ripe old age, though."

"And what," Hank asked after a few more steps, "would you have said if Cready'd told you Frank James had talked about his family?"

"Something. I'd have thought of something. I've taken classes in improvisation—it's important when you work with video. I guess I'd have said I was Frank's cousin...don't imagine that would have been nearly as effective, would it?" she added with a smile.

Hank shook his head, wondering how a woman as beautiful as Erica could be so clever, as well. "I've got to give you credit, Erica. You're amazing."

"Thanks. It's just too bad," she teased, "I don't know a danged thing about either Indians or time travel. If I did, I'd be perfect."

Too bad she didn't know a danged thing about time travel? Too bad? Hank wasn't at all sure he agreed with that.

In fact, he mused as they hurried after Cready, there was a tiny hope growing in the back of his mind that maybe, given a little longer, she'd stop caring about traveling through time ever again.

They walked a mile or so, mostly downhill, into the mountains surrounding Honey Lake Smith's. Finally, John Cready stopped at the top of a rise and turned back, waiting for Hank and Erica to catch up.

"See there? By the gully?" He pointed down the hill to a tent sitting in the clearing near a large, dry ditch. "That's Clemens's."

"Much obliged, Cready."

The man nodded, taking a few steps back in the direction of the inn. "Remember me to your brother, ma'am."

"I'll do that Mr. Cready. I'll be certain to tell him how helpful you've been."

They waited until Cready disappeared back over the far side of the hill, then started down to the tent. It was a nondescript little shelter of dirty gray canvas.

Hank paused fifteen feet in front of it. "Sam? Sam Clemens? You in there you buzzard? It's Hank Lockhart."

"Hank?" a muffled voice shouted from inside the tent.

Erica stared at its opening. She was about to get her first glimpse of the legendary Mark Twain.

But the figure that scrambled from the tent bore no resemblance to the image she had in her mind—undoubtedly recalled from a book's dust jacket.

Her mental picture was of a debonair-looking, elderly gentleman—elegantly dressed, sporting a full head of salt-and-pepper hair and a bushy, gray mustache.

The man emerging before her certainly had a full head of hair. Its waves and long curls would rival a rock star's. And he had a mustache, although it was only a minor part of the bushy beard that hid most of his face.

But both Sam Clemens's hair and beard were fiery red. And he was far from elderly. He was younger than she was. He couldn't be more than twenty-six or twenty-seven.

And there wasn't a hint of anything debonair about him. He had either a black eye or a large smudge of dirt on what was visible of his face.

Atop his unruly long hair perched an extremely battered, brown slouch hat that didn't even pretend to coordinate with his rumpled blue shirt.

A large revolver was stuck jauntily into the waistband of a pair of pants. They were so stained that their original color was impossible to determine. His pant legs were crammed into the top of scuffed boots.

"Hank!" he hollered, tucking the tail of his shirt in and striding toward them.

HANK WATCHED SAM'S EXPRESSION across the campfire as Erica told her story, trying to read his young friend's thoughts. There was no clue to betray them.

"And the next thing I knew," Erica concluded, "I woke up in Hank's office...in 1862."

She sounded, Hank thought, awfully despondent. And justly so.

When they'd broached the subject of time travel to Sam and he'd claimed never to have heard of it, Hank had expected Erica to break into tears of disappointment right then and there.

She'd surprised him. She'd simply suggested she tell Sam her story, raised the possibility he knew something that might help her.

"Maybe," she'd said, "the term *time travel* doesn't exist yet. But maybe you've read something...or heard something..."

Hank didn't have much hope that was the case. He no longer believed Sam would be able to help them. Perhaps, though, having told her story to someone else, Erica would feel a little better.

He glanced at her, sitting beside him, and felt a rush of tenderness. She looked so vulnerable in that thin white cotton dress.

The light was growing dim; the mountain air had cooled. She pulled the rough wool shirt Sam had lent her a little more tightly about her shoulders, not taking her gaze off Sam's face—as if she could stare him into telling her how to get home.

Sam took a long drag on his pipe, then grinned broadly at Hank.

"I knew you'd try to get back at me for bamboozling you with that story about the petrified man. And having Miss James do the telling was a stroke of brilliance. You almost hornswoggled me! Almost.

"Especially starting off by asking if she could call me Sam and telling me I should call her that crazy name . . . Erica! You made only one mistake."

"Of course, most men wouldn't have caught it, Hank. But you and I have discussed this before. Doesn't matter whether you're telling a tale or writing it. A good story can't be so far-fetched it's impossible to believe. There's got to be a chance it's the truth."

"But you, Miss James," he added, smiling over at her, "you were superb. I've been known to spin some pretty far-fetched yarns and sound sincere doing it. But I swear to Moses you make me envious. You're a natural-born storyteller. I'm amazed to hear a woman tell a story at all, let alone so well."

A sudden stream of tears gushed down Erica's cheeks. She brushed furiously at them, making a small animal noise in her throat, clearly trying to choke back a sob.

Sam glanced frantically at Hank. "What did I say? I was complimenting her! What did I say wrong?"

"It's a long story, Sam. We'll get to it."

Hank looked back at Erica. The flow of tears was accelerating at a frightening rate and she'd given in to the sobs. He swallowed hard. To hell with what Sam thought and to hell with propriety. He wrapped his arm around Erica's shoulders, pulled her against his chest and began to gently stroke her back.

"I—it sure does look like a storm's brewing," Sam mumbled, leaping up and scurrying off into the twilight.

"I've got to collect some more wood for the fire," he called over his shoulder.

Hank glanced at the large stack of wood beside Sam's tent, then gazed down at Erica once more. Her unhappiness was tearing at his heart.

He brushed a strand of tear-dampened hair off her cheek, trying to sort through his feelings. He'd seen his share of misery. He'd seen patients die... and his parents... seen his own wife die.

After that had happened, he'd thought he was through hurting for others... except for Billy, of course.

But here he was, hurting for a woman again, wishing there was something he could do to take away Erica's pain.

Possibly there was. Possibly, White Cloud...

He shook his head, not wanting things to come to that, not wanting to be forced to trust the shaman... not wanting to trust her with Erica.

But there was another solution. The longer Erica was with him, the more it seemed the perfect one. Despite their differences, if Erica stayed in 1862, stayed with him, they'd be happy.

Every minute he spent with her convinced him more and more of that. All he had to do was convince her.

He held her until she was cried out. He could have gone on holding her forever. But, finally, her sobbing ended. After a few minutes she drew back a little and wiped at her face.

Hank pulled his handkerchief from his breast pocket and handed it to her.

She dabbed at her eyes with it, managing a tearful smile. "A handkerchief. That's so gentlemanly. It's sad handkerchiefs went out of fashion."

Hank merely nodded. This didn't seem the appropriate time to ask how science had overcome man's need to blow his nose.

"I'm sorry, Hank," Erica murmured. "I'll be fine now. I'm thinking logically again. I'm just sorry I embarrassed you in front of your friend."

"You didn't embarrass me, Erica. I understand. You were counting on Sam knowing something helpful and you were disappointed."

Erica sniffed. "We'll have to explain this all to him. Otherwise he'll think I'm a big baby. It was only that suddenly, when I realized he thought I was telling him an impossible tale, it seemed like the end of the world.

"That was silly though, wasn't it, Hank? Sam's not our last resort. We have White Cloud. We can go back to the Paiute camp and talk with her. I'm certain she knows how time travel works. The fact she knew I wasn't where I belonged was plain as day."

"Well...there's still Harvard, Erica. The folks there might come up with what we need."

"Hank, the more I think about that possibility, the more unlikely it seems. If there was information about something as incredible as time travel sitting in a major library, don't you imagine someone would have come across it? Publicized the details? No, Hank, I suspect White Cloud's my only hope. And you said, if worst came to worse, you'd talk to her. Well, I think we've reached worst. You *will* talk to her once we get back to Mountainview, won't you?''

Hank nodded slowly. He had promised. Like a danged fool, he'd promised. "I'll tell you what. Tomorrow, we'll stop in Aurora on our way through and I'll send another telegram to my friend at Harvard—ask him to let me know whether they've found anything to send us.

"If they haven't, I'll talk to White Cloud. After that, you and I can discuss your options—decide what's best."

"There won't be a lot to discuss, Hank. If White Cloud's my last resort and she says she can help me get back, I'm going to have to trust her. That's about the last of my options."

Hank swallowed hard, organizing words in his mind, ordering his voice to sound casual. "There's another option, Erica... You could stay here."

He held his breath, waiting for her to reply.

She gazed steadily at him for a long moment. Finally, she shook her head. "That's not an option, Hank...not a viable one...not as long as there's a chance I can get back."

Hank tried to shut out her words, not wanting to hear. She continued speaking.

"Hank, my life is in 1989. My home, friends, career—everything I have is there. And my parents.

"Hank, you're a father. What if Billy suddenly vanished from the face of the earth? You'd spend the rest of your life wondering and worrying about what had happened to him.

"If my parents arrive back from Europe in August and I've disappeared, they'll be frantic."

Hank nodded slowly, trying to accept what he didn't want to. Erica was obviously telling him, as nicely as she could, that life with him wasn't something she'd consider. He'd damned well have to keep that fact frontmost in his mind, regardless of all else.

"Hank?"

He glanced down. She was gazing up at him, her blue eyes still luminous from crying. Even with a red nose and a tear-stained face, she looked absolutely beautiful. He wished to hell she didn't.

"Hank...thank you for being so understanding."

Erica leaned up, sliding one hand around the back of his neck. She drew his head toward her and kissed him, kissed him like he'd never been kissed in his life.

Sizzling bolts of lightning surged through his veins. His body threatened to explode at the soft warmth of her mouth on his. She tasted incredibly good.

And she was touching him! Her fingers began playing with the hair on the back of his neck, sending urgent waves of desire swirling wildly down his body.

Her other hand was slipping across his chest, under his jacket, smoothing his shirt, making his heart pump madly beneath her caress. And, oh, Lord! Her tongue was...!

Hank pulled her closer, wanting nothing but the touch of her body against his, the taste of her mouth, the captivating scent of her.

No! That wasn't all he wanted. He wanted to make her part of his world—to make her his.

And she wanted him. He could feel that. Despite what she'd said, she wanted him as much as he wanted her.

Hazily, he recalled there was a fact he'd intended to keep frontmost in his mind, regardless of all else. Something about her not willing to consider life with him?

No! That definitely couldn't have been it! But what was it exactly?

He neither knew nor cared. It must have been just a silly thought...dissolved into nothingness at the wonder of Erica's kiss.

CHAPTER SEVEN

SAM CLEMENS SHOOK HIS HEAD for the hundredth time, and light from the campfire caught glints in his long red hair.

"Your stories about the future are unbelievably good, Miss James! I'm pretty fair at telling tales, but you're damnable marvelous!"

"You're pretty fair at cussing these days, too, Sam," Hank added with a trace of a grin. "When you first arrived in Nevada, you couldn't swear in the presence of a lady without looking the other way."

Erica laughed. "I'm afraid, in 1989, ladies hear a lot worse swear words than *damnable*."

"Well, I mean it, Miss James, you're by far the best yarn spinner I've ever met. You've almost got me convinced you really are from the future." Sam turned her purple plastic rat-tail comb over in his hand once more.

Erica wished she had her video camera along. That's what had turned the trick with Hank. She glanced at him. He was sitting beside her, smoking his briar pipe, smiling between puffs, obviously enjoying Sam's astonishment.

Hank caught her gaze and held it.

His deep black eyes, she'd decided some time ago, were the most gorgeous eyes in the world. And his mouth was the most sensual. Even the dark whiskers framing his lips had worked soft, tantalizing magic against her skin when they'd kissed earlier.

When they'd kissed. Erica forced her eyes away from Hank.

She might have managed to convince herself that first little peck on the cheek in the hallway of the Shamrock hotel had been innocent. But there was no way she'd fool either of them about the second kiss. It had shaken her to her toes.

She'd been astonished by its intensity, by the hot flames of desire it had ignited inside her. Her body had responded primitively to Hank's. He couldn't possibly have misread her reactions.

Talk about sending a double message! One minute she'd been telling him she wouldn't consider staying in his world and the next, she'd been kissing him as if leaving was absolutely the last thing on her mind.

But it wasn't. It had been the first and foremost thing on her mind since the instant she'd started believing what had happened to her.

She couldn't stay in 1862. Not if there was any possible way of getting home. Everything she'd told Hank had been true, every bit of her reasoning made sense. She had to go back to her own life, back to her family, back to where she belonged.

If only, when Hank held her, she didn't feel she belonged in his arms.

Well she didn't! So she had to shape up. Immediately. She was the one who'd be leaving—White Cloud willing. And since she was the one who'd be leaving, she was the one who had to draw the line.

She couldn't let this impossible relationship get any more impossible. She was certain her leaving was already going to be painful for both her and Hank.

She'd be a fool to do anything that would make the pain worse.

The last thing she wanted was for Hank to be hurt, for either of them to be hurt. So she'd damned well better keep her eyes—and all the rest of herself—off him.

She'd take his help. She had to take that from him. But nothing more. She wasn't about to take his heart.

She looked studiously away from Hank, over at Sam.

"Let me have another glance at those shoes, Miss James."

"Please call me, Erica."

"No, no I couldn't. Even if I wasn't convinced you two just concocted that crazy name, calling you by it wouldn't seem proper."

"I'd never remember to do it anyway, not with everything else you're telling me that I'm trying to cram into my head. Even if none of it's true, you're giving me wonderful ideas for stories."

Erica uncurled her legs, stretched one of them toward Sam and pulled her dress modestly up to her ankle.

"And you say they're . . ."

"Reeboks, Sam. And you're sure it's all right if I call you Sam?"

"Fine. Fine. Call me whatever you want. Just keep on with your stories."

Erica smiled, still trying to adjust her mental set to a youthful Mark Twain. Calling him anything more formal than Sam would seem strange.

"Well, Sam, Reeboks is just the brand name. The generic word is *sneakers*."

"Brand," Sam repeated, reaching over and running his finger hesitantly over the word *Reebok*. "Like

a brand on cattle. You want me to believe that in the future people brand shoes like cattle? Why on earth would they do that? Shoes aren't likely to wander off onto someone else's land, not without their owners wearing them. You don't have shoe rustlers in 1989, do you?''

"No," Erica told him, laughing. "The brand name on shoes isn't exactly the same as brands on cattle. It doesn't signify ownership. I mean, Reebok isn't *my* name. It's the name of the company that made the sneakers. I guess putting it on their product is a form of advertising.''

Sam shook his head for the hundred-and-first time. "Advertising on people's feet. Imagine that. But what's the use of advertising that gets covered by a dress?''

"This is a dress Hank bought for me in Mountainview. Dresses get a lot shorter. In the 1920s, then on-and-off over the years after that, women's dresses don't even reach their knees.''

In the glow of the fire Erica couldn't be certain, but she thought Sam began blushing at that news flash. She hurriedly changed topics.

"Sam, would you like me to tell you what becomes of you?''

"Of me? How would you know what becomes of me?''

"You're going to like the answer to that one. I know because you become famous—a famous writer.''

He stared at her skeptically. "Now you're playing to my vanity—just telling me that because Hank's mentioned I write, probably said I have higher aspirations than scribbling for the *Esmeralda Star*.''

"Yes, he did. And you make it, Sam. You make it right to the top. Your name becomes a household word."

"Samuel Clemens a household word?"

"Oh. Well, not exactly. You see, you're going to start publishing under a pseudonym."

"Really? You know . . . this may just be the strangest coincidence, but I've always thought Sam Clemens isn't a good name for an author. It's too ordinary. I've already published bits under various names—used Thomas Jefferson Snodgrass, then W. Epaminandos Adrastus Blab, for a while."

Erica laughed at the easy way the absurd names rolled off Sam's tongue. "I take it you've decided against those?"

"Yes. I need something shorter. Something people will remember easily. I've started using Josh for the odd piece. But maybe that's too common. I've been considering something more colorful. What do you think of . . ."

"Yes? What?" Erica held her breath. The pen name Mark Twain was about to be born. And she was a witness.

"What do you think of Huckleberry Finn?"

"Oh. Well, yes, that's certainly colorful—an interesting name. But you decide to save it for a character in one of the books you'll write. You choose something more solid sounding as your pen name."

"I do? What is it?"

Now what? How on earth did time travel work? Did she get to decide this little piece of American literary history? Give Mark Twain his name?

Since nobody else was saying anything, that must be the case.

"You go with Mark Twain. That's the name that becomes a household word."

"Mark Twain? Now I know for sure you've been joshing me! Mark Twain's not a name—it's a depth."

"A what?"

"A depth! Two fathoms—twelve feet. Takes me right back to my days as a riverboat pilot on the Mississippi."

Sam closed his eyes. "I can hear that leadsman now—standing at the bow of the *Paul Jones* with his line, testing the water's depth, shouting his findings back to the pilot house.

"He'd call out *M-a-r-k three* when the water was three fathoms deep—eighteen feet. Then I'd listen for his next call. If it was *M-a-r-k twain,* we had only twelve feet, and I knew we had to be mighty cautious because riverboats draw nine feet of water."

Sam shook his head once again. "Mark Twain's two fathoms, Miss James, not a danged name."

"Sam," Hank said, chuckling, "if Erica says you change your name to Mr. Two Fathoms, that's what happens."

"Nope. I'd never use a name as queer as Mark Twain. I might as well call myself Mr. Five-foot-nine.

"You've just overplayed your hand, Miss *Erica* James. You won't convince me any of these fantastic stories are true."

"All right, Mr. *Samuel Langhorne* Clemens," Erica told him with a grin. "Just remember you won't become famous until you're known as Mark Twain."

"What did you call me?"

"Pardon?"

"I said what did you call me."

"Mark Twain."

"No! No, you used my real name."

"I—I'm sorry. I don't know what you're getting at."

"My name! You used my middle name."

"Langhorne?"

"Langhorne?" Hank hooted. "I didn't think I could have heard you right the first time, Erica. Langhorne? What in blazes kind of name is that? Sounds like a breed of poultry."

Sam glared at Hank for an instant, then turned back to Erica. "How on earth did you know my middle name? Listen to Hank's reaction. That name's the last thing about me I'd admit to anyone. Yet you know it! How?"

"Well...Mark Twain's the name you used, but people do know your real name. In fact, I remember trying to find one of your books listed in a library catalog and having to look under Clemens, Samuel Langhorne. I'm not sure why. I guess librarians just like making things difficult."

"Well I'll be! Nobody in Nevada knows my middle name except my brother, Orion. And he's sworn to secrecy. So you must really be—"

"Sam," Hank said after a moment, "if I didn't know better, I'd think you're speechless."

"Mighty near, Hank. Mighty near." He stared at Erica curiously. "What about Hank? Does he become a famous writer, as well?"

"Hank? Why would Hank become a famous writer?"

"He hasn't told you he writes?"

"Well, he did mention something about it but—"

"My writing's nothing special, Erica," Hank interrupted. "Not like Sam's."

"Don't you believe him, Miss James. Hank's a wonderful writer. That's how we got to be friends.

"I was in Mountainview one day and dropped into Hank's office because...well, it's not important why. But the next thing I knew we were talking about writing and Hank was showing me some of his work. It's good. Damnable good. He should be trying to sell it."

"Really? I'd like to read it when we get back, Hank."

"Sam's exaggerating, Erica. It's not that good— just something I do as a hobby. I'm a physician. I enjoy writing stories but I just don't have time to sit doing it. Tell Sam more about what's going to happen to him."

"Well, I'm starting to feel like a fortune-teller but at least what I can tell you is good, Sam. You'll write several books. The best known of them is called *The Adventures of Tom Sawyer*. And you'll be in demand as a public speaker."

"Public speaker? I've never thought about that idea! A speaker. I like that."

Erica laughed. "You should. You become a successful humorist. And a lot of things you say during your talks, as well as things you write, become famous quotes."

"Really?" Sam's chest puffed up a little. "For example?"

"Well, I'm a Bostonian and one thing I recall striking me as humorous goes, 'Tomorrow night I appear for the first time before a Boston audience—4,000 critics.'"

Sam stared at her blankly. "I've never even been to Boston."

"Sam!" Hank admonished. "You'll say that sometime in the future. You're going to be in Boston in the future. That's how this works."

"Oh." Sam looked doubtful. "You mean I'll say that and people will actually think it's funny?"

"Extremely," Erica assured him.

"I'd best remember to say it then." Sam pulled a pencil and small notebook from his shirt pocket and wrote a few lines.

"What else do I say that's memorable?"

"Let's see...there's something about the difference between a starving man and a starving dog is that if you make the dog prosperous he won't turn around and bite you."

Sam nodded and scribbled. "That needs some work but I can use it."

"And one of my favorites is a play on an Aesop's fable. 'Familiarity breeds contempt—and children.'"

Sam made a little choking noise.

"I really say that? It sounds terribly indecent. I'm...I'm surprised a good woman like yourself would have heard it, would be repeating it."

"Maybe you say it quite late in life, Sam. As I recall, you live well into the twentieth century. You're going to see a lot of changes in the world. Good women become far less sheltered."

A rumble of thunder rolled across the sky.

"Wretched climate," Sam muttered. "A lady who goes visiting in Nevada should take her fan under one arm, her umbrella under the other and strap snowshoes to her back."

"I'm afraid I didn't come properly equipped," Erica teased. "I only brought my Reeboks."

"Well, we're going to be rained on for sure, Miss James. How about a mug of slumgullion? Then we'll fix up my tent for you."

"Slumgullion?" Erica shot Sam a hesitant smile. The greasy rabbit stew he'd served for dinner hadn't said much for his culinary skills. "Is slumgullion really something I might want a mug of?"

Hank laughed. "No, it isn't. But it also isn't what you're likely to get. Sam's just fond of the word—picked it up at some station stop on his trip from back East. But *his* slumgullion tastes a lot like coffee."

"You should be glad it does," Sam muttered. "The slumgullion I was served pretended to be tea, but there was too much dishrag and sand and old bacon rind in it to deceive the intelligent traveler.

"And it was served with week-old bread, as hard as pavement, and condemned army bacon. The United States wouldn't feed that bacon to its soldiers in the forts, so the stage company had bought it cheap for the sustenance of their passengers and employees."

"Sounds like a gourmet's delight," Erica offered, suspecting she'd just been treated to a Mark Twain tall tale.

Sam took his gun from his waistband, placed it on a nearby rock and bent to prepare his slumgullion.

Erica gazed at the large weapon. "When we were in Honey Lake Smith's," she admitted to Hank, "I was wishing you had ten guns that big instead of the little thing you carry."

"That little thing can do what's necessary," Hank told her. "And," he added, raising the level of his voice and checking to be sure Sam was listening, "just because a fellow totes a revolver doesn't mean he's a marksman."

Sam glanced over, grinning. "Can't keep secrets, can you Hank?"

Hank pretended not to hear. "Sam likes to dress the part, though. He'd as soon be seen without his trousers as without that navy revolver."

"It's not dressing the part at all!" Sam hollered defensively. "It's a simple matter of self-preservation.

"I admit I can't shoot worth doodle-d-squat, Miss James, but I have to wear that thing in deference to popular sentiment. Without it I'd be offensively conspicuous, a subject of unkind remarks. Why, if I stopped by Honey Lake Smith's for a drink without my navy, I'd be target practice.

"If it wasn't for that, I'd carry a pistol in my pocket like Hank does. It's safer. I doubt Hank's ever shot himself with his own gun."

"Ever done what?"

"Well, much as I hate to admit it, that's how Hank and I met, why I first dropped into his office. That damnable Colt got in my way, then turned on me in a temper and shot me in the leg.

"Just a flesh wound. But you notice," he added dryly, "I've learned to take the danged thing out of my waistband before I bend over."

Erica bit her lip, certain she shouldn't laugh.

THUNDER BEGAN RUMBLING louder and more frequently while they drank their coffee. An occasional lightning bolt flashed across the sky.

Sam drained his mug and grinned over at Erica. "How'd you fancy my slumgullion?"

"Best I've ever drunk."

"I like your way with words, Miss James. I surely do. And you weren't exaggerating about my becoming famous?"

"Not in the least."

"Well, Hank, if your lady friend's right, I'm going to make my fortune after all. That'll sure ease the pain of Higbie and me losing the Johnson. That claim was

guaranteed millions, and we were such fool dunder-
heads we—"

Lightening slashed the sky again—a blazing streak
of brightness splitting the black night.

Erica silently counted, waiting for the accompanying thunder's roar. Six seconds after the flash they
heard an enormous boom. The storm had progressed
to within a mile of them.

Sam moved the battered coffeepot away from the
fire. "We'd best get settled for the night. It looks like
we're about to be drenched."

Erica sighed, knowing Sam was right, yet wishing
she could sit by the fire all night listening to his stories.
She was dead tired. But she and Hank would be leaving in the morning and there was still so much she
wanted to learn.

She'd had no chance to ask about Orion Clemens—how he'd come to be territorial secretary of
Nevada. She hadn't even known Mark Twain had a
brother until a few days ago, let alone a brother with
political power.

And now she was curious about what had happened with Higbie and the Johnson claim. If she
ever...no...*when* she got home, she'd buy a collected works of Mark Twain. Maybe that would give
her the answers.

"You'll take the tent, Miss James. Hank and I'll be
fine out here by the fire."

"Oh, no! You'd get soaked. We can all share the
tent."

Erica caught the look Sam gave Hank and silently
groaned. She was being unseemly again.

Well, to hell with being seemly. In her world, you
didn't let your friends sit out in the rain. And, even in

someone else's world, she'd feel awfully guilty doing it.

"Erica," Hank said quietly, "I realize you're just trying to be kind, but it isn't—"

"I know what it isn't, Hank. But I'm not merely trying to be kind. Really. I'm being selfish, as well. What would I do if you caught your death of cold?"

"I won't."

"But just suppose you did! What would I do then? Wander back to Honey Lake Smith's on my own? If I could even find the way? Then hitch up Barleycorn and drive her back to Mountainview?

"Hank, aside from having to face that crew at the inn—those charmers with glints of rape and murder in their eyes—I don't know a harness from a rein. And, even if I did get back, I couldn't talk to White Cloud on my own."

"I need you, Hank! And the world needs Mark Twain. I don't want either you or Sam dying of exposure."

"People don't die of exposure in July," Hank pointed out with infuriating logic.

"Shucks, Hank!" Sam interrupted. "Don't be so all-fired certain. This *is* Nevada. I reckon men have died of exposure every month of the year in this godforsaken territory."

"Tarnation, Sam! Mind your own pot! Aside from any other considerations, I doubt there's room for three people in that danged tent of yours."

"It is a mite small," Sam agreed. "Tell you what, Miss James. Hank and I will start off out here. If the storm gets really bad, we'll squeeze in with you for a bit. Then you can tell me more about, the future."

"Well..." Erica glanced at the tent. It was awfully tiny. "Well...you both promise to come inside if it does anything more than spit?"

"Spit? Spit?" Sam asked, glancing from Erica to Hank. "She certainly does have an interesting way with words, doesn't she?"

Sam vanished into the tent for a few moments, then reappeared with a couple of blankets.

"She's all ready for you, Miss James. Have a good night's sleep."

Erica settled in, only banging her head once against the low roof. But what did a five-foot-high roof matter? She was too tired to stand anyway.

She snuggled under the blanket, wondering how long it took to get used to sleeping in a dress, glad she wouldn't be in the wilderness long enough to find out.

The air inside the tent was stale. She shifted a little so her head was nearer the opening. Even an occasional breath of fresh air would be welcome.

She squirmed about uncomfortably; there was no soft spot to be found. Lying on a canvas sheet spread over the ground was far from luxury. But at least she wouldn't get wet.

Erica propped herself up onto one elbow and peered out, smelling the impending rain.

Hank and Sam had bedded down between the fire and the tent's opening.

"Good night," she called to their shadowy forms.

"'Night," two voices echoed.

She sank back onto the floor, aching from head to toe, certain sleep would come instantly.

Instead, she lay awake, staring into the darkness of the stuffy little tent, anticipating the storm. From outside, she could hear Hank and Sam chatting quietly—could just make out what they were saying.

She told herself not to listen to their conversation. Her ears ignored her, straining to catch Sam's next words.

"I'm plum sorry I'm no help with this time travel, Hank. Are you serious about going back to see White Cloud?"

"I promised Erica I would. I won't have any choice unless my friend in Boston comes up with something."

"Think the old woman knows anything that could help?"

"I suspect she does. Erica said White Cloud looked mighty smug when she saw those shoes... as if she wasn't the least bit surprised... as if she already knew the entire story.

"And that old shaman's amazed me before this, Sam. She knows about the dangedest things. She must be at least a hundred years old, and she's had all the tribal secrets passed on to her."

The men fell silent.

A few moments later, Sam spoke again.

"How's the boy, Hank?"

"About the same."

"No improvement?"

"It's hard to say. Sometimes I think he's growing stronger. Then he has a bad spell and I start wondering, all over again if there's really any hope."

Erica wriggled closer to the opening. They were obviously talking about Billy! But what—

"I'm certain," Hank went on, "he's better than he'd have been if we'd stayed in Boston. The mountain air's good for him. But, beyond that, I'm not certain at all."

"Sorry to hear that," Sam mumbled. "He's a fine lad."

"He is," Hank agreed so quietly that Erica could barely hear him. "And with my being a physician it seems there should be something more I can do, some way I could manage to... I'd give anything to make him well..." His words trailed off.

Erica waited in the darkness, listening for one of the men to speak again, her heart aching for Hank. The pain in his voice had been obvious.

She'd thought Billy was smaller and paler than he should be. But what was wrong with him?

Outside the tent silence reigned, broken only by the chirping of crickets and sputters from the fire.

Somewhere in the distance a coyote wailed. Or was it a wolf? A wolf that howled like Billy's dog?

Finally, she shifted away from the opening a little. The conversation had ceased. She wasn't going to learn any more tonight.

NOISE ERICA couldn't identify awakened her, but when she opened her eyes all she could see was blackness. She didn't know where she was. Her senses finally identified the surroundings as an ancient basement—cold and damp.

Then, gradually, her brain defined reality more accurately. She was lying on an incredibly rough and soaking wet sheet. Her backside felt like a block of ice.

She leapt up quickly, bumping her head against a roof of sloping canvas. It released a stream of cold water that poured down her back. She shrieked.

Muttering under her breath, she pulled the blanket up and rubbed it over her wet hair.

Being treated to a freezing shower was a terrific memory aid. She was inside Sam's tent—inside Sam's sopping wet tent.

Puddles had spread across most of the floor. And if the canvas was saturated, Hank and Sam must be wrinkled as prunes.

Erica scrambled into a crouching position so only her sneakers and the hem of her dress were in water. Raindrops pelted noisily down onto the tent—hundreds of them sploshing against the fabric every second.

She hiked her dress up and duck-walked a few steps to the opening, still puzzled by the curious cacophony of sounds.

The sight outside was even stranger than the noises. Through the darkness and the rain, she was just able to make out a line of human figures moving along the ditch by Sam's camp. She rubbed her eyes, trying to see more clearly.

Indians! The people were Indians. Men, women and children. There were at least thirty of them slopping along, single file, through the mud swamp beside the ditch. Every one of them was loaded down with bundles.

Several of the men were leading horses carrying packs. One of the animals, she was certain, had a collapsed teepee strapped to its back.

A large dog moved into her line of vision, pulling a sled of some sort through the muck. That, too, was loaded with belongings. Another sopping dog ran loose alongside its companion, barking frantically.

The overall picture was one of noise and confusion. The Indians seemed in a desperate hurry.

Erica hesitated by the tent's opening, staring at the huge, muddy expanse of ground before her, deciding whether she wanted to brave the full force of the elements, whether seeing this parade up close would be worth getting even wetter... and dirtier.

Then she spotted Hank and Sam, splashing along beside one of the braves, talking to him.

She waddled backward from the opening, still able to see the Indians but out of range of the driving rain. Whatever was going on, she'd wait inside to hear about it.

Hank and Sam continued walking with the little line of soaked humanity until Erica lost sight of them.

The last of the Indians passed by. She peered anxiously after him, waiting for Hank to reappear.

When he finally did, he, then Sam, crowded into the dark tent without waiting for an invitation.

They could barely move inside but, apparently, a downpour changed their definition of what was seemly.

"Well?" Erica demanded, breathing shallowly. Both men reeked of wet wool. "What's going on? Who are those Indians? What are they doing out there?"

"They're a band of Shoshoni," Hank answered. "Members of Chief Qudazoboeat's tribe. They were camped beside the Walker River but decided it's going to flood. They're heading for higher ground."

"In the middle of the night?"

"Erica," Hank said dryly, "floods don't wait for daybreak."

"I know that! The world does still have floods in 1989! But is the river really going to overflow? How far away is it from here?"

Erica peered at Hank in the darkness, wishing she could see his face more clearly.

He was pressed closely against her. His suit was drenched and cold but, already, she could feel the warmth of his body beneath it.

Oh, Lord! How could she possibly be finding his nearness arousing at a time like this?

"How far's the Walker from here?" Hank repeated her question to Sam.

"Well . . . I think it's a fair piece."

"What do you mean, you think?" Hank snapped. "Don't you know?"

"'Course I know!" Sam shot back through the darkness. "I just told you. It's a fair piece."

"Well, I'm certainly relieved to hear that precise an answer."

"Dammit, Hank! I'm a writer and I'm a prospector. But I'm not a danged surveyor. The Walker's far enough away that we're safe here. Does that satisfy you?"

"Then, as long as we're safe," Hank said evenly, ignoring Sam's final question, "we might as well get as comfortable as possible and try to sleep."

He wrapped his arm around Erica's shoulder. "Lean against me, Erica. That sure won't keep you dry, but at least you'll feel warmer."

Hank unbuttoned his jacket and drew her closer yet, so that her body curled against his, so that her cheek was resting against his shirt, against the wet warmth of his chest. She could feel his heart beating, precisely attuned to the deep, throbbing ache of desire that had begun within her.

She tried to remind herself she didn't belong with Hank . . . would be leaving his world soon . . . couldn't let this impossible relationship get any more impossible . . . that would only hurt them both.

She'd convinced herself of all those things earlier tonight. Hadn't she? She wasn't certain. At the moment, she couldn't seem to think straight. The only thought in her head was that Hank had been right. Leaning against him was making her feel warmer... much warmer... hot, in fact.

She shut her eyes, telling herself it was merely the way the three of them were crowded into the tent that was making her hot, hoping she could will herself asleep before her blood began to sizzle.

CHAPTER EIGHT

"JUMPING JACKRABBITS!" a man screamed.

Erica exploded from sleep, uncertain whether she'd merely dreamed the shout.

She blinked in the darkness, awake but not alert, grasping for reality, not quite able to catch it. She wasn't in her bed in Boston. She wasn't in a bed at all. And she wasn't alone!

Her mind began chugging. But it was processing stimuli in slow motion while her senses whirred in fast forward.

She could hear the rush of Niagara Falls, smell a rain forest, feel the warm, reassuring body beside her jerk away, leaving her instantly frozen.

Then strong arms surrounded her once more, pulling her to her feet.

Her head hit soaked fabric. It drained water onto her. Dimly, she realized that had happened before.

"Erica! Wake up!"

A man was shaking her. Hank! Details rushed into clarity. The Broken Hill Mine and Hank and 1862 and Sam Clemens and the Sierra Nevada.

And . . . and, oh, Lord, water inside the tent, ankle high and reaching rapidly for her calves.

"Come on!"

Hank shoved her toward the opening. Sam was already scrambling through it. She followed him blindly into the night—into the shallow lake that surrounded the tent.

Hank scuttled out after them, muttering obscenities under his breath.

The three of them stood, for a shocked moment, simply staring at the scene greeting them.

The storm had ended; the sky was clearing. Moonlight illuminated water. Water everywhere, lapping higher, tickling icily against the backs of Erica's knees. Her dress clung to her legs, pulling heavily with the water's weight.

The deepening water around them rippled calmly. But, to their left, what had earlier been a dry ditch was now a channel filled to the brim with raging water.

The torrent churned along, foaming wildly, sweeping ahead at furious speed, carrying dark shadows of brush and logs and heaven only knew what else.

Along stretches of the ditch, water roared forward level with the bank. But, in a hundred different places, it was overflowing, turning the land that sloped down to the tent into a water slide.

"You camped in a damned hollow, Clemens!" Hank yelled. "And I'd wager that ditch is carrying runoff from the Walker. Those Shoshoni were right! We're in the midst of a flash flood! Let's get the bejesus out of here!"

Hank grabbed Erica's hand, wheeled around and started sloshing in the opposite direction from the ditch. Erica pressed through the thigh-high water after him.

Ahead of them, outlined in the moonlight, was the hill they'd descended after John Cready had left them yesterday.

"My tent!" Sam shouted over the water's rush.

Hank paused. Erica stopped beside him. They glanced back. The water was almost lapping Sam's waist.

"Never mind your damned tent!" Hank bellowed. "Worry about your damned hide! Or do you aim to drown?"

Sam stared at his tent for a final second then turned and waded after them, uttering a string of the most unseemly words Erica had heard since she'd arrived in the nineteenth century.

The water reached her chest at the same moment she felt the hill's incline beneath her feet.

They scrambled all the way to the top, then turned back, sinking to the ground, breathing hard, dripping wet. Erica scuffed out of her sneakers and began wringing the bottom of her dress.

She'd practically frozen in the water, but the exertion of escaping it had started her perspiring. Now, in the cool night air, she was undoubtedly a candidate for pneumonia.

She watched Hank and Sam tugging off their boots. They each poured out about a gallon of water. She revised her thought. There were three candidates for pneumonia here.

The moonlight had grown brighter and the water level higher. Below, only the roof of Sam's tent was still visible.

As they gazed down, the little structure gave up its hold on the ground, floated to the surface in a ragged canvas sheet, and began drifting away like an uninflated rubber raft. Sam's battered coffee pot bobbed along after it.

"Everything I owned was inside that tent!" Sam exclaimed.

"Don't worry about what you owned," Hank snapped. "Losing it won't matter for long. You're going to be a rich, famous writer. And the sooner that happens—the sooner you stop playing at being a prospector—the better!

"Otherwise, Sam, you're going to kill some unsuspecting friend with your blamed idiocy! In a hog's eye we were camped a fair piece from the Walker River. Didn't it occur to you that where there's a hollow looking like a creek bed, there's sometimes water. Especially after a storm? A whole *lot* of *cold* water?

"We're all chilled to the bone! You go on to be Mark Twain. But maybe Erica and I end up dying of exposure after all—in July in this damned territory!"

"I can't die," Erica muttered wearily. "I've been giving that some thought. I can't possibly die because I haven't been born yet. I was born in 1958. If I was born in 1958 I can't die in 1862."

"Does that logic make sense to you?" Sam looked quizzically at Hank, apparently eager to deflect the subject of conversation from his idiocy.

"About as much sense as anything's made to me in the past little while. And it seems both you and Erica survive. But that still leaves me." Hank shivered.

Erica eyed him closely. He looked even colder and wetter than she felt—definitely appeared to be the prime pneumonia candidate. And his absurd reasoning might even make sense. She knew her future—and Sam's. Whereas Hank...

"You can't die either, Hank. I need you, remember?" She instinctively moved closer and snuggled against him. "And what *you* need is a little body heat." She reached for one of his hands and began rubbing it between her own.

"What you both need," Sam muttered, "is a bundling board."

"A what?" Erica asked.

"You tell her." Sam shoved himself up and strode off into the darkness.

Erica glanced a question to Hank.

"What Sam was implying," he said quietly, "is it isn't proper for us to be sitting like this...touching...you taking my hand the way you did."

"Oh. The old *seemly* chestnut again."

"What?"

"Nothing. Nothing. Hank. I'm sorry. You're right."

Of course he was right. What on earth was the matter with her? How many times was she going to have to tell herself to keep her hands off Hank before she started listening to herself.

"You just looked so cold," she mumbled, sliding away and letting go of his hand.

He quickly grabbed her wrist and drew her back to him. "Look, Erica, I was telling you what Sam was implying, not what I was thinking. Not what I was thinking in the least."

"I like you sitting beside me. I like your body heat. It...well, you take me by surprise sometimes, that's all. I understand things—customs—are different in your world, but I don't know how to react when one of those differences sneaks up and hits me. I mean, well, I know how I react. I just keep thinking I shouldn't... You see, Erica, you do things no virtuous woman would do. Yet I'm certain you are—virtuous, I mean—if that's what it's still called in 1989."

"Well, the word isn't used all that much," Erica murmured, embarrassed. "But, by 1989 standards, I imagine I'd qualify as virtuous."

"I knew you would." Hank smiled. "But you see, today, men and women who aren't married or engaged don't hold hands, not unless they're dancing. And even then their bodies don't touch.

"I realize everything becomes very different, Erica—even clothes. You said women expose their knees in your world. Here, even a woman's ankle is a sight to behold."

An ankle, Erica thought, conscious of her dress's high neckline. She'd better not elaborate on what else was routinely exposed in 1989.

"I understand things change, Erica. But there's so much I'm not certain of. I know what a kiss or holding hands means in 1862. I'm not sure what they mean to you."

Erica gazed at Hank, incredibly touched by his effort at expressing his feelings. Considering the era of the sensitive male was generations away, Hank was taking a great shot at being sensitive.

But she was at a loss about what to say. Kissing Hank meant an awful lot more to her than she wished it did. Probably a lot more than she should admit to him.

She was so tempted to let nature take its course while she was in Hank's world. But a tiny voice of sanity kept screaming at her to be careful about things she did.

It was *his* world, after all. Perceptions of "nature's course" had apparently changed considerably since 1862. What she considered virtuous enough was undoubtedly promiscuity in Hank's view.

She tried to think. It was difficult with Hank sitting so close beside her. She'd be best to avoid talking about the two of them while her emotions, rather than her brain, seemed to be in control.

"I...let's discuss this tomorrow, Hank. After we've left Sam. You were about to tell me what a bundling board is."

"Bundling's an old custom."

"Yes?" Erica looked at him closely. He appeared extremely ill at ease with this topic. "What custom?"

"Well...unmarried couples, courting couples that is, can be in the same bed. Fully dressed, of course. But there's a board between them...so..."

Erica nodded her understanding, only too aware that if she was ever in a bed with Hank she wouldn't want to be fully dressed. She wouldn't even want to be unfully dressed. And she wouldn't want any darned board between them.

But things weren't going to go that far.

Although Sam, she mused, had thought she and Hank looked like a courting couple.

Were their feelings that obvious?

They must be.

Did that mean her emotions were winning the battle against her tiny voice of sanity?

She didn't know.

And what about Hank? He'd said that in 1862 men and women didn't even hold hands unless they were engaged. And he was an 1862 man. On the other hand, he *was* definitely very much a man. Sooner or later, despite the century, wouldn't he...?

Erica stared into the darkness, willing Sam to return and chaperon her and Hank for the remainder of the night.

HALF AN HOUR after they'd collected the buggy and left Honey Lake Smith's, Erica realized she was breathing more easily. Despite the reassuring brightness of the morning, she'd half expected one of the disreputable characters from the inn to follow them and waylay them along the trail.

But by now surely they'd traveled far enough to be safe from that threat.

And Hank had said they could make it all the way to Mountainview by dark. The route back was mainly down hill. Despite the rocky trail, Barleycorn was having a far easier time than she'd had pulling the buggy yesterday.

Erica gazed ruefully at her dress once more, certain it would never be white again, that it would forever remain the grayish-brown color of flood water.

She didn't even want to imagine what condition her face and hair must be in.

She folded her hands into her lap, trying to hide her dirty fingernails. She'd washed her hands at Honey Lake Smith's but that hadn't done much good. The water in the bucket had been far from clean.

She glanced at Hank. He could pass for a man who'd spent the past week ploughing a wet field.

Her dress was filthy, but at least the cotton had dried. She could smell that Hank's suit was still damp, and little clots of dirt clung tenaciously to the wool. There were even specks of mud in his beard. And his hair was standing every which way. He looked worse than a panhandler in the Boston Common.

So why did she have an almost uncontrollable urge to slide across the buggy seat and sit closer to him?

She forced herself to shift a few inches farther away.

If she kept her distance from Hank and pretended the chemistry between them didn't exist, they'd both

be far better off. Because she'd be going home soon.
She just knew she would!

Hank had said he'd stop in Aurora to send another
telegraph to his friend at Harvard. So they'd know
soon if there'd be information coming. With any luck,
a reply would reach Mountainview tomorrow.

And if there was nothing about time travel at Harvard, Hank would take her to see White Cloud.

White Cloud knew the secret. Erica had been certain of that from the start. And, after Hank's conversation with Sam last night, she was sure Hank thought
so, too.

White Cloud knows about the dangedest things,
he'd said. *She's had all the tribal secrets passed on to
her.*

So, failing Hank's Harvard connection, White
Cloud would help them . . . she hoped.

If that wasn't the case . . . well, there was no point
worrying about that possibility unless it became reality.

Hank glanced over at her. "What are you day-
dreaming about?"

"Uhh . . . I was just wishing I'd had more time to talk
with Sam. I'm curious about his brother—what he's
like, how he ended up with a political appointment in
Nevada."

Hank chuckled. "Orion's about as different from
Sam as he could possibly be. He's ten years older,
pious and priggish. Sam originally came along with
Orion to be his private secretary. But that only lasted
about two weeks. Orion was driving Sam so crazy that
he packed up, left Carson City and headed south, determined to become a Nevada Nabob."

"A what?"

"That's what we call fellows who get rich by mining."

"Oh. Well, if Orion's such a jerk—"

"A what?"

"That's what we call fellows who are pious and priggish and drive their brothers crazy."

Hank rewarded her with a grin.

"Anyway," Erica hurried on, trying to ignore the little rush that engaging grin sent through her bloodstream, "if Orion's such a jerk, how did he get to be territorial secretary? It sounds like a pretty impressive position."

"It is. The appointment was a reward—for Orion's work during Lincoln's presidential campaign. Orion's an abolitionist, and he owned a newspaper back East. It gave Lincoln a lot of support."

"I see." Good grief. Even Honest Abe had practiced political patronage.

"Was there...were you thinking about anything else, Erica?" Hank gazed at her expectantly.

She bit her lip, not wanting to bring up the subject but, yes, there was something else she wanted to talk about.

That conversation she'd eavesdropped on last night had been repeating itself in her mind—the entire conversation, not merely the bit about White Cloud. Something was wrong with Billy's health.

She didn't know much about medicine, but there'd been so many advances since 1862. Possibly, she knew something Hank didn't.

She hesitated, uncertain how he'd react, yet wanting to ask about his son. If there was anything she could do to help, it would make up a little for all Hank had been doing for her.

"Hank...I overheard you and Sam talking last night...about Billy."

"Oh?" Hank stared straight ahead.

"I—I guess it's none of my business...I just thought...There've been a lot of discoveries over a hundred and twenty-seven years. And a lot of changes in medical treatment. I—I probably don't know anything about what's wrong with Billy, but I might."

"I guess you might," Hank admitted, glancing at her. "I wasn't really trying to cut you off. Well...maybe I was. I don't talk about this much. I want Billy to live as normal a life as possible. Don't want him to start thinking he's an invalid."

"He seems healthy, Hank—the way he races around."

"He's fine most of the time. Then he has an attack. They're only occasional bouts but, each time, it takes him a little longer to recover. And, each time, the recovery doesn't quite bring him back to where he was."

Erica pictured Billy running out the door with Cheyenne at his heels. He was such a sweet little boy. She swallowed hard. "What does he have, Hank? What's wrong with him?"

"Consumption. He's had consumption since he was four. That's what his mother died of."

Hank's voice was steady and controlled. Erica sensed, rather than heard, his pain.

"Consumption," she murmured, recalling the deep way she'd heard Billy cough the other day. "That's the same thing as tuberculosis, isn't it?"

Hank glanced over at her again. "Yes. Most people still call it consumption. The word *tuberculosis* is becoming more common, though.

"And you obviously know about it, Erica. I guess that means it's still prevalent in 1989. I—I'm sorry to learn that. I've always hoped there'd be a cure...before it was too late for Billy."

"But there is a cure, Hank. I mean someone does discover one. Tuberculosis isn't a serious problem anymore—at least not in developed countries."

Hank reined Barleycorn to a rapid halt, staring at Erica with excitement in his eyes. "A cure? What? When?"

"I—I'm not certain. I know tuberculosis isn't common anymore. And it's curable. Let me think for a minute."

Erica ordered her brain to focus on its tiny store of knowledge about T.B., praying her memory was retaining something more than she'd already told Hank.

He was watching her with obvious impatience, waiting for her to continue.

"Antibiotics!" The word popped into her head and out of her mouth simultaneously. "I think that's it, Hank. They use antibiotics to cure tuberculosis."

Hank's shoulders sank visibly. "Anti...biotics," he repeated slowly. "Which are?"

"Oh." Erica felt her own body sag, felt a sudden hollowness in the pit of her stomach as she realized antibiotics didn't exist yet. She racked her brain, searching for more information.

"Antibiotics are drugs." She spoke slowly, not wanting to run out of words. Hank was clearly hanging on each one she uttered.

"And when? When are they discovered?"

"I'm not sure I know. I don't think...I'm certain they weren't around during the first world war. They were discovered sometime after it ended."

"The first world war. I remember you telling me a little about the world wars but I can't recall... The first one isn't any time soon, is it Erica?"

She shook her head, not trusting herself to speak.

"When? What year?"

She took a deep breath, feeling as if she was about to deliver a death sentence. "World War I began in 1914."

Hank merely turned away from her and stared at the scenery.

"I see," he eventually murmured, clicking Barleycorn's reins.

They started off along the trail once more.

Erica's eyes were blurred, her throat was stinging. A mental argument was going on inside her head.

One imaginary voice was telling her to leave well enough—or bad enough—alone. A second was saying she should go ahead and ask what she wanted to know. Sooner or later she'd ask. Or Hank would volunteer the information. They might as well get it over with now.

The second voice won.

"Hank...is consumption fatal?"

The silence lasted forever.

"Eventually it most always is," he finally said.

ERICA STOOD IN THE TWILIGHT, waiting while Hank fetched Billy.

They'd left Barleycorn at the livery stable, then walked through the cool evening to the McCully's house.

Hank had suggested Erica come inside with him but she'd declined. Whtever impression the locals of Mountainview had formed of her from a distance, meeting people while she was covered with mud wouldn't enhance it.

The McCullys' door opened. Hank reappeared, his features barely visible in the faint light. He was alone.

Erica's heart skipped a beat. Something had happened to Billy while they were away! She took an involuntary step forward, then paused. From what she could make out, Hank didn't look upset.

She waited for him to reach her. "Is Billy all right?"

"Fine. But he's fast asleep."

Fine. Of course he was fine. Hank had said Billy suffered occasional attacks. But most of the time he was fine. She had to keep that in mind, had to keep treating him like a normal little boy. She couldn't dwell on what would become of him . . . not when there was nothing she could do about it.

They started the short walk, along a footpath, toward the back of Hank's house.

"The boys had a busy day," Hank added. "Mrs. McCully suggested Billy'd be better off staying where he is. If I woke him, he'd be awake half the night, wanting me to retell Sam's latest stories.

"Besides, it's better for you if he stays there till morning. I imagine you'd like another bath. You wouldn't fancy Billy bursting in on you."

"Oh, I wasn't going to ask about a bath. That's so much work. I thought I could just make do with a basin of water."

They'd reached the house. Hank opened the kitchen door, shooting her a wry glance that was barely discernible in the growing darkness. "It would have to be a danged big basin."

Erica laughed. "I guess I must look like a mud **wrestler.**"

"A what?"

"It's...mud wrestling's a sport, sort of.... It's...just what it sounds like."

Hank lit an oil lamp, shaking his head. "People wrestle in mud?"

"'Fraid so."

"You live in a very strange world, Erica. I'll just go out to the shed and fetch the tub. I could do with a bath myself."

"Let me help get the water, Hank. Otherwise you'll be lugging it in all night."

"No. No, we'll use the same water. Ladies first, of course."

"That hardly seems fair! You'll get stuck with cold, dirty water. In my strange world, we'd probably share the hot, clean—"

Oh, Lord! She could barely keep from slapping her hand over her mouth. What had she been saying? How had that suggestion almost slipped out? It was a Freudian slip if she'd ever made one.

She could feel herself growing hot under Hank's gaze, suddenly certain her brain was fighting a losing battle, that her heart and body had ganged up to defeat rationality.

Every hour she spent with Hank, she was falling deeper in love. Every time he looked at her, the sexual tug she felt grew stronger. She wanted nothing more than to make love to him.

She felt so alienated in his world. But whenever she was close to him, that world seemed better. And the closer he was, the better it seemed.

Kissing Hank had started her imagining how fantastic being really close to him would be.

But if Hank truly thought their kissing was improper, he certainly wouldn't...

So she'd better make a major effort to curb her imagination—not to mention her longing.

But what if—she didn't even want to think about this—but what if it turned out she wasn't able to leave. She could be here for weeks yet—or months or years.

Her thoughts spun wildly. She wasn't certain what made sense any longer. All she was certain of was she wanted to make love to Hank Lockhart, that being in his arms made everything seem perfect. And that, when he looked at her with his warm black eyes, she wanted him more than she'd ever wanted any man.

She knew what she wanted. She just didn't have the slightest idea how what she wanted fitted into these bizarre circumstances.

Clearly, in 1862, nice girls didn't. But perhaps...people in their thirties...both previously married...feeling the way she and Hank did...in the incredible situation they were in? Did any of those factors change the ground rules?

She had no idea. But they were in Hank's world. And he was a gentleman. The only rational thing she could do was follow his lead.

She wanted Hank to continue believing she was virtuous. She'd begun caring desperately about what he thought of her. So she'd have to be extremely careful about what she said and did from now on.

She'd sit on her hands before she'd initiate anything further—before she'd instigate anything else he could possibly think was unseemly.

Yet if Hank pushed, even a little, she knew she'd give in to love, give in to what she wanted so badly that it was making her ache.

If Hank wanted to make love to her, if he made that clear, she certainly wouldn't fight the idea. Not when it was what she wanted too. She glanced back up at him, catching his gaze.

Hank stared at Erica, trying to decide if she was joshing about sharing their bath. She must have been. In her world men and women surely didn't...did they?

"Is that another 1989 custom, Erica?" he managed, his voice sounding reasonably normal to his ears. "Do men and women bathe together? Even men and women who aren't married? I mean do you—did you—bathe with men?"

"Well...not really... I mean people do...it isn't considered outrageous...but I didn't mean... I don't know why I even mentioned..." She shrugged and stopped babbling.

Hank continued to eye her closely. Despite the dirt on her face, he could see she was blushing.

"Not really." What in tarnation had she meant by that? Did women from the future bathe with men as a matter of course or not? Virtuous women? Was that the kind of thing that went on in her world?

Did Erica James bathe with men? Yes, that was the specific question he wanted an answer to. Because, if she did...if she thought it proper...

It just might be he hadn't been giving her world its due. Maybe he should make an effort to stop comparing everything she told him about 1989 with the way things were in the present.

Maybe he shouldn't be dismissing everything about her world as unseemly in comparison to his.

The idea of men and women bathing together was a perfect example. Perhaps it had merit. Aside from everything else, she'd made a good point. He wouldn't have to make do with cold, dirty water.

But the mere thought of Erica naked—of her naked with him—was sending throbs of pleasure along his manhood. He turned to the door. He'd better get that tub while he was still able to walk upright.

Somehow, Hank made it through the next hour—fetching the tub, building a fire in the stove, drawing water from the well, heating it. Erica had hovered about, chatting anxiously, then had disappeared upstairs to get towels.

Hank poured the last of hot water into the tub, called up to her that the bath was ready and retired to his office.

His thoughts, earlier, had been verging on the insane. They'd caused him physical discomfort and embarrassed Erica. He'd almost forgotten he was a gentleman. But he was. And, in 1862, a gentleman gave a woman her privacy.

He sat at his desk, thinking and listening. His ears strained at the faint sound of Erica coming down the stairs.

He heard—or was he merely imagining—the rustle of her dress dropping to the floor.

He definitely heard a little splash. Erica was in the tub.

He swallowed hard. The image floating before his eyes was driving him crazy! His body was screaming its desire. He wanted Erica James so badly it pained him. If only he knew what she wanted. If only he knew what she'd think, what she'd do if he— But he couldn't!

His thoughts raced wildly, each one in total conflict with the one before it. How could he be thirty-five years old and suddenly not know right from wrong, proper from improper?

How could he and Erica have learned two totally different sets of rules? Why didn't he know what hers were? Why hadn't he asked more questions about her world, gotten the relationship between 1989 men and women clearer in his mind?

How could he be sitting here not knowing what he should do?

But he did know! That realization struck with crystal clarity. He should do whatever it would take to keep Erica in his world—forever. Do whatever it would take to make her want to stay with him.

He wanted her to stay. He desperately wanted her to stay. If only he knew what he should do to keep her here.

He loved her. He wasn't certain when in blazes it had happened but, sometime during the past few bizarre days, he'd fallen in love with her.

And she loved him. He was certain she did. Maybe social customs had turned topsy-turvy over the years but human emotions just couldn't have changed that much.

The way she looked at him . . . the way she touched him. And that kiss she'd given him yesterday. Lord! That kiss had curled his toes and straightened other parts of him. Her kiss had promised things he'd never even imagined.

Yes, she loved him. But she didn't want to admit it—that was clear. Maybe she didn't even realize it. He'd suspected she was fighting her feelings for him. He was beginning to figure out why. If she gave in to them, she'd have to consider staying here with him. Wouldn't she?

Yes. That made sense. So he had to make her aware she loved him, had to convince her she didn't want to leave.

He had to! Because he couldn't lose her. He'd lost too many people he'd loved…and he was going to lose Billy. He had almost resigned himself to that sorrow.

But Erica! He'd never loved anyone as he loved her.

He'd loved Billy's mother, of course. But it had been a quiet affection, not the exhilarating, wild, emotional storm of his love for Erica. Just being near her sent his feelings whirling like a tornado.

He couldn't lose her. Even if there did turn out to be a way for her to go home, she had to decide she didn't want to leave. And he had to do what he could to make her decide that. But sitting here at his desk was doing absolutely nothing.

Maybe he should start acting more like the men she was accustomed to—make her believe his world wasn't so different from her own.

If only he knew precisely how men acted in 1989—knew what a man might do to make her want to stay with him.

If only he didn't feel so in the dark. He didn't want to do the wrong thing. But he had to do something soon because he might not have much time.

He had a horrible sense White Cloud actually did know the secret of time travel. If she did, he'd be obliged to ask her to help Erica go back.

And White Cloud was such an ornery old crow, she just might decide to help when he didn't really want her to!

Yes, he had to do something. But it had to be the right thing. And how was he supposed to figure out what that was?

He felt as if he was walking on quicksand. If he made a wrong move...

Erica had said bathing with men wasn't considered outrageous. Not considered outrageous. That left a whole lot of uncertainty in his mind about exactly what it *was* considered—what she considered it. But he'd have to take a chance.

Hank pushed back his chair and rose. He forced his legs to move to the door, took a deep breath and knocked.

"Erica?"

"Yes?"

"Erica...I was wondering if you'd like me to scrub your back."

"I...I haven't any clothes on, Hank."

"I know."

CHAPTER NINE

"JUST . . . JUST A MINUTE, HANK." The sound of Erica's voice came through the door between them in a mere whisper.

Hank swallowed, feeling twelve years old, imagining Erica in the tub. He could hear the sound of water sluicing. She was undoubtedly taking this moment to modestly cover herself with her hands. Oh, Lord! She had such tiny hands!

He had half a mind to flee out the front door of his office. But the other half was intent on him joining Erica in that bathtub.

He suddenly pictured how small it was. They couldn't possibly both fit into it! But she'd said, *in my strange world we'd probably share . . .*

Share. She'd definitely said share.

So there must be a way. He just wasn't thinking clearly enough to figure it out.

But if there'd been all those advances in medicine, there'd undoubtedly been advances in mechanics, as well.

Erica had used that tub before—knew its size. And she'd said share.

"Come in, Hank."

Come in! He grabbed the door handle, began turning it. It slipped in his grasp.

Frantically, he wiped his palm against his muddy trousers and tried again.

The door opened!

He heard a tiny choking sound escaping from his throat and hoped Erica hadn't.

He pushed the door fully ajar and stepped into the kitchen. His entire body turned rigid.

Erica was standing beside the tub, in a small puddle of water, with a white towel wrapped around her body.

Around *some* of her body. Erica was half naked! And totally beautiful! Naked from her toes to her ankles and up her legs. Oh! Her legs were incredible! And her creamy shoulders were exposed...and the swell of her breasts.

She'd washed her hair again. It was hanging wetly over her shoulders. That incredibly arousing long hair...lying on her bare, luscious shoulders.

Damnation! He'd been having sexual thoughts and physical reactions just imagining Erica in here. But hellfire! Reality bettered his imagination like an Arabian stallion would better a Mexican plug.

Except for that towel. Part of Erica was covered up by it.

He hadn't realized he owned such a large towel.

She smiled shyly at him. "I'm done, Hank. I didn't think you were going to join me. My back's already scrubbed. But I'll be happy to do yours."

"Mine?"

Oh, no! His voice had cracked. His voice hadn't cracked in fifteen years!

"Yes. Of course, yours. Hurry up before the water gets cold."

Hurry up? Hurry up and do what? Why had his brain stopped functioning?

"Come on, Hank. Get out of that suit. It's filthy."

Get out of that suit? Right here? In front of her? But she had that danged towel and he'd have nothing! And, in his present condition, he more than ever needed something to cover himself with!

"No. No, it's fine, Erica. I can scrub my own back. You go on upstairs."

"I don't mind, Hank."

"No. No, you needn't bother."

"Have you ever had your back scrubbed, Hank? By someone else, I mean?"

"No. No one else. My mother. There was my mother. But not since then."

"Well try it. You'll like it. A bath was what you came in here for, wasn't it?"

He glanced at her face again. Her smile didn't seem as shy as it had been. In fact, she looked as if she was quite enjoying this little scene. Brazen hussy!

He quickly reminded himself not to be judgmental. She wasn't a brazen hussy in 1989. In the future this would probably be a perfectly normal evening's activity.

And didn't he want Erica to feel at home in his world? Hadn't that been part of his marvelous plan to make her want to stay with him?

At the moment, he couldn't seem to remember what his plan had been at all.

But Erica obviously expected him to take off his clothes and get into that tub... in front of her.

He cleared his throat. If his voice cracked again he'd die of humiliation.

"Would you mind turning around, Erica?"

She grinned broadly, then turned her back to him.

Hank scrambled out of his jacket and shirt, his eyes never leaving Erica. The sight of that damp towel clinging to her behind was causing him excruciating discomfort.

He jerked his boots off, dancing first on one leg, then the other. Then he unbuttoned his trousers and stumbled out of them, moving as fast as he could, certain Erica would peek any moment.

She didn't.

He lowered himself into the tub, strategically arranged his hands, then sat in the water, not knowing what to do next, feeling as if he'd just stuck his head into a noose.

"I...do you scrub my back right away or after I finish the rest of me?"

Erica turned, her eyes flashing with apparent amusement.

He didn't see that anything about this sudden turn of events was the least bit funny. It was downright mortifying. He couldn't remember feeling so uncomfortable in his life.

How could anything remotely resembling what was happening be a normal activity in Erica's world? In anybody's world?

And how had he become the only one of them with absolutely nothing on?

"Why don't I scrub your back first, Hank? Then, if you like that..."

He forced a weak grin. Grinning was mighty hard to do under the circumstances but, given the look on Erica's face, she was obviously trying to be funny. Humor, he'd realized some time ago, had also changed a heap.

She gazed into the tub. "Hank, I need the soap. I'm afraid I left it in the water. It must be sitting on the bottom."

Hank stared down at his strategically placed hands.

The soap was on the bottom of the tub. And Erica wanted it. And his brain couldn't figure out how that soap was going to get from where it was into Erica's hand unless one of them fumbled around the bottom of the tiny tub for it.

He tried to decide which of the two available options for locating it would be worse. Either he had to move his hands or she—

"Oh," Erica murmured. "I brought a second wash rag down. I'll just get it while you find the soap."

She turned away.

Hank dove both hands to the bottom; his fingers touched the soap. It scooted away like a slippery fish. He cussed under his breath but finally managed to grasp it and bring it to the surface.

One hand holding the soap, the other covering what it could, he glanced at Erica.

She was heading back toward him, rag in hand, smiling calmly, as if this bath was an every day occurrence.

Of course, she'd said that in her world she showered every morning. She was accustomed to being naked and wet. But he wasn't.

And that was the least of what he wasn't accustomed to that was happening at the moment.

Erica knelt down beside the tub, took the soap from him and swirled the wash rag in the water for a moment. Then she swished it up his back.

Warm water streamed down from his shoulders. She rubbed his wet skin with the soap, then rinsed the suds off with the rag.

He hadn't realized his back was itchy, but it must have been. That rough rag scrubbing against it felt mighty good.

But far more delightful than that feeling were the sensations Erica's hand was igniting. It swirled softly and gently along its soapy path, yet his skin tingled with a burning awareness of her touch.

She leaned closer to the tub, stretching to reach the far side of his back.

She was so close Hank could smell the soapy-fresh scent of her skin, could feel the towel she wore brushing against his arm.

He turned his head slightly and gulped. Her breasts were pressed against the edge of the tub, their naked fullness pushing up above the top of the towel mere inches from his eyes.

That T-shirt had clung to her breasts in an incredibly suggestive way. But this towel was actually exposing their bare flesh! And what if the towel slipped when she moved back?

"How does that feel, Hank?"

His gaze flew straight ahead once more. What? How did what feel? He felt as if he was about to explode.

If he didn't touch Erica within the next ten seconds he was going to die. He tried willing his body under control. His willpower had apparently died already.

"How does the back scrub feel, Hank?"

"Oh. Oh, the back scrub. Yes. Very nice. Very nice indeed."

"Would you like me to wash your hair for you?"

"Uhh . . . sure." Why not? As long as he was experiencing this twentieth-century debauchery, he should experience the entire process. Otherwise, he decided as Erica pushed his head forward, down into the water, he wouldn't be a fair judge of evenings in Erica's world.

Her fingers began working their magic on his scalp. He closed his eyes, protecting them from the soap, wishing he could peek at Erica again, wondering if she was peeking at him.

She pushed his head back down and scooted water through his hair, rinsing it.

She let go of his head.

He sat upright and opened his eyes.

"Well, Hank? Want me to do the rest of you?"

The rest? Of his body? Tarnation! There was only so much a man could take! Limits to how much debauchery he could stand in one evening! Did she want him to jump right out of his skin?

"No! I mean, thank you, but no. I reckon I can manage the rest of me just fine." He grabbed the wash rag from her hand before she could decide he merely wanted coaxing and started swishing water over his chest.

Erica stood up. "I left another towel on the dry sink. I'll get it for you."

Hank looked at her as she turned away. Oh, Lord! Sitting down in the tub, he could almost see up under the bottom of that towel she had on. If his eyes were just a little lower...

He fended off the ungentlemanly urge to sink farther into the water and concentrated on washing the rest of himself while Erica wasn't watching, certain he was setting a new time record for bathing.

Erica walked back across the kitchen, unfolded the towel and held it out, like a flag, in front of her.

"You done, Hank? I'll dry you off."

He stared at her in disbelief. She clearly wasn't holding that towel out for him to take from her while he sat in the tub. She was holding it waiting for him to stand up!

"Erica. I—"

There was a muffled thud at the outside door.

Erica froze.

Hank glanced from her to the door, waiting for another sound. The first one hadn't been a knock but there was definitely someone out there.

"Who could that be?" Erica hissed.

"Don't know."

"It's not Billy, is it?"

"No. Mrs. McCully would never let him come home this late. Maybe it's a patient looking for me."

"At the back door?"

"Could be. If he got no answer at my office. Give me the towel, Erica."

She quickly passed it to him. "Hank, I have no clothes on!"

"Yes. I'm aware of that." He wrapped the towel around himself as he rose, suddenly seized by vengeful pleasure at Erica's obvious discomfort.

"Hank, I can't let anyone see me standing here in a towel!"

He looked at her quizzically. "You're letting me see. Aren't I anyone?"

"Hank! You know what I mean!"

Ah-ha! So he definitely wasn't just anyone. And his thoughts about the two of them—about how she felt toward him—hadn't been just wishful imagining.

Erica was permitting him intimacies she wouldn't accord most men. Well hallelujah for that!

And if scrubbing his body, if standing around practically naked in front of him was acceptable, then some of the other 1989 customs she'd told him about...some of the courting customs...with not even a bundling board between them . . . He felt himself reacting to the mere idea.

"Hank, I'll run upstairs. Don't unlock the door until I'm out of sight!"

"Unlock the door? It's not locked. Nobody locks their door in Mountainview."

Erica shot him a look of total dismay, then turned and dashed for the stairs.

Hank tugged his trousers on, unable to stop grinning.

ERICA HUDDLED BENEATH the sheet wondering who'd been at the door. She'd heard Hank opening it as she dived into bed but hadn't heard voices.

What if it was a burglar? That would explain why the noise had been more a thump than a knock. But Mountainview mustn't have burglars. Otherwise, people would lock their doors.

What if it was a drunk, then? A mean drunk? One of Mountainview's barroom brawlers? A drunk might have thumped. What if it had been a mean drunk and he'd stuck a knife into Hank?

No. That was crazy.

No it wasn't! It would explain the lack of voices. What should she do? Get up, throw on some clothes and head back downstairs?

Yes. If anything was wrong, if Hank needed help...

She jerked the sheet down. Then she heard footsteps starting up the stairs and yanked it back up to her shoulders.

She sat staring into the hall, feeling as if she'd been plunged into a *Friday the 13th* movie. The doorway was barely visibly in the darkness. Stray shafts of moonlight afforded the only illumination.

If it wasn't Hank who was coming up the stairs, what on earth would she do?

The footsteps reached the upstairs hallway and started along it.

Erica opened her mouth, gearing up to scream.

A shadowy figure turned into the room.

"Hank!" Relief flooded her.

"Who were you expecting?"

"I—I wasn't sure. I didn't hear you talking to anyone downstairs."

"No. Cheyenne and I don't have many conversations." Hank fumbled with the candle on his dresser.

"Cheyenne? That noise at the door was Cheyenne?"

"Yes. He wanted to come inside. Mrs. McCully probably turned him away." The candle flickered to life, sending a faint, warm glow into the bedroom. "She doesn't mind Billy staying there in the least, but Cheyenne makes her a mite nervous."

"I can't imagine why," Erica lied.

She eyed Hank. He'd only taken time to put his pants on before letting the dog in. The dim light was casting shadows onto his naked chest, catching glints in his still-damp chest hair, defining the firm musculature of his shoulders. Minutes ago, she'd been washing those shoulders....

Bathing Hank had certainly tested her resolve not to instigate anything with him. The back scrub had seemed like a hilarious idea when he'd tapped on the kitchen door. But it had almost been her undoing.

She swallowed hard, extremely aware she was naked under the thin sheet, wondering if Hank was even half as conscious as she of the tinyness of this bedroom, wondering if the room had really grown incredibly hot or if it was her.

"I reckon," he mumbled, "I should get along to Billy's room now...get bunked into his bed...."

His words trailed into silence but he didn't move. He merely stood, watching her, his presence filling the room.

His nearness was overwhelming her senses. He was so close to her that with a single step he could . . .

He did!

He stepped across to the bed and tentatively sat down on the edge of the mattress. His glance lingered for a moment on the towel she'd been wearing. It was lying in a heap on the floor.

His gaze drifted to Erica's face, then he reached out, brushed a lock of damp hair back and cupped her chin with his hand.

She felt her entire body dissolving into liquid desire.

She shivered. Or was it a tremble?

Hank ran his fingertips along her cheek, sending a second tremor through her.

"Do you feel cold, Erica? You didn't catch a chill standing around in that skimpy towel, did you?"

Cold? Did she feel cold? Lord, no! She felt as if she was in the midst of an inferno.

She merely shook her head, not trusting her voice, not certain what direction Hank intended to take this scene, not entirely sure she was reading him accurately.

Her body was crying out with longing for him. He couldn't possibly be having any problems reading her.

Yet he simply sat, gazing at her in the faint light, making no further advance.

"Do I look sick?" she finally tried. "Is this a professional examination?"

He smiled the sexiest looking smile she'd ever seen. "No, you don't look sick. Not in the least. But you were shivering."

"Are you uncomfortable about me being in here, Erica? Are you nervous with me sitting on the bed?"

"A little," she whispered.

"If we were in your world—in your bedroom—would you be?"

"I—I don't think so."

"Then don't be anxious here. You're still you, Erica. And I'm just me." Hank softly stroked her cheek.

All she was aware of were physical sensations—the gentleness of Hank's touch, the deep, rich timbre of his voice, the way her skin was tingling under his caress, the firm arousal of her nipples, the aching throb in her private place and the clean, enticing, masculine scent of Hank.

There was no smell of bay rum. There was only the raw, sexy, animal smell of Hank Lockhart.

She wanted to press her nose against his skin, breathe in his intoxicating, personal allure. She forced herself to remain still.

"Hank, I guess...I guess what's making me nervous is that I know I don't belong here."

"But you do, Erica."

His fingers channeled a stream of heat down her neck, began a feather-light circular motion on her shoulder.

She felt a rush of liquid warmth and bit her lip, biting back a moan.

"You do belong here, Erica. You definitely belong here—with me." He paused for an eternity. "I love you. You belong with me because I love you."

Hank's whisper filled the room, echoed in the recesses of Erica's mind.

He loved her! But, under the circumstances, that was absolutely terrible. Wasn't it? Wasn't it every bit as terrible as the fact she'd fallen in love with him? Yes! It was awful.

So why was his declaration thrilling her to pieces?

"Oh, Hank." Her heart, she realized, not her mind, was speaking. And she was helpless to silence it. "Hank, I love you, too. But time can't stand still and—"

Hank placed a finger against her lips. "Erica, if I love you and you love me, then whether it's 1862 or 1989 or any year in between simply doesn't matter.

"The only thing that matters is us. We're both here—now. And all that matters is this tiny magic pocket of time we've found together. It's our time, Erica. Yours and mine."

He trailed his hand slowly down her arm, fanning the flames of the fire smoldering within her.

"Erica . . . if we were in your world . . . what would I do now? What would you want me to do?"

"I—I don't imagine you'd think it seemly, Hank."

"Let's take that chance. I might surprise you."

Erica gazed into Hank's soft black eyes, seeing the moment of truth reflected in them. If she made love with Hank, would she be passing the point of no return? Would she still want to go back to her own world?

Because she had to. If she could, if there was a way home, she would still have to go back. Her mind knew that. But at this precise moment in time, her mind clearly didn't have much say about things.

"If we were in my world now, Hank," she whispered, half afraid to tell him, "you'd take your trousers off."

Hank made a funny little choking noise in his throat. "Would I snuff the candle out first?"

"You might."

He rose and stepped over to the dresser. A second later, the room was in darkness once more.

Erica watched Hank's shadowy figure return to the bed, heard him fumbling with his pants, heard them drop to the floor.

And then he was sitting beside her again, naked in the stray moonlight—naked and gorgeous and so evidently wanting her.

"All right, Erica," he murmured, "what would we do next if we were in your world?"

Erica took a long, deep breath, wanting Hank more than she'd ever wanted any man.

Slowly, she reached across the space between them and circled the back of his neck with her hand. Slowly, she pushed aside the sheet. Slowly, she lay back, drawing him down beside her.

"Oh, my god," he whispered.

His body pressed the length of hers, hard against her softness, cool against her heat, his skin alive against her skin, his nearness making her quiver with anticipation.

Erica smoothed her palms down the muscles of Hank's back, relishing his body, loving the feel of his maleness.

Hank lay perfectly still for a moment, then shifted up a little and traced Erica's lips with his fingers.

She kissed his fingertips.

His mouth found hers in the darkness; his hand slipped gently down to her shoulder.

Hank's lips moved demandingly, sending ripples of delight through her. His beard brushed softly against her face.

His tongue teased, but only until she teased him in return. Then his kiss became deeper—searching her mouth, possessing it with his own.

Erica stroked the back of Hank's neck, playing with locks of his hair, her fingers drawing him ever closer, wanting him to kiss her even more deeply.

His hands lingered on the swell of her breasts, stroking them, tantalizing her.

Her body arched closer to Hank's, not needing guidance from her mind, responding with pure, primitive instinct. Her nipples were alive with desire for his touch. They brushed against his chest—hard, aroused buds, pressing into him, demanding his attention.

And then his hands slid over her breasts, cupping their fullness while his fingers began grazing slowly back and forth across her nipples, making her gasp with pleasure.

Clearly, she thought fleetingly, Hank needed no further instructions about what he'd do in her world— about what he'd do in any world.

His caresses were sending pulsating waves of liquid fire rushing through her body. And, lower, his hard arousal pressed its message of desire against her, sending her own longing soaring to an incredible height.

The throbbing ache within her was becoming painful.

Erica smoothed her hands down Hank's sides and grasped his hips, wanting him so desperately, she'd die if he didn't enter her soon.

His hands followed hers lower. He broke their kiss, and his lips nuzzled a warm, moist trail to her breasts. His tongue began teasing an impossibly fierce arousal from her taut nipples.

Erica moaned, pressing her hips to Hank's, her entire body screaming its need. Breathing was becoming difficult. There wasn't a fraction of her being, not a nerve ending in her body that wasn't being overwhelmed by the excruciating pleasure of Hank's lovemaking.

He began slowly stroking her inner thigh, his hand slipping infinitesimally higher with each leisurely caress.

Erica clutched his hips desperately, feeling herself losing control, loving his incredible touch but wanting more, needing all of him, needing him to be part of her.

She was verging on orgasm, yet Hank still didn't enter her, continued caressing her into an ever more luscious frenzy, touching her everywhere but not touching her with all of him. Touching her so exquisitely that she could hardly bear it but not as exquisitely as she knew he would.

Her mind screamed a garbled message about her dying from desire.

Even as it was screaming, Hank was moving over her, entering her, making them one, making her complete.

Her mind relinquished all semblance of awareness. Only her senses were focused—attuned to Hank's every movement, to each deep thrust that was bringing her closer and closer to the brink.

And then her senses exploded. With a final thrust, Hank drove her over the edge of conscious perception, sending her body shuddering into a series of deliciously indescribable spasms.

The explosions continued within her, wracking her body again and again, until she was totally lost in love.

Gradually, the shudders began to weaken. Finally, they faded, leaving her drained, leaving her in a haze of incredible reality.

Hank's body lay hot and heavily on hers. She wouldn't want him to move for the world.

Finally, Hank shifted his weight and cuddled Erica to him, sliding her slick body into perfect harmony with the shape of his own.

She pulled the sheet across them and snuggled against him.

"I love you, Erica," Hank murmured. "And that was the experience of my life. To think that's what happens to lovemaking in the twentieth century!" He paused to nuzzle her neck. "How could something so basic to life have changed that much...improved so vastly?"

Erica shook her head slowly. "I don't think what we just shared had anything to do with the twentieth century, Hank. At least, not with anything I ever experienced in the twentieth century."

Hank raised himself on his elbow and gazed down at her in the dimness. "You mean you..."

Erica nodded, turning toward him and giving his chest a quick kiss.

He lay back; she rested her head on him, her cheek against his soft chest hair, her ear listening to the rhythm of his heart.

"You mean," Hank hesitantly began again, "even when you were married...even with your husband?"

Erica heard a smile in Hank's voice and realized she was smiling into the darkness herself.

"I mean never and nobody, Hank. Now or then or whenever. I guess what people feel when they make love depends entirely on who they're making love with. And as far as this person goes, I've never felt anything remotely like what I just felt with you.''

"Then," Hank offered tentatively, "then I guess we have some talking to do in the morning...have to talk about you staying.''

He cradled Erica to him and softly kissed her neck. "'Night, love.''

She closed her eyes, not wanting to speak, not wanting to spoil the perfection of the moment for Hank, even though his words had spoiled it for her.

She should have known that would be his reaction. She *had* known, dammit! She just hadn't accepted it, just hadn't been able to resist what she'd wanted so badly.

But, deep down, she'd known that to Hank's 1862 male mind love meant commitment. And sex undoubtedly sealed the bargain. And she'd still been fool enough to let sex into the equation between them.

Now Hank thought she wanted to stay. But she didn't. Well...her rational side didn't. And it was constantly reminding her about her parents and friends—reminding her that her entire life was in another time.

As long as there was the possibility of getting home, she had to keep searching for the way.

She loved Hank. There was no doubt she loved Hank incredibly. But she could never be happy in 1862—could never stay here if there was any way back to 1989.

Women in this world were sheltered, restricted, second-class citizens. Lord, they couldn't vote, let alone work! She might have Hank's love if she stayed, but she'd have no place in the 1862 world at large.

If only Hank's love didn't feel so perfect. If only...

Her mind began racing through a litany of things she could never adjust to. Never mind *could*! She'd never *want* to adjust to this primitive past where electricity and running water didn't exist, where epidemics killed people and antibiotics hadn't been discovered, where children like Billy died of consumption and women routinely died in childbirth and couldn't do much to prevent pregnancy and . . . and a million other things she couldn't live with when she knew how much better life would become!

She blinked fiercely, forcing back tears, intensely aware of Hank's body pressing firmly against her own, of his arm securely around her.

They'd just shared an incredible moment in time. But this wasn't her time. It was his. And no time would ever be theirs.

CHAPTER TEN

ERICA SLEPT RESTLESSLY through the night, occasionally aware of Hank disentangling his body from hers and leaving the bedroom.

Now and then, while he was gone, muffled sounds of voices drifted upstairs. Vaguely, she realized nighttime patients must be in Hank's office.

But then he would return, warm and real to cuddle her lovingly against him once more, to make the night wonderful again.

Except, even in the warm afterglow of making love, even through the haze of sleep, an intrusive little voice kept reminding her everything was far from wonderful...that being here with Hank was far from reality...that, fantastic as making love with him had been, it had also been a dreadful mistake.

Now Hank was under the impression she wanted to stay. Come morning, how painful was clearing up that misconception going to be?

Eventually, the black velvet curtain before her closed eyes warmed to pale gold. She moved her arm, searching for Hank and realized she was alone in his bed.

She opened her eyes a crack. Sunlight was streaming through the window. Gradually, her other senses wakened. The aroma of coffee was wafting up from the kitchen, and she heard the faint sizzle of something frying.

From directly below the bedroom, she could hear Hank speaking quietly. Billy's reedy little voice chimed in with a childish snippet of conversation.

Of course. Billy had come home from Mrs. McCully's. That meant her talk with Hank would have to wait. She couldn't decide if the temporary reprieve made her feel better or worse.

But maybe she'd been imagining things last night. Maybe Hank didn't really think their lovemaking had changed everything, didn't really think she'd be content staying in his world. Maybe...but she doubted it.

She heard Billy pounding up the stairs and pulled the sheet decorously up around her neck.

His footsteps slowed as he neared the doorway. He paused in the hall.

"Good morning, Billy," she called.

He peeked shyly into the room. "Good morning, ma'am. Pa says to tell you breakfast is almost ready."

"Thank you. Tell your pa I'll be along as soon as I get dressed."

"Yes, ma'am." Billy vanished.

Erica waited until she heard the little boy start back down the stairs, then quickly put on the navy cotton dress Hank had bought when she'd arrived.

As soon as breakfast was finished, she'd have a shot at washing the white one. She should have done that when they got home last night. But last night...

She hurried down to the kitchen, trying to ignore her nervousness about seeing Hank this morning, about what his reaction would be when he saw her.

She stopped at the bottom of the stairs. All traces of their baths had disappeared. And her other dress was hanging in the corner—wet and amazingly white once more.

Hank was standing at the wood stove, his back to the stairs, putting the final touches on breakfast.

On top of all the problems she'd been causing, she thought guiltily, she was being useless as a housekeeper.

"Morning, Hank. Sorry I slept in. Can I at least help you serve?" Her voice sounded normal; she breathed a tiny sigh of relief.

And then Hank turned, wished her good morning and treated her to the most lovestruck gaze she'd ever seen.

Her feeling of relief evaporated instantly. Her guilt took a quantum leap.

Hank was looking at her with distinct pride of ownership.

Making love had definitely been a mistake! And she was totally to blame. Hank would have stopped anytime she'd told him to. But she hadn't told him to.

"No need to help," Hank assured her. "Everything's done. Just sit down with Billy."

Erica slipped into a chair and sat quietly while Hank served breakfast, wishing he'd wipe that adoring look off his face. It was making her feel like Delilah.

It's not as if you set out to betray him, a little voice reassured her fiercely.

"So," she asked, avoiding Hank's gaze and focusing on Billy, "what did you do while we were off visiting Sam?"

The little boy grinned at her, apparently pleased by her attention, and began to ramble on about not being able to locate Three-finger Jack.

Erica tried to concentrate on what Billy was telling her. It was impossible to do with Hank staring at her as if she was a chunk of double-deluxe chocolate cake.

"But you and Pa had more excitement than me!" Billy exclaimed loudly.

Erica dared a glance at Hank. "You told him about our adventures?"

"An edited version."

Billy turned to his father. "Will you be writing a story about your trip, Pa? About the flood?"

"Possibly. Perhaps I will sometime."

"Are you going to let me see some of your work?" Erica asked, eager to get Hank thinking of anything other than her. "Sam talking about how well you write made me curious."

Hank grinned. "Sure. Bottom left-hand drawer of my office desk. You can look at it whenever you like. If you get a second to yourself during the remainder of this century, that is."

Erica tried to ignore the implication in Hank's remark, tried not to see the expectant look on his face.

She had to get this issue cleared up. Absolutely had to, because she was feeling like a complete and utter jerk. A complete and utter jerk with an enormous lump in her throat and tears threatening to spill every time she looked at Hank.

The last thing she wanted to do was hurt him. But she wouldn't let him go on thinking what he was clearly thinking. And the sooner she got her explanation over with the better. Lord, he was liable to say something inappropriate in front of Billy if she didn't speak up. She had to say something.

"Maybe," she suggested, forcing a smile and trying to sound casual, "I'll have a look at your writing when you go to the telegraph office."

Hank stared at her blankly, still wearing his guilt-provoking grin. "Telegraph office?"

"Yes." She ordered herself to keep gazing at Hank as she spoke. "When you go to check for the reply to that telegram you sent from Aurora yesterday. An answer might have come from Boston already."

Hank's smile faded before her eyes.

"But . . . but it doesn't matter now. If there's a telegram there, and I don't pick it up, someone will bring it along. And we don't really care about the reply anymore."

He eyed her closely. "We don't care about it anymore . . . do we?"

Billy was looking, with obvious interest, from one adult to the other. "Care about what?" he asked.

Erica shot Hank a cautioning look, then stared uncomfortably at her hands.

"I still have to know, Hank," she murmured. "I still have to know what my options are."

Silence chilled the air, broken only by Billy slurping his milk.

"I see," Hank finally said.

Erica snuck a glance at his face. It was expressionless.

"I see," he repeated evenly, his voice ice-cold.

He turned to Billy. "Fancy taking a walk with me to the telegraph office, son?"

Billy nodded eagerly and drained his glass.

Hank shoved back his chair, rose and wheeled away from the table. He strode across the kitchen and out the door without another word.

Billy raced after his father, pausing in the doorway to call goodbye to Erica.

"Bye, Billy," she managed.

The door slammed, shattering Erica's final shred of self-control. She buried her face in her hands and surrendered to a therapeutic cry.

ERICA SAT AT the kitchen table, Hank's manuscripts spread in front of her. She'd gotten them from his desk out of curiosity—curiosity and the desire to take her mind off what had happened, off the way he'd stomped out of the house.

But now she was totally engrossed in his writing. It was incredibly good! She turned another page, fascinated by the story.

The back door opened.

Hank strode into the kitchen, looking every bit as angry as he'd been earlier.

Erica's gaze riveted on the neatly folded piece of paper he was holding. The telegram! They'd gotten a reply from Boston.

She stared at it, dying to know what it said—whether or not there was anything about time travel in Harvard's library.

Hank shoved the door closed and stood looking at her, saying nothing. He was holding her fate in his hand and was clearly in no rush to tell her what it was.

Erica ordered herself to be patient. Hank was upset. She'd hurt him. He was going to punish her for that.

Well, she undoubtedly deserved his anger. And, since she'd waited this long, she could wait a few minutes longer—not make him absolutely certain the only thing she cared about was getting out of his world.

"Where's Billy?" she asked casually.

Hank tapped the telegram against his thigh. Erica's nerves jumped at each tap.

"He met up with some of his friends and decided to go off with them."

"Oh." Erica sat quietly, keeping her gaze on Hank's face, not allowing it to drift to that piece of paper she was itching to get her hands on.

"I see you've been reading my stories."

"Yes. And they're wonderful, Hank. Sam was right. They're first-rate."

Hank eyed her as if he was deciding whether or not she was lying.

"As Sam said, you should be trying to sell them."

"What's the point?"

"What do you mean?"

"I mean, we know I don't become a successful writer. If I did, you'd have recognized my name the same way you did Sam's. So, since I know I'm not going to succeed, what's the point of trying to sell them?"

"Oh . . . well . . . I can't imagine my not recognizing your name means much. Sam becomes incredibly famous. That's why I knew about him. But I'm far from a literary expert. And maybe you do what Sam does. Maybe you decide to use a pen name."

Hank shook his head. "I'd never do that. Henry Lockhart was my father's name. And he'd have been proud to have an author carry it on."

"Well...well I still don't think what I know or don't know about literature means much."

"It means I'm not going to waste any more time writing garbage!" Hank stepped forward, gathered the manuscripts up under one arm and started toward his office with them.

"Oh, by the way," he said, pausing. "Your telegram came."

Hank tossed the piece of paper onto the table in front of her and stalked out of the kitchen.

Erica stared down at the telegram, wanting and not wanting to read it. Finally, she picked it up and focused on the hand-printed words.

Her gaze flickered over Hank's name and rested on the message.

Extensive reference search done. Stop. No information time travel. Stop. No related concepts. Stop. Regards. Stop. Walter Bonnery.

No information. The two words burned themselves into Erica's mind. *No information.*

She hadn't really expected there'd be any. So why was the confirmation of that making her stomach roil?

Because, she silently answered herself, she was now down to her last chance. White Cloud.

But White Cloud was only a possibility if Hank was willing to talk with the old woman.

Erica crumpled the telegram into a tight little ball, pitched it across the table, then sat waiting for Hank to come back out of his office, feeling more alone than she'd ever felt in her life.

Minutes that seemed like hours later, he walked into the kitchen again. He looked less angry than he'd been. In fact, he looked almost contrite.

"I . . . Erica, I'm sorry there was nothing."

"I didn't really think there would be." She paused, longing to ask about talking to the shaman but afraid to push.

"I reckon you'll be wanting to visit White Cloud."

Erica could feel her body sagging with relief. Hank was still prepared to help her.

"I guess that's what we're left with, isn't it, Hank."

"Guess so. Since you can't abide my world."

"Hank . . ." Erica swallowed over the lump in her throat and tried again. "Hank, please sit down with me for a minute. Please let me try to explain."

"Shoot, Erica! What in blazes is there to explain? I love you. And last night you said you loved me. Was that just sweet talk?"

"No! Hank, I do love you. I love you so much that part of me does want to stay here with you."

"Part of you!" Hank snorted. "Is that another thing that happens in the future? Do people's minds become divided up into little parts that all want different things? Must make life mighty confusing!"

"Hank, please!"

Hank stood staring at her for a moment, his distress so apparent it tore at her soul.

She wished with all her heart she'd never come to Nevada, had never heard of the Broken Hill Mine, never explored that damned tunnel, never met Hank.

No...despite the pain it had led to, she'd never want to wish away her time with Hank.

He slumped into the chair opposite her. "Erica, I don't understand this. I love you. You say you love me. I want you to stay with me. And at least part of you wants to stay. So why see White Cloud?"

"Oh, Hank, sometimes the part of me that wants to stay with you makes me forget the reasons I have for going back. But there are my parents... Oh, Hank, there's my entire life!

"I simply have got to learn if White Cloud knows the secret—if she'll help me."

"And what if she doesn't know anything, Erica? Or what if she won't help? What then? Will you spend the rest of your life trying to find someone who'll help you leave me?"

"Oh, Hank, I'm sorry! I know this isn't fair to you." Erica paused, thinking how dangerous split-second decisons could be. But she owed Hank...and she loved him.

"Hank, I have to talk to White Cloud. But I truly believe she's my last chance. If she doesn't know or if she knows and refuses to help, then I'll stop trying, Hank. I'll stop trying to go back...because I do love you...so very much."

"So very much," Hank repeated slowly. "So very much but not enough to keep you from wanting to see White Cloud, from wanting to leave me."

"Hank, it's not leaving *you* that I want. That's the *last* thing I want. Every time you hold me, I'm incredibly happy. If I could spend the rest of my life in your arms, I wouldn't ask you to take me to see White Cloud again.

"But it isn't that simple, Hank. You know it isn't! You couldn't devote the rest of your life to making me happy. I couldn't expect you to.

"You've spent the past few days helping me, being with me. And I'm more grateful for that than I could ever express. But you have a life aside from me. You have your work and Billy and your friends.

"Hank, if I can't go back, if I have to stay here, I'll have no life aside from you. My world will be inside these four rooms. The biggest event in my day will be shopping for dinner."

"I...Erica, what if I packed up my things and we moved to Boston? I think about that idea now and then. It's so much more civilized. Maybe..."

Erica shook her head sadly. "It isn't the town, Hank. It's the time. It's the way women are forced to live in this century. If I don't go back, if I can't go back, I'll end up trying to live through you. Trying to live my life through someone else when I'm accustomed to a world where I have a life of my own. Hank, imagine how much I'd miss my life."

"Apparently, more than you'd miss me!"

Erica brushed away a stray tear. "That wasn't fair."

"Fair? Tarnation, Erica! You have the gall to talk about fair? Are you being fair? Have you given life in my world half a chance? What do you see 1862 as? A primitive abyss without a single redeeming virtue?"

"Oh, Hank!" Erica reached across and covered his hand with her own.

She thought, for an instant, he was going to jerk away, but he left his hand beneath hers.

"Hank, I didn't mean to sound so critical of your world. I was only trying to explain why I have to see White Cloud. Why I have to make this one final effort at going back. I certainly wasn't trying to imply your world was a purgatory! And, when it comes to redeeming virtues you... you are the most redeeming virtue I've ever had the joy of meeting... in either world."

"But I'm not enough."

"Hank—"

"No. Don't say anything more. You've made yourself perfectly clear. If White Cloud doesn't help you, you'll stay with me. But it'll be because you have to. Not because you want to. How do you think that makes me feel, Erica?"

"Hank..." She didn't know what else to say.

ERICA SAT IN HANK'S BUGGY, her gaze frozen on his distant figure. He stood under White Cloud's arbor, talking with the shaman, gesturing about something.

Erica wished she could hear what he was saying. He was still angry with her. But he wouldn't let his anger stand in the way of helping her. She just knew he wouldn't!

Erica consciously unclenched her fists, trying to relax. It was impossible. Her body was a mass of tension. No doubt her entire future rested on the conversation those two were having.

Finally, Hank nodded to White Cloud and started back to the buggy.

Erica tried to read his expression. Impossible. He was too far away. She held her breath as he walked. He drew closer. She still couldn't tell whether his news would be good or bad.

Hank stopped beside her and extended his hand. "White Cloud wants to speak with you, Erica."

The shaman wanted to speak with her. Erica's spirits soared. "Does she…does she know how to get me home, Hank?"

"I'm not certain. She does know about time travel."

White Cloud knew about time travel! Then everything was going to be fine! Wasn't it? Erica tried to contain her excitement, forced herself to listen to the rest of what Hank was saying.

"And you were right. White Cloud had realized you were from the future. But she wouldn't tell me whether she has the knowledge to help you get back. She wants to talk directly to you."

Erica gathered her skirt, clutched Hank's outstretched hand, and swung anxiously down from the buggy.

Her heart pounded more loudly with each step she took toward the arbor.

The shaman sat gazing at them in silence, her piercing black eyes revealing nothing. She looked even older than Erica had remembered her.

By the time they reached White Cloud, Erica could feel perspiration pouring down her body. She suspected she should wait for the Indian to speak first; the wait was torture.

"The white doctor," the old woman murmured eventually, "has told me you do not like our world."

"No . . . I mean—I mean it's not that I don't like it. It's just that I want to go back to my own."

"Then go."

"I—I can't. I don't know how. I need help, White Cloud."

"And the white doctor will not help you?"

White Cloud smiled the cruel-looking smile Erica recalled from their first meeting.

"As I told you," Hank said, his words measured and precise, "I don't know how to help her."

White Cloud's smile grew. "How can that be true? The white doctor knows everything."

Hank shook his head. "White Cloud, it's Miss James who wants to leave. Not me. If you know how to help her, please don't punish her because of your dislike for me."

"Dislike. I dislike no one."

"I'm glad to hear that, White Cloud. Then I know you'll help Miss James if you're able to. Can you? Do you know how she can get home?"

"Perhaps." White Cloud shot Hank a look that dripped malice.

Erica bit her lip, holding back tears of frustration at the realization she was in the middle of a cat-and-mouse game. And she definitely wasn't the cat.

"I must hear only the truth," White Cloud murmured, still focusing on Hank. "If I do not, I will know. If I hear a lie, I will listen no longer."

Hank nodded slowly. "What do you want me to tell you?"

"This woman wishes to leave?"

"Yes."

"And you wish her to leave?"

Hank didn't answer.

"The truth, white doctor."

"No. The truth is I don't wish her to leave."

A fresh smile spread across White Cloud's round face. "I see. You will not be happy?"

"No," Hank muttered. "I will not be happy."

White Cloud's eyes dismissed Hank. She looked at Erica. "Tell me how you came here. Tell me exactly."

Erica recounted her story. Her words wanted to race, but she spoke slowly, trying to relate events in their proper order.

She finished and stood staring at White Cloud, silently begging the shaman to say something positive.

The old woman picked at an invisible spot on her dress. Slowly, infuriatingly slowly, she smoothed the buckskin.

"It is as I thought," she finally whispered. "You came on the second shadow of the first blue moon."

"I—I don't understand."

"The blue moon," White Cloud repeated. "The first blue moon."

"Yes, yes I heard that." Erica paused, feeling her anxiety level rising. "But I don't know what a blue moon is."

White Cloud looked off into space for such a long time that Erica wanted to shake her. Didn't the old woman realize how important this was? Of course she did. She was a damned sadist.

"Only one year in three," the Indian finally murmured, "or one year in four, the full moon comes two times in a month. Those are blue moons."

"Some time away from each moon, before and after, are its shadows. Shadows have magic. You traveled here on the after-shadow of the first blue moon this month."

Erica's mind raced, trying to understand what the old woman was saying. *Once in a blue moon*—she knew the phrase, of course. Now she'd learned what a blue moon was.

But what did blue moons mean as far as her particular predicament was concerned? She screwed up her courage, afraid to ask the question she so desperately wanted the answer to.

"White Cloud...is there a way for me to go back?" Erica waited, not breathing, for the shaman's answer.

The Indian nodded slowly.

Erica breathed again.

"But there is only one way for you to return, only one time you can leave. You must go back the way you came."

"What do you mean? Through the mine shaft?"

White Cloud nodded again.

"But I tried that! I told you! Nothing happened! How exactly do I go? What exactly do I do? When?"

"You must travel back on the before-shadow of the second blue moon.

"The second blue moon. Do you mean the next full moon? Do you mean all I have to do is wait until the moon is full again and I'll be able to go home?"

Erica automatically glanced at the sky as she asked her question. Pointless! It was the middle of the afternoon. But she had no idea what phase the moon was in.

"Not the moon," White Cloud murmured. "The shadow."

The shadow? What on earth were these shadows the shaman kept mentioning? Erica looked frantically at Hank, hoping he knew what the woman was talking about.

He was watching White Cloud with suspicion written all over his face.

Erica caught his attention. Her eyes asked him what he was thinking.

"Erica...the only way there can be two full moons in the same month is if there's one in the first day or two and one in the last couple of days. And it seems to me the moon is waxing now, that it'll be full again a little after the middle of July. So there can't be two full moons this month."

Erica's gaze flew back to the shaman. Was she simply playing a cruel joke?

"No, white doctor. The two full moons are in this Paiute month. Not the white man's month."

"Paiute month?" Erica whispered. Blue moons! Shadows! Paiute months! Was any of this going to start making sense? She looked questioningly at Hank again.

He shrugged an apology. "Sorry. I didn't think of it, but Indians don't divide the year up the same way our calendar does."

"Different calendars!" Erica practically moaned the words. "But, White Cloud, regardless of whose calendar we're using, are you saying that if I came on the first full moon this month—"

"Shadow," White Cloud whispered.

"Yes. Of course. Shadow. But if I came on the first moon's shadow, can I go back on the second one's? Is that how it works?"

"Yes."

Yes! Erica almost cheered.

"You have traveled back in time on a shadow. To return to where you came from, you must use the next shadow. Only the next shadow."

"Only the next shadow. Right! So I go to the mine shaft at the next shadow. Right?"

"Yes."

"And the next shadow comes when? You said before the next full moon. But exactly when?"

White Cloud smiled slyly. "There is the time of the shadow to know. And there is the rest of the magic."

"The rest of the magic," Erica repeated dully, feeling her spirits plummeting. She eyed White Cloud, desperately wishing she was certain the old woman was telling the truth, not spouting hocus-pocus.

"Will you...will you tell me the time of the shadow, White Cloud? Will you help me with the rest of the magic? Will you help me to get home?"

The Indian's gaze drifted from Erica to Hank, then back. "Perhaps."

Erica swallowed hard. "What will make you decide?"

The shaman glanced at Hank once more. "The white doctor. The white doctor will make me decide."

"And precisely what," Hank muttered, "is that supposed to mean?"

"We will talk more after I rest." White Cloud closed her eyes.

Hank glared at her.

She sat motionless. Her eyes remained closed.

"Look, White Cloud," Hank finally snapped. "How do we even know there *is* any magic? And, even if there is, how would we be sure Miss James would end up back home? That she wouldn't find herself someplace else entirely?"

Erica frantically signaled Hank to be quiet.

White Cloud opened her eyes and gave him a look of pure derision. "The second moon's before-shadow will take her exactly where she came from. That is the only place it will take her.''

"A blue-moon shadow is not the only way to travel through time, white doctor. It is not the easiest way. But it is the only way back for Miss James. She made the journey here on the first moon's after-shadow. She must return on the second moon's before-shadow.''

"And that's the honest to Moses truth, White Cloud? Miss James would be safe? She'd end up back in 1989?''

"You doubt me, white doctor. Talk to Chief Numaga while I rest. He knows the secret of time travel. He will tell you what I say is true. The next moon shadow will take Miss James to the place and time she started from.''

Erica stared at Hank, certain he must just have realized the same thing she had. If Chief Numaga knew the secrets then he could help her. They didn't need this evil old woman.

White Cloud stared at Erica, making her shiver, making her suddenly certain the shaman could read minds.

"Chief Numaga knows the secrets,'' the Indian whispered, her words barely audible. "But he does not have the magic. Only I have the magic.''

CHAPTER ELEVEN

As though with a mind of its own, Erica's gaze strayed across the ten feet to the arbor.

White Cloud was still resting in her Buddha-like pose. Her eyes remained closed.

Erica looked down and concentrated on smoothing out a tiny crease in the Indian blanket she and Hank were sitting on, ordering herself not to look at the shaman again.

Staring at the old woman wasn't going to wake her...if she was actually asleep...if she wasn't merely playing games with them.

"Try to relax," Hank said quietly.

"She'll probably sit there forever, Hank. She'll probably sit like that till she dies. She'll probably never wake up, never talk to us again."

"Just be patient. You're going to get home. All there's left to do is convince White Cloud to give you the magic."

"All there's left to do?" Erica moaned. "*All?* Hank, you were the one who told me that old woman isn't to be trusted. And she might decide not to help me anyway. And what is this magic? Did Numaga tell you?"

Hank shook his head. "He doesn't know precisely. Only White Cloud knows that. But he knew enough to assure me everything she told us was true. The next shadow will get you home safely."

He eyed Erica with a hopeful look. "You starting to have doubts? Are you still sure you want to go back?"

"Yes. Yes, I'm sure. I'm a little frightened. That's all." Erica answered quickly, forcing a smile, hoping she looked and sounded more certain than she felt.

She couldn't stay and didn't want Hank to think she was wavering. But the idea of relying on White Cloud was making her more anxious by the minute.

"I think it's this talk about magic that's scaring me, Hank. I didn't have any magic to get here, so why do I need it to get back?"

"Erica, I reckon we're never going to understand exactly how you got here. But it doesn't matter much at this point. What matters is that you're here. And if both White Cloud and Numaga say you need magic to get back, then I expect you do."

"Oh, Hank, I don't even believe in astrology, let alone magic. That's just sleight of hand, something people do in theaters or on television. It's simply entertainment."

Hank reached over and took her hand. "Erica, you've traveled through time. How can you doubt the existence of true magic or its power, after doing that?"

"Well, I guess you have a point. But listening to White Cloud talking about blue moons and their shadows doesn't exactly inspire confidence."

"Surely you didn't think you were going to get home by stagecoach or train, or that one of your Boeing 747s was going to whisk you into the sky."

Erica managed a smile. "You'd better be careful about flaunting your knowledge of the future, Hank. Start talking cars and planes and space shuttles to the wrong people, and they'll have you carted away.

"But as far as my getting home goes, I don't know exactly how I thought I'd manage it. I certainly never imagined a moon shadow as the transportation, though. I'd never even heard of moon shadows. That makes it awfully difficult to believe White Cloud knows what she's talking about—or that I can trust her."

"Erica, she's the only one who seems to understand how you got here, the only one we know has the knowledge to get you home. And you'll be safe. In this instance we can trust her. Numaga wouldn't lie to me. Everything will be fine. Remember when you were first trying to convince me you were from the future? How you showed me all those things from your backpack?"

Erica nodded.

"Well, initially I thought they had to be products of magic. But they were actually products of science. I guess magic is simply science we don't understand."

"That's . . . that's very insightful, Hank. And very supportive."

Hank's blank look told her she'd used a twentieth-century term.

"Very . . ." She searched for another word. "It was a very reassuring thing to say. Thank you," she added quietly. "Thank you. I know this isn't easy for you. I appreciate everything you've done."

Hank squeezed her hand but didn't meet her gaze.

Erica caught herself looking at White Cloud again and quickly turned back to Hank. "She said you'd be the one to make her decide whether she'd help me or not, Hank. What do you suppose she meant by that."

"Lord knows. Whatever she's got on her mind, though, I can't imagine I'm going to like it."

"But . . . but you'll go along with it. If you can, I mean. If it isn't something too awful."

"Yes, Erica," Hank snapped, dropping her hand. "Yes, I'll go along with it if it isn't too awful. I'll probably go along with it even if it is too awful.

"You don't think I'd want to be responsible for you having to spend the rest of your life in this godforsaken century, do you? Not when you want to get out of it so almighty much!"

"Hank, I—"

"Stop, Erica. Just stop trying to be so danged nice to me. Do you think that's going to make me feel any better about this? You aim to leave. You've made that perfectly plain. So I'll help you. I love you, so I'll help you leave me, although the logic of that makes me question my sanity.

"But I'll keep on helping you, Erica. Just stop telling me things like I'm *supportive* and *reassuring*! And for gawd's sake stop looking at me as if you don't really want to leave when I know you do!"

"Hank—"

Hank shoved himself up from the blanket and stalked off in the direction of Numaga's tentlike *Karnee*.

Erica gazed after him, uncertain if she should follow.

"The white doctor truly does not want you to go."

White Cloud's voice drifted across the space between them, startling Erica.

She glanced at the old woman, wondering how long she'd been listening with open ears and closed eyes.

"I wish to speak again," White Cloud continued. "I wish to speak to both of you."

"Hank?" Erica called anxiously at his retreating form. "Hank, White Cloud has finished resting."

He hesitated, then turned and started back. The black expression on his face made Erica wince.

When he reached the blanket, he silently offered her his hand and pulled her up.

Together, they walked to the arbor and stood in front of the shaman.

"You have talked with Chief Numaga, white doctor?"

Hank nodded.

"And you believe the way back is safe for your friend?"

"Yes. I believe she'll be safe. May I ask a question about the trip, White Cloud?"

The old woman slowly nodded. Sunlight caught glints in her long, silver hair.

Silver glints. No doubt, Erica mused, moon shadows were silver. Or were they blue? The blue shadows of blue moons? That would explain the shimmering blue light she'd followed down the mine tunnel on her way into the past.

She heard Hank speaking again, and her mind shoved aside the issue of what a moon shadow might look like.

"White Cloud, could someone else travel with Miss James? Could someone from this world travel to the future with her and live there? Would that be possible?"

Erica's gaze flashed from the shaman to Hank. What was he saying? She stared at his even profile. She'd heard him ask if he could go back with her!

And now he was standing beside her, looking cool as the proverbial cucumber, while her heart had begun leaping in deliriously happy flip-flops.

Hank would go back with her if he could! Why hadn't the possibility that he could do that occurred to her? But, even if it had, she'd never have thought he'd consider the idea. Yet he was!

She realized White Cloud was saying something and forced every ounce of her attention onto the Indian's words.

"You would leave my world, white doctor?"

The old woman's voice betrayed her surprise. And her face no longer wore its expressionless mask. She'd clearly like nothing better than to see Hank leave.

"Please." Erica whispered under her breath. "Please say he can come with me."

"You would leave my world?" the shaman repeated when Hank didn't answer. "You would leave Chief Numaga with only me to counsel him once more?"

"You haven't answered my question, yet, White Cloud. Would it be possible for someone to travel with Miss James, to live the rest of his life in her world?"

A gleeful little grin possessed the old woman's mouth. "Yes, it would be possible. It would be simple!" The shaman's words were bubbling out.

"If I give Miss James the magic, you must only hold her hand...or merely stand very close to her. The magic will flow from her."

"I see."

Erica forced herself to remain still, steeled herself against the urge to throw her arms around Hank. How could he look so calm when she was so excited that she was about to explode?

"Then tell me, White Cloud," Hank said slowly, "how can I make you decide to help Miss James?"

The shaman glanced at Erica. "Leave us."

"I...but I..."

"Do as she says, Erica. Wait in the buggy while White Cloud and I talk."

"But Hank, this conversation is about me! About my future! I have a right to know—"

"Dammit, Erica! You're a stranger in my world! What gives you the *right* to know anything?"

Erica bit her lip, trapping the words that were struggling to escape. She wanted so desperately to stay exactly where she was, to hear what White Cloud was going to say, whether or not she was going to help.

But Hank apparently wanted to deal with White Cloud alone. He wanted to travel to the future, though! That was what really mattered!

It was just that there were so many questions! What about Billy? Surely if she held on to Hank with one hand and Billy with the other...

She realized both Hank and White Cloud were glaring at her and she began backing away. Hank would think to ask about Billy. Of course he would. Hank would think of everything. And he'd do whatever was necessary to convince White Cloud to help.

Erica turned and fled to the buggy.

WHEN HANK FINALLY LEFT White Cloud, Erica clutched the edge of the buggy's seat to keep from leaping down and running to meet him.

She could feel a dozen different emotions surging inside her, running the gamut from joy to despair. And, depending on what the shaman had said, each one was ready to dominate her.

Erica willed Hank to walk faster, willed him to at least flash her a victorious smile that would tell her they'd be traveling to her world.

He did neither. He strode, stiff-backed and straight-faced to the driver's side and climbed in.

Erica stared at him, desperate to know whether White Cloud would help them or not—whether they'd be going or staying.

"Well? You aren't going to keep me in suspense, are you, Hank?"

He clicked Barleycorn's reins, and they started off. "Wait until we round the bend—until White Cloud can't see us."

Erica tried to conceal her impatience.

The bend was only a hundred yards ahead. But why was Barleycorn walking so slowly? They'd be an hour reaching that damned curve in the trail.

They turned the bend; the Paiute camp disappeared behind trees. Hank reigned the mare to a halt and looked at Erica.

"Well?" she demanded. If he didn't tell her what had happened this very minute she'd kill him.

"Well...White Cloud will give you the magic to travel with if I do something for her first."

The old woman would give them the magic! They could go! But Erica's relief was tinged with trepidation. What was the something?

She offered up a silent prayer that it wasn't a major something, then tried to speak evenly to Hank, as if the shape of her future didn't depend on what he was about to tell her.

"How awful is what White Cloud wants you to do, Hank?"

"It isn't awful. The problem is it's not something I'm sure I can do."

"But Hank, if it's not awful you can do it!"

He shook his head. "It might be impossible."

Impossible? A little ring of fear tightened around Erica's heart. "What is it, Hank? What does White Cloud want from you?"

"She wants my help with something."

"With what!" *Get to the point, Hank!* a little voice shouted inside Erica's head.

"Well, a group of tribal chiefs are setting out for Carson City tomorrow. They've arranged a meeting with Orion Clemens about the whole problem that's developed between the Nevada settlers and the Indians."

"The whole problem?" Erica could feel her sense of trepidation growing. Her fear that the something Hank was supposed to do was a major something jumped several notches.

"Yes," Hank continued. "The basic problem is the huge number of miners who are coming west—and the herds of cattle being driven here as their food supply.

"The Paiutes don't raise crops. They simply gather whatever grows wild, and they hunt, of course. But the settlers are hunting, too, and the local game is becoming scarce. Besides that, the cattle are destroying the land—grazing it barren."

"And what does White Cloud expect you to do about all that?"

"Head for Carson City tomorrow and ask Orion if I can sit in on his meeting with the chiefs. Do what I can to influence him to agree to their demands."

"The shaman's a better person than I was giving her credit for being then," Erica murmured. "It never even occurred to me she'd want something from you that would help her tribe. I thought it would be selfish."

Hank smiled ruefully. "Don't be so quick to commend White Cloud's altruism. She'll only help us if the Indians get a satisfactory response from Orion.

"And there's one other little detail to my bargain with her. If the meeting's a success, I have to give her the credit for making it succeed. Have to tell Numaga that all my ideas were her ideas—maybe tell him she cast a spell on me, giving me the power to sway Orion.''

"Oh, Hank, that's ridiculous. Numaga would never believe it.''

"Yes he would, Erica. There's no point thinking about this from your twentieth-century Bostonian perspective. This is 1862 Nevada. And the Paiutes have great faith in the powers of their shamans. If I told Numaga that White Cloud had affected the outcome of the meeting, he'd be happy to believe me. And White Cloud's power would be stronger than ever.''

"Well, do you think you can manage what she's asking, Hank? Can you influence Orion?''

"I don't know. I can't imagine he'll object to my sitting in on the meeting. But how much I'll be able to sway him will depend on what the Indians want and what the settlers have been telling him. And probably on how Orion and the other government officials at the meeting are feeling that day.

"Problem is, the Nevada government isn't exactly composed of the most reasonable men around. In fact, the territorial legislature is commonly referred to as the 'asylum.' ''

The asylum! Terrific. Talk about inspiring confidence. Erica's head had begun throbbing. She managed a smile.

"But you'll try, Hank? You'll go to Carson City? And—and you'll be able to make it back to Mountainview before the next moon shadow?''

"Yes. I'll go. I'll try. I'll make it back in time. There's a good horse I know I can borrow. If I ride, instead of taking the buggy, the trip will be faster.''

"Oh, and I'm sure you'll succeed with Orion, Hank.'' Erica reached over and took his hands in hers.

"I'm sure you'll succeed and White Cloud will help us."

She slid across the seat, unable to contain her feelings any longer. She wrapped her arms around Hank's neck and clung to the secure warmth of his body. He'd manage to influence Orion. She just knew he would. And the thought of Hank going home with her—the knowledge she'd be able to hold him like this forever—was almost making her weep with joy.

"Hank, you've made me the happiest woman in the world—in either world. And you won't regret this. I promise you won't. I won't let you. I know it'll take you a little time to adjust to life in 1989 but once you do, you'll be so—"

"Not me, Erica."

"What?"

"It's not me that's going with you. I want you to take Billy."

"What?" she repeated frantically. "I mean of course we'll take Billy but—"

"I want *you* to take Billy, Erica. *We* won't be taking him. That's your part of this bargain. I help White Cloud. White Cloud helps you. And you help me."

"But, Hank!" Erica stopped, realizing she was so upset that she could barely speak. She couldn't possibly be getting this straight! Hank had said he wanted to go back with her. She'd heard him!

She could repeat what he'd said word for word. *Could someone else travel with Miss James? Could someone from this world travel to the future with her and live there?*

Oh Lord! He'd said *someone.* And he wasn't the someone he'd meant! What an idiot she was! He didn't want to go with her. She untangled her arms from around his neck and slunk to the far side of the seat.

Her throat was so constricted, she doubted she could say another word. And her eyes were burning. Hank didn't intend to go back with her! She wouldn't have everything she wanted, after all . . . couldn't have both Hank and her own world.

"Is it an agreement, Erica? Will you take Billy to the future with you?"

"Hank." Speaking his name hurt her throat. She wasn't certain if the pain was physical or psychological. Well to hell with the pain. This couldn't wait.

"Hank, that idea's absurd. I can't take your son away from you."

"Erica, if Billy stays here he's going to die."

Consumption. The horrible word began flashing in Erica's mind like a bright neon sign. She hadn't been thinking about Billy's illness. She'd been focusing entirely on the issue of White Cloud helping them.

She gazed across the buggy at Hank. He'd made the statement about his son with no apparent emotion, as if it were merely a statement of fact. Of course. That's what it was. Fact.

In 1862, people who had consumption died of it. And in 1989 they didn't.

But she'd seen enough of Billy and Hank together to imagine how very difficult he'd find giving up the little boy.

"Hank . . . that just wouldn't work, not for any of us. You can't send Billy with me and not come yourself. You'd miss him something awful. And he'd miss you. And I don't know anything about bringing up a little boy. Not a danged thing."

Hank clicked Barleycorn's reins and the buggy began rolling forward once more. "You can get some practice bringing up a little boy while I'm in Carson City.''

"But, Hank—''

"Erica, listen to me. I'm a physician. I have absolutely no doubt Billy is going to die if he stays here. I've always clung to the hope there'd be a cure soon. But, according to you, that cure—those antibiotics— aren't going to be discovered for decades.''

"But, Hank, you—''

"Erica, do you know much about consumption?''

"No. I don't know much at all. It isn't a significant disease in my world, Hank.''

"Well, it's a mighty significant disease in mine. Three million people die of it every year.''

"Three million?''

"Yes. Let me tell you a bit about it. What's happening inside Billy's lungs....'' Hank's voice sounded strained. He paused.

When he began speaking again, he'd clearly forced himself from an emotional mode to a clinical one.

"Billy's lungs, Erica, are gradually filling with tubercles—small, round bodies that increase in numbers until they completely solidify portions of the lungs.''

"So—so he has trouble breathing,'' Erica murmured.

"That's the eventual effect. What causes the problem at this stage, though, when he has his spells, is the linings of his lungs becoming inflamed.''

"And what caused the inflammation? The spells?''

Hank shrugged. "It often isn't clear. But Billy's lungs are gradually degenerating from the strain of those bouts. They ulcerate, liquid discharge results, he coughs it up and his lungs are reasonably clear again for a time. But the ulceration leaves cavities that further weaken the organs. The process is a slow one. But eventually Billy's lungs will be reduced to the consistency of cheese.''

"Oh, Hank! That's such an awful disease for a little boy to have.''

"That's why you have to take him with you,'' Hank said quietly. "I'd rather lose Billy to the future, so he'll have a future, than keep him with me for a few years more and watch him die.''

"But, Hank, I just can't understand the losing part. You don't have to lose Billy at all. If we get the magic then the three of us—''

"No, Erica. The two of you. After all you've told me about your world, I know I couldn't possibly adapt to it.''

Little streams of tears trickled down Erica's cheeks. How had everything gone from so right to so wrong in minutes?

"I'll raise what money I can, Erica. I'm not a rich man, but I'll buy as much gold as I'm able for you to take with you. I know it won't be enough to pay for Billy's entire upbringing but—''

"I'm not worried about money,'' Erica murmured, lapsing back into silence. Her mind raced. Hank was undoubtedly right as far as Billy's health was concerned. If she got the magic, she'd have to take Billy with her. She couldn't leave him here to die.

But what on earth would she do with a little boy in her life? How would she explain him? How could she deal with the responsibility? And how could she stand the prospect of Hank not being there with them?

She couldn't. If she and Billy went back, Hank had to come, as well. He could adapt. She had to think of a way to convince him of that.

Not a single good idea came to her.

"Well?" Hank finally asked. "Do we have a bargain?"

"Hank...I never thought about it being possible for anyone to go back with me. But, now that we know it is, don't you think you..."

She couldn't finish what she was asking, didn't want to hear what Hank would say. Only a masochist would want that. He'd told her he didn't intend to go with her. She'd be an idiot to think he'd had an instant, miraculous change of heart.

Hank eyed her closely. She suspected her plea was written all over her face.

"That's not an option, Erica. Billy is young enough to adjust. And it'll mean he'll be healthy. But my going is out of the question."

She'd been right! She'd known he'd tell her again that he wouldn't go. How could being right be so awful? She didn't want to live without Hank!

Well, if she didn't want to live without him, she had to make him change his mind. And to do that, she had to control her emotions, had to convince him in a rational, reasonable manner.

"Hank, if you're certain it's what you want, I'll take Billy with me. Of course, I will. But why is your coming with us out of the question? It makes perfect sense. We'd all be together. And Billy would be cured."

Hank merely shook his head.

"Oh, Hank! Are you trying to break my heart?" She paused in frustration. So much for rational and reasonable. She was simply too upset to manage that.

"Hank, you thought it would be perfectly fine for me to live here. Well, I think it would be perfectly fine for you to live there. In fact, I think it would be wonderful.''

"Think with your brain instead of your heart," Hank said softly. "What would I do in your world? How would I earn a living? You could have managed to fit in here. But I'd be an anachronism there."

"Well, you could..."

"Would I take along my medical diploma? My medical diploma dated 1851? Would I smudge the date, set up a practice and start treating patients with methods that are more than a hundred years behind the times?"

"Don't be sarcastic, Hank."

"Lord, Erica! If I wanted to be sarcastic I'd have my choice of a thousand different things to say. I'm simply pointing out that I wouldn't know a thing about practicing my profession in 1989. I'd never even heard of those commonplace antibiotics until a couple of days ago.

"And what other career could I have in the future, Erica? I don't even know how to drive a car or work a computer. Hellfire! I wouldn't even recognize cars or computers if I saw them. All I know about things in the future is what you've described.

"I don't have any of the skills people in your world take for granted. What could I be happy working at? How could I earn enough money to support us?"

The answer struck Erica in a flash of brilliance. "Hank, there's your writing! You said you enjoy writing. And you're good. Damned good. You could be a writer in my world."

"I'm not good enough."

"You are, Hank!"

He gave her a wry look. "Are you the same lady who told me, only this morning, that you aren't a literary expert?"

"Hank, I may not be an expert, but I recognize quality writing when I see it."

"Quality? I suspect your judgment of my work's quality is tainted by your emotions."

"No! That's not true. Videos need dialogue and narration. I've worked with scriptwriters. I know good writing. And yours is first-rate. Even Sam said that, and he *is* an expert."

"Sam was being kind. I'm not good enough to make a living at writing, Erica. We established that before. If my work was really good, you'd have recognized my name, same as you did Sam's."

Erica's thoughts whirled. Hank was right about not having the credentials or experience to make it in most careers in her world. But his writing was a definite possibility.

"Hank, I might not have recognized your name for a hundred different reasons—none of them related to the quality of your writing.

"Maybe I hadn't heard of you because you didn't sell any of your work in the nineteenth century. Maybe you travel to the twentieth century and become published then. If you're living in the future with Billy and me, maybe you'll become a rich and famous author."

She held her breath, watching Hank's face, praying he'd buy that bit of hope.

"Maybe. But maybe isn't exactly a guarantee, is it, Erica?"

"Hank, there are no guarantees in life. You know that as well as I do. But you have the potential. You write so well. And you know so much about life in the eighteeen hundreds. You could write all kinds of historical material—novels or articles or scripts.

"Hank, the possibilities are endless. And I have associates at Boston University who are writers. They'd help you find a publisher, help you market your work."

Hank shook his head slowly. "And what if I couldn't succeed, Erica? There'd be no chance of me coming back. White Cloud would be overjoyed to get rid of me. She'd never give me a return passage. What if I couldn't support myself and Billy and you?"

"I earn a good salary, Hank."

"And I'd be a parasite? I'd let a woman support me? That would be totally unacceptable. I'd shoot myself first!"

Yes. Yes, of course it would be unacceptable, Erica admitted silently. Hank's ego could never permit it. In his world, women didn't even contribute to household finances, let alone support their men.

Hank flicked the whip lightly across Barleycorn's flanks. The bay shifted to a trot.

Erica stared into the distance, her vision blurred by threatening tears, trying desperately to think of an argument that would convince Hank he could make it in her world.

HANK DRANK ANOTHER large swallow of whiskey, slapped the glass back onto the table and stared at the kitchen window once more.

Erica's gaze followed him across the dimly lit room. It was pitch black outside. Hank couldn't possibly see any more through that window than she could.

Apparently, he simply didn't want to look at her...or talk to her. Every time she said anything, she got a short, grunted reply.

.And every time she brought up the subject of him going back with her, she got a black look.

She had to admit they'd argued the issue into the ground—discussed it all the way back from the Paiute camp. They were both sick of the topic.

But how on earth was she going to convince him she was right when he refused to discuss the matter any further?

And, come morning, he wouldn't even be in Mountainview to be convinced. He'd be on his way to Carson City. She could feel tears of frustration lurking again. She hated crybabies! Yet every time she looked at Hank, every time she thought about—

Why wouldn't he agree to go with her? It was their only possibly happy ending. Why was he being so damned stubborn?

But she kept getting ahead of herself. They still had no guarantee she was going back. If Hank didn't succeed with Orion, she'd have to stay here. Maybe that wasn't—

But then Billy would die. She didn't want that to happen.

Billy... Erica glanced over at Hank. "What do I do if Billy takes sick while you're away, Hank?"

"He'll be fine. He seldom has spells in the summer."

"Seldom. But what if..."

Hank shrugged. "There isn't a whole lot you can do. Basically, you bring down his fever and try to relax him as much as possible. Massage his back. If liquid forms in his lungs, he has to cough it up. But nothing will happen. And Mrs. McCully's always around. She knows exactly what to do. Don't worry."

Don't worry, Erica thought morosely. She'd worry from the moment Hank walked out the door tomorrow until he returned—whenever that would be.

Hank took another gulp of whiskey.

"I didn't realize you drank," Erica murmured for lack of anything else to say.

"It's medicinal," Hank snapped. "I prescribe it for myself now and then."

"It's not medicinal! It turns out not to be good for your health at all! Neither's smoking your pipe, for that matter."

Oh, Lord! Her nerves had her snapping back at Hank when that was the last thing she wanted to do. But she hadn't really sounded as bitchy as it had seemed to her own ears, had she?

Hank's glare told her she had. "Well, thank you for that twentieth-century medical update, Erica. So smoking and drinking will kill me. I'll likely die before you do. But that won't be any great surprise, will it?"

"Oh, Hank, don't!"

He gazed across the table at her, the angry look in his dark eyes softening. "Erica, I'm sorry. I don't mean to be short with you. I'm just so danged frustrated. I feel so damned helpless being caught in the middle of this impossible situation."

"I know, Hank. I feel the same way."

Hank shoved the whiskey bottle aside. "Erica, I don't want to lose you. But since I've thought about the possibility of leaving my own world and trying to live in a strange one, I understand a little better why you want to go back. And now that we know Billy can go with you, part of me wants you to go, to take him.

Part of me wants you to go, Erica, and part wants you to stay.

"Oh, Hank."

"Rationally, I know that your going is the only solution. It's just difficult accepting the idea of never seeing either you or Billy again."

One of those damned lurking tears made good its escape. Erica quickly brushed it dry. "There's a simple solution, Hank. And you know how much I want you to come with us."

Hank slapped his palm against the table top. "I can't, Erica. I've tried to convince myself it could work, but I just can't. I'm too old to try and start my life over. And...and I'm too danged uncertain I would make anything of myself in the future. Even you admit writing's a risky profession. And there'd be so much I'd have to learn in your world."

"Oh, Hank, you could do it."

"Erica, here I'm a respected adult—the town physician. There I'd be like a child. I'd have to grow up all over again, have to learn about every single thing that's changed over a hundred and twenty-seven years.

"I couldn't do it, Erica. I'm a thirty-five-year-old man. I couldn't go back to being a child. I couldn't take the chance that I'd never be a real man again, that I'd end up always needing your help."

"There's nothing wrong with needing someone's help, Hank. Think about how much I've needed yours."

"That's different, Erica. You're a woman. It's all right for a woman to need help. And you've only needed help for a short time. Not for the rest of your life."

"Hank, maybe I won't need your help for the rest of my life, but I'll need you. I don't want to lose you any more than you want to lose me or your son.

"Hank, if we go...if we go and you don't come with us, I'm going to miss you every day for the rest of my life.

"I know your coming with me would be taking a risk. But can't you see it's a risk you have to take? Can't you see that your coming with us is the only way?"

"No, Erica. It's not the only way. I can stay here where I belong."

"Hank what happened to you and I belonging together? You said I belonged to you because you love me."

"I—I guess I was wrong, Erica. Guess I wasn't considering all the facts."

"Hank—"

He shoved back his chair and rose. "It's late. I want to get an early start. I'm going up to bunk in with Billy, now."

"With...Billy?" She hated the unsteady way her words came out.

"Let's not make your leaving any harder than it's already going to be, Erica." Hank turned away and climbed the stairs without looking back, leaving Erica in tears.

CHAPTER TWELVE

ERICA HAD BEEN CERTAIN the night would last forever but, half an hour ago, pale gray fingers of dawn had begun creeping through the window.

She listened to Hank moving about in the other bedroom. He spoke quietly to Billy for a few minutes. The child murmured sleepy-sounding responses.

Then she heard Hank go into the hall. She closed her eyes, not wanting him to know she hadn't slept. But surely he'd come in and tell her he was leaving. Surely he'd say goodbye.

He didn't. His footsteps faded down the stairs. The kitchen door creaked open, then closed.

She resisted the urge to leap up and peer out the window after him. Seeing him walking away wasn't going to make her feel the least bit better.

In fact, she didn't imagine there was anything in the world that would make her feel better. Unless Hank changed his mind, of course. And the odds on that were probably a zillion to one.

She lay in the early morning dimness, trying to force her mind to go blank, not wanting to think any of the thoughts that were muddling around in her brain. The thoughts continued to boil up, not letting her rest.

Whatever happened in Carson City would determine her future. But, regardless of the outcome of that meeting, her future was looking far from ideal.

If the Indians were happy after their meeting with Orion Clemens, she'd be going home. She no longer had any choice about that. Not when it meant the difference between life and death for Billy. But they'd be leaving Hank behind.

And, if the Indians weren't happy, she'd be staying here, in a world she didn't want to live in, where she and Hank would watch Billy die. If Hank would even have her with him, that was, knowing she'd wanted to leave him.

But she hadn't! Leaving Hank was the last thing she wanted. If only he could see his way clear to—

She rolled over and buried her face into the pillow. She had to stop letting that wish obsess her, because there was nothing more she could do to convince Hank to come with her.

She'd given him every argument she could think of. He certainly knew how she felt. But she couldn't *make* him come. If he came, he'd be the one in a different world. The decision had to be his.

Erica shoved the pillow away and rolled out of bed. There was nothing to be gained by lying there feeling sorry for herself. She was in charge for the next little while. She had Billy to look after. *To look after.* What if...?

She tried to push the fear from her mind. Billy would be fine while Hank was away. He'd told her the boy's sick spells were infrequent, that he seldom had one in the summer. And, if anything awful did happen, Mrs. McCully would be nearby. Still, Erica wished she'd pressed Hank about what to do if...

She grabbed her navy cotton dress, threw it on and fumbled in annoyance with its numerous buttons.

Then she tugged her ridiculous petticoat on under it and pushed her feet into her Reeboks.

She'd get breakfast started. Maybe for once she could manage unburned biscuits for Billy.

He hadn't gotten much attention the last little while. She should try to make up for that, should start getting to know him better.

The little boy popped out of his room the moment Erica stepped into the hall. He was fully dressed, and his expectant grin said he'd been waiting for her to get up.

"Morning, Billy."

"Morning, ma'am."

Ma'am! That made her feel as if she was a hundred and seven years old. She certainly wasn't going to have Billy calling her ma'am forever. But what? She should have asked Hank about that before he left.

There were undoubtedly a whole lot of things she should have asked Hank before he left. But she hadn't. So she was about to begin learning childcare by trial and error.

"What would you like for breakfast, Billy?" she asked, starting down the stairs after the child.

"Pancakes? With maple syrup?" He looked back up at her hopefully.

"Pancakes." Pancakes from scratch. The only pancakes Erica had ever made had come out of a box of mix. She imagined they were a lot more difficult to make when Aunt Jemima's smiling image wasn't sitting encouragingly on the kitchen counter.

And getting maple syrup probably required the cook to go outside and tap a tree.

"I—I don't suppose you know how to make pancakes, do you, Billy?"

"No, ma'am. I don't know how to cook."

"No...no, I guess you wouldn't."

Erica stopped in front of the cast-iron stove and gazed unhappily at the stack of firewood beside it. Cooking pancakes in an electric frying pan with a Teflon surface was undoubtedly easier than—

"Don't you know how to make pancakes, ma'am?" The incredulous tone of Billy's voice clearly implied that was impossible.

"Well, they're not my speciality, Billy."

"What's your speciality?"

"Ahhh...boiled eggs?" She couldn't possibly go wrong boiling eggs. Not even on this stove. "Do you like boiled eggs?"

Billy's hesitant nod suggested he might not like boiled eggs in the slightest. But Erica didn't imagine she had a chance of producing palatable pancakes.

"And biscuits, too?" the child asked hopefully. "My pa always makes biscuits with eggs."

"Yes. Yes, of course we'll have biscuits." And she'd make a batch that didn't burn if it killed her.

"Do you want me to fetch the eggs from Mrs. McCully, ma'am?"

"Is that where you usually get eggs?"

"Yup. She keeps hens. Johnnie and I sometimes collect the eggs."

"Well...yes, I guess you'd better get the eggs, then."

"And some water? I can get fresh water from the well, too."

"Yes. Thank you, Billy. You're being a wonderful help. You get the eggs and water." And I, she added silently, will get this beastly stove going and try to remember all the ingredients for those damned biscuits.

By the time Billy returned, Erica's fire was blazing and the stove's... She searched her mind and realized she didn't know the pre-electricity word for the metal cooking circles on the stove...but, whatever they were called, they were growing warm.

Warm, not hot, she reflected ruefully. It would likely be noon before she got breakfast on the table. And, by then, the stove would have made the kitchen even hotter than the scorching July day would be outside.

She put some of the water on to boil and stuck the tray, dotted with soggy lumps of biscuit dough, into the oven. It wasn't terribly hot yet, either. But meat was better if it was cooked slowly. With any luck, that held true for biscuits, too.

Billy plopped down at the table and watched Erica for a moment as she began squeezing oranges for juice.

"My pa said he's going to be gone for days. Maybe more than a week."

"Mmm. I guess Carson City's a fair distance away."

"He said I didn't have to stay with the McCully's. He said you'd look after me."

"Yes. Of course I will. I'm looking forward to spending some time with you."

"He said you'd look after me and I'd look after Cheyenne."

"That sounds like a good deal to me, Billy."

The child sat quietly for a minute, one short leg swinging back and forth in front of his chair.

"My pa said you remembered where you're from. That you're from Boston...same as us."

"Mmm-hmm," Erica murmured, wishing Hank had taken the time to let her know exactly what he'd told Billy.

"Do you have any little boys at home in Boston, ma'am?"

"No. No, I don't."

"No. My pa told me you didn't. No girls, either? Right? And no dog?"

Erica glanced over at Billy's inquisitive expression. So this was how children checked up on the truth of what adults told them. She fleetingly wished she wasn't an only child. Even having a niece or nephew would undoubtedly have given her some idea of the ground rules.

"No...no girls, either, Billy. No children and no dog."

"Don't you like little boys?"

"Oh, yes. I like little boys fine. Dogs, too." She smiled at Billy's obvious relief. "I especially like nine-year-old little boys. That's a good age. I just don't have any children because I don't have a husband."

"My pa told me that, too." Billy lapsed into silence.

"Mrs. McCully," he finally offered, "Mrs. McCully said that was mighty pre...prec...precoolar."

"Peculiar?"

Billy nodded.

"What did she say was mighty peculiar?"

"That you don't have a husband. She said a woman who looked like you without a husband was precoolar."

"Mrs. McCully said that to you, Billy?"

The little boy shook his head fiercely. "No. She said it to Mr. McCully. But Johnnie and me heard."

"I see." Erica turned to the stove, wondering what else Johnnie and Billy had overheard.

"Me and Johnnie are going to the hills after breakfast. Mrs. McCully said she'd make us a lunch—so we could have a picnic. Is that okay, ma'am?"

"Yes. Of course. I could..." Erica paused, having rapid second thoughts about offering to pack something for the boys herself. Johnnie's mother had seven children. She undoubtedly knew all about what good picnic lunches consisted of; she undoubtedly didn't include boiled eggs in them.

"I could get some housework done while you're on your picnic, Billy. It's about time I cleaned the house."

Erica glanced across the kitchen at the sound of the door opening. A little boy, sturdier-looking than Billy and several inches taller, stood in the doorway peering at her. He was holding a ragged brown knapsack.

Cheyenne pushed his way in past the child and trotted over to flop by the stove.

The boy continued to stare.

"Hello," Erica tried.

"Good morning, ma'am," he offered politely. He looked questioningly at Billy. "Ain't you done breakfast yet?"

"Nope. Miss James is boiling the eggs I got."

The boy who Erica assumed was Johnnie made a face. "I didn't know you was going to have to eat 'em for breakfast."

"They'll be good." Billy assured him staunchly. "Miss James is making them...and biscuits, too."

Erica managed not to laugh. "You must be Johnnie McCully."

The boy nodded, eyeing her closely again, making her suspect she'd been discussed extensively in the McCully household.

"I was just about to pour Billy a glass of orange juice, Johnnie. Would you like one as well?"

"Yes, ma'am!"

Erica looked at the small amount of liquid she'd managed to squeeze from half a dozen oranges. Her hands were already sticky, orange colored and sore from pressing the fruit.

She decided she didn't really want any juice after all, divided what little there was into two glasses, and took them over to the table.

Johnnie dropped his knapsack onto the floor and grabbed a chair.

With her peripheral vision, Erica caught sight of Cheyenne silently rising and skulking over to the knapsack. She gestured at it. "Is your picnic lunch in there, Johnnie?"

The boy leaped off his chair and snatched the sack from under Cheyenne's nose.

"We'll give you some at lunchtime," Billy solemnly assured the dog.

"Ma'am?" Johnnie said, slurping his juice down in one large gulp.

"Yes, Johnnie?"

"Ma'am, I think your biscuits are done."

Erica glanced toward the stove, suddenly aware of an unpleasant smell in the kitchen. Her spirits plummeted at the sight of dark smoke spiraling from the oven.

ERICA PEERED INTO the cooled oven, trying to decide whether or not cleaning it would be worth the effort.

She couldn't imagine it would. Hopefully, most of the black, charred bits coating it had been there long before she'd begun trying her hand at baking.

She'd gotten the rest of the house in reasonable order. Surely she deserved a break. She contemplated the coffeepot, weighing her desire for a caffeine fix against the effort brewing coffee would take, and decided a glass of water would be more refreshing.

She reached for the bucket, knowing the water in the well would be far cooler than the remainder of what Billy had brought in this morning. Her hand paused midreach as the kitchen door flew open.

Johnnie McCully rushed in, terror written across his face.

Erica stood staring at him as he skittered to a halt in front of her. The instant he'd appeared, her heart had begun racing wildly; she was suddenly unable to swallow. Something awful must have happened to Billy!

"You gotta come, ma'am," Johnnie hollered breathlessly. "You gotta come! Billy's having one of his spells!"

Oh, Lord! Her worst fear was reality.

Johnnie was already rushing back outside. Erica gathered her skirt up and raced after him.

They ran past the few houses behind Hank's, then into the open plain that surrounded Mountainview, heading in the direction of the hills that lay south of town.

With every step, Johnnie seemed to be pulling farther ahead of Erica. She hadn't realized children could run so fast. She wanted to ask exactly where Billy was, how bad his spell seemed, how it had started.

But Johnnie was too far ahead to ask him anything. And she was already almost breathless. She wiped her sleeve across her face. Her entire body was dripping with perspiration. She tried to run faster, cursing the hot sun beating down on them.

A sharp pain stabbed her side. She forced her legs to keep moving, telling herself the hills weren't far. But how long had the boys walked for? How much farther before she reached Billy?

They started into the hills. The going suddenly became more difficult. Erica was certain she was about to collapse when Johnnie slowed his pace and looked back.

"Billy's down there, ma'am." The boy pointed in the direction of a cleft between two hills. "We were going to picnic by the stream down there."

Johnnie turned away and began running again.

Erica stumbled after him. The pain in her side was lodged permanently now, stabbing like the blade of a knife with every step. And her throat felt raw. Each breath of air painfully seared its lining.

The sound of a dog howling echoed amidst the hills. Cheyenne! A moment later, Erica spotted him. He was a hundred yards or so away, staring directly at them.

Even at this distance, Erica could see his hackles were raised. He was standing protectively in front of Billy.

The child lay, a crumpled heap, on the ground.

Fresh fear set Erica's heart pounding even harder as she rushed to Billy, praying he wasn't dead.

The little boy was curled into a ball, lying on one side, gasping harshly for breath as if it had been he, rather than Erica, who'd just run more than a mile. But he wasn't dead.

Cheyenne continued to stare at Erica as she approached, his yellow eyes unblinking.

"It's okay, Cheyenne," she whispered as she drew near.

The dog hesitated, then moved from in front of Billy and stood watchfully beside him.

Erica knelt at Billy's side and wrapped her arms gently about his quivering body. His pitiful frailness brought tears to her eyes. This just wasn't fair! Not to happen to a sweet little boy like Billy.

"I'm here, Billy," she whispered, uncertain if he was even conscious. "I'm here to look after you. You're going to be fine."

The child opened his eyes for a moment and murmured something incoherent. At least he was conscious. That had to be a positive sign. Didn't it? But his breathing was noisy, rapid and shallow, as if he was fighting for every bit of air.

And his face and lips were a livid red. Perspiration drenched his skin. Erica touched his forehead. It burned beneath her palm.

She glanced frantically at Johnnie, unable to remember a single word of what Hank had told her about dealing with this situation. This situation he'd assured her wouldn't come up.

"Do you know what to do, Johnnie? Have you seen Billy like this before?"

Johnnie nodded, wide-eyed. "My mother rubs his back, ma'am. And you have to get the fever down."

Erica forced her mind into recall. Hank had talked about liquid on the lungs. Yes, rubbing Billy's back was right . . . much like burping a baby. It would help him cough up that liquid.

She maneuvered Billy's head onto her lap and could feel his fever burning through to her body. She pulled up the hem of her dress and ripped at her petticoat, managing to tear off a large strip of the cotton.

She thrust it at Johnnie, ignoring the way his eyes had grown even wider. "Run to the stream, Johnnie. Get this dripping wet and run back with it."

Johnnie took off like an obedient jackrabbit.

Erica shifted Billy's head slightly, turning his face to one side and began massaging his back, praying she was doing it the right way.

She ran her palms gently along either side of his spine, then across his back, beneath where his lungs would be.

Billy emitted a tiny, gurgling noise. It frightened her half to death, but she smoothed her hands down his thin back again. He coughed a dry-sounding little cough. That was a good sign. Wasn't it?

Johnnie raced back to them, the rag of her petticoat a sopping ball in his hands.

"I need your help, Johnnie. I want you to wipe Billy's face with that cloth. Have you seen your mother do it?"

The child nodded.

"Good. Then you know how. I'm going to keep on massaging Billy's back, and you're going to get his fever down."

Johnnie squatted beside Erica and tentatively patted at Billy's face with the wet fabric.

"That's fine, Johnnie. Keep wetting his entire face. And the back of his neck. And when the water in the cloth starts feeling warm, run back and wet it in the stream again."

Erica began murmuring a string of reassuring phrases to Billy, continuing to massage his back, praying they were doing the right things.

Johnnie made so many trips back and forth to the stream that Erica lost count.

Her words gradually became babble to her ears but she kept speaking, hoping she sounded reassuring. Her arms began aching. She continued stroking Billy's back.

"He doesn't feel so hot," Johnnie whispered.

Erica paused to touch Billy's forehead. "You're right, Johnnie. You've done a good job. What— Do you know how long I should keep rubbing his—"

Billy suddenly erupted into a violent coughing spell that set his little body shuddering. The coughs shook it mercilessly.

Erica stared down at him in horror, not knowing what to do in the face of this loud, painful-sounding hacking.

These body-wracking coughs were nothing like the few dry ones that had preceded them. These were liquid, choking coughs that were causing Billy to gag, that were threatening his breathing. And he was sobbing between coughs!

Oh, Lord! He was going to choke to death! Terrified, Erica gathered the child into her arms and held him tightly to her, rocking him, hoping the solid warmth of her body against his would somehow ease Billy's torment.

The shuddering little boy felt so frail, Erica was certain he was going to die in her arms. She couldn't let him! Hank had entrusted Billy to her care. Billy had to survive.

She hugged him even more closely, suddenly fully understanding how Hank could give up his son, why he was insisting Erica take the boy to the future. And her few lingering doubts about the wisdom of that plan vanished. It offered the only way for Billy to live.

Suddenly, Billy retched to one side and began coughing up liquid. Erica stroked his heaving back, feeling utterly helpless.

The child coughed for a painful, heartrending eternity. Then, mercifully, his hacking began to diminish. Gradually, his shuddering lessened.

Erica took the rag from Johnnie and wiped Billy's face clean. She glanced at the damp white cotton. It was stained red with blood.

She closed her eyes and hugged Billy to her once more. Hank simply had to succeed in Carson City. White Cloud simply had to give them the magic.

Erica sat, holding Billy, until he was completely still, until the last weak tremors had subsided.

Eventually, he drew back a little. His face was tear stained. His complexion had turned from red to white.

"I'm okay now, ma'am," he assured her weakly. "I won't cough any more."

"Well...well, I guess we should get along home then," Erica murmured with false cheeriness. "How about I give you a ride?"

Billy merely nodded and cuddled back against Erica's shoulder.

She easily managed to stand up with the child in her arms. He seemed to weigh nothing at all.

Johnnie picked up his knapsack, and the three of them started back to Mountainview, Cheyenne trailing at Erica's heels.

"Johnnie," Erica murmured as they neared Hank's house, "would you mind going home and asking your mother to come by? When she can. When she has a moment. Tell her what happened."

"Yes ma'am. She'll come right away, ma'am. I know she will. But Billy will be fine now, ma'am. You'll see. After a couple of days in bed he'll be fine again. Just like before."

Johnnie scurried off in the direction of his own house.

Erica opened the kitchen door and carried Billy upstairs. Quickly, she undressed him, rubbed his skinny body with a towel, then pulled a nightshirt over his head and tucked him into bed. She kissed his forehead gently.

Billy smiled weakly at her as she drew away.

"I want you to try to sleep now, Billy." The words were clearly unnecessary. Billy snuggled his head into the pillow, looking as if he'd be asleep before Erica even left his room.

He'd be fine, Erica firmly reassured herself. Johnnie had sounded certain of that. And Mrs. McCully would come by and tell Erica exactly what she should do for Billy.

But she knew, without any doubt, the little boy would only be fine until his next spell seized him.

Erica stood in the doorway, watching Hank's son, knowing Hank would do everything he possibly could to assure the meeting in Carson City ended with Numaga and the other chiefs satisfied.

BY RIDING HARD, Hank had taken only two days to travel through the mountains that lay between his home and Carson City. Now, he gazed down at desert. A few more hours would bring him to his destination.

But between here and Eagle Valley, where the capital was nestled near the Carson River, uninhabitable land stretched before him, surrounded on all sides by snow-clad mountains.

Hank clicked the reins. The black gelding he was riding started down the trail.

As they descended, trees became scarcer. By the time they reached level ground, sagebrush was the only vegetation. Gray sagebrush, covered by the same powdery alkali dust that made this desert look like solid ash.

The dust hung visibly in the air. Thick clouds of it billowed up with each clop of Baron's hoofs. The horse snorted, clearly dismayed at leaving the fresh mountain air.

As they progressed across the desert, the gelding's coat gradually turned gray. Hank glanced at his clothes. By the time they reached Carson City he'd look like a ghost rider.

Animal skeletons dotted the landscape on either side of the trail. Some had obviously lain there for years and were gradually turning into dust, becoming one with the desert.

Other carcasses still had dry skin clinging to them. The only signs of life, other than Hank and Baron, were ravens sitting tearing at the dead remains.

After half an hour or so, Hank's eyes started burning. Dust particles were clogging his nose, irritating his throat.

Eventually, Carson City appeared in the distance. Baron trotted on, finally reaching the outer end of the main street.

The city was no more impressive a capital than Hank had recalled. Its population was only about ten thousand and, aside from scattered housing, it consisted of four or five blocks of tiny frame stores, packed closely together and fronted by a boardwalk.

All that visibly differentiated Carson City from a dozen other small Nevada towns was its dearth of saloons. Likely, that was because this area had once been part of the adjacent Mormon state of Utah.

Hank rode to the middle of town where its open plaza lay. A few teamsters were camped in the large, unfenced area. On one side of the plaza was a livery stable.

With Baron entrusted to a stablehand, Hank walked, bone-tired and saddle-sore, to Mrs. O'Flannigan's boarding house, where the territorial secretary lived.

With any luck, there'd be a spare room. A wash and a sleep would put Hank in shape to talk with Orion Clemens tonight. The more time he and the secretary had to discuss the Indians' problems before the meeting tomorrow, the better.

THE FOLLOWING MORNING, sitting over coffee with Orion in Mrs. O'Flannigan's parlor, Hank was hopeful the meeting would be a success.

He'd expected several government officials would be meeting with the chiefs but, until his arrival, Orion had apparently intended to deal with them alone.

He'd seemed relieved at the idea of Hank sitting in, had appeared only too happy to rely on Hank's advice about the issues of whites hunting and grazing cattle on land the Indians considered theirs.

Orion's reliance, Hank reflected ruefully, would benefit everyone involved. From what he'd been able to gather, despite Orion's evasiveness, the secretary hadn't had a whole lot to do with the Indians in Nevada.

Orion hadn't met a single one of the four chiefs who were coming to Carson City. And he obviously didn't have much of a grasp of the "Indian problem," as he called it. Worse, he apparently didn't care much about its resolution.

Hank's opinion of Sam's older brother had sunk steadily lower as they'd talked last night. The secretary didn't expect to be in Nevada much longer. He was vying for a more prestigious government posting back East. And his major concern was that the duration of his stay in Nevada run as smooth a course as possible.

He'd undoubtedly agree to any Indian demands that Hank assured him would keep the tribal hostilites from escalating in the near future. So, as long as Orion's willingness to listen to Hank lasted through the meeting, Hank knew he could succeed. He could negotiate an agreement that would make the chiefs happy.

At least it would make them happy for a short time. But Hank suspected that, whenever Orion moved on, any treaties he'd negotiated would turn out to be worthless. They'd be broken at the whim of the new territorial secretary.

Hank tried to ignore the guilt he felt about that . . . and his general guilt about what white settlers were doing to the Indian way of life.

He was only one man. And he was a physician, not a politician. How could he expect to have any lasting effect on policies? How could he hope to do any better than improve the Paiutes' situation for a little while?

According to Erica, none of the treaties had lasted . . . none of the Indian tribes had fared well for long.

Hank glanced across the breakfast table at Orion, thinking how unlike his younger brother this sober, self-centered man was. What had Erica called Orion? When Hank had told her Sam's brother was pious and priggish and drove Sam crazy?

A jerk. Yes, that was it. Hank smiled, thinking of Erica's strange words, thinking of Erica. Lord! How could it be he seldom thought of anything else? What on earth would he do when she was gone? When both she and Billy were gone? They were all he cared about in the world.

He tried not to dwell on that fact, because, whenever he did, he wondered if Erica wasn't right . . . if he shouldn't consider going with them.

But he couldn't. He knew he'd never be able to succeed in a future that sounded so completely different from life as he knew it. And he couldn't be a failure in Erica's eyes . . . or in his son's.

Being a memory, and having memories, was preferable to being a failure.

"So," Orion muttered, "I guess we have to meet in the legislature, seeing as how these fellows are chiefs. I doubt the townsfolk are going to like having Indians in there."

"Actually, Orion, the chiefs would probably prefer to meet in the plaza. Our buildings make them uncomfortable. I imagine they'd be far more at ease if you met with them outside. They'd take it as you making an effort to meet them on their own turf."

"Meet them on their own what?" Orion stared across the table, his expression curious.

"Uhh..." Tarnation! Now he was starting to use phrases from the future. Erica was right. If he wasn't careful he'd say something that sounded so strange he'd be carted away.

"What I mean, Orion, is if you were meeting with them in one of their villages the meeting would be outside...around the council fire. I reckon they'd consider the plaza the closest thing you've got to a council fire."

Orion almost smiled. "Good. That's a good idea, Hank. The Indians will think I'm being considerate of their customs and the townsfolk will think I'm keeping the Indians out of our legislature. The plaza it'll be. Couldn't have come up with a better plan myself, Hank."

Hank stared into his coffee, refraining from pointing out that Orion couldn't have come up with a plan half as good, let alone better.

What did it matter? If the Indians were pleased with the results of this meeting, Hank had to give most of the credit to White Cloud. He might as well give the balance of it to Orion.

"I noticed there were a few teamsters camped in the plaza yesterday, Orion. Might be a thought to have them cleared out before the chiefs arrive. Might be a thought to decorate the plaza's liberty pole, as well— make them believe you've put a lot of effort into welcoming them."

"Good ideas, Hank. Good ideas. Couldn't have come up with better myself."

Orion passed Hank's suggestions along, in the form of commands, to one of his assistants, then turned back.

"Why don't we stroll on down to the plaza, Hank? Make sure the boys get everything in order. I must admit to being mighty curious to see those chiefs arriving—to watch the townsfolks' reactions when a bunch of naked redskins ride down Carson Street."

CHAPTER THIRTEEN

IT WAS ALMOST NOON before a cloud of dust in the distance announced the Indian chiefs' arrival.

Hank stood beside Orion in front of the plaza, watching as the chiefs entered town and rode, single file, along Carson Street, looking neither right nor left.

Each of the four men sat tall and upright on his pony. Each head of long, straight black hair bore traces of desert dust.

Despite the midday heat, the chiefs were formally dressed in buckskin leggings and beaded leather vests. None of them appeared to be armed.

On the boardwalk, residents of Carson City watched the procession with apparent apprehension. Several men checked that their pistols and rifles were ready.

Hank prayed there were no itchy trigger fingers in the crowd.

At the head of the group rode Chief Numaga, an impressive figure with his ramrod-straight back, broad shoulders and muscular chest.

Orion cleared his throat. "That first one looks like a redskin to be reckoned with."

"That's Chief Numaga, Orion. He's a reasonable man. All he wants is a chance to tell you the Indians' side of the issue. All he wants you to do is treat them fairly.''

Hank glanced back at the riders. ''The chief behind Numaga is Maungwadaus, next is Sasagon and, finally, Chief Kahkewaguonaby.''

''You don't expect me to remember those names, do you?'' Orion sputtered. ''The message I got about this meeting was from Numaga. His name I can pronounce, but the others—''

''I'll help you with the others, Orion,'' Hank snapped. ''In fact, it might be best if I do most of the talking. They'll accept that. In tribal meetings, the chief—the man in charge—often doesn't say much.''

Orion smiled. Obviously, he liked being thought of as ''the man in charge.''

''You go right ahead and talk, Hank. You just might do better than I would. I've never really met with any Indians face-to-face like this.''

''What? Never?'' Hank stared at Orion in disbelief. How could he not have mentioned that little detail before this? In time for Hank to have covered protocol with him?

Hellfire and damnation! If Orion made some idiotic mistake, if he insulted one of these chiefs, the meeting would end instantly...and with it, Hank's hopes for Billy's future.

''Orion, are you serious? How could you never have met with any Indians in all the time you've been in Nevada?''

The secretary shrugged. ''I delegated. Indians make me nervous. This meeting just came up so suddenly I didn't have a chance to—''

"Orion, listen to me! Indian chiefs are extremely easy to insult. Say the wrong thing and you're liable to see Carson City attacked."

Orion's face lost three shades of tan. "But—but—"

"Follow my lead, Orion. Don't do anything I don't do. And don't say anything unless there's no way 'round it. We'll just listen to the chiefs. Then you and I will talk about what they want in private. All right?"

Orion nodded quickly.

Hank could almost see visions of Carson City under Indian attack dancing in the other man's head.

The chiefs reined their ponies to a halt in front of the plaza. Numaga recognized Hank's presence with an almost imperceptible nod, and the four Indians dismounted.

"Have someone picket their ponies," Hank hissed to the nearest of Orion's assistants.

The man hurried to obey.

Hank stepped forward. "Welcome, honored guests. I would like to present the territorial secretary, Orion Clemens. Sir," he continued, turning to Orion, "this is Chief Numaga."

Numaga nodded formally.

Hank prayed Orion would have the brains to do the same.

He did.

Hank breathed again and went on, "Chief Maungwadaus... Chief Sasagon... Chief Kahkewaguonaby."

Hank gestured to the large pipe slung, on a rawhide strip, over Numaga's shoulder. "You have brought your peace pipe. That is good. We will be able to have a proper ceremony."

Hank led the way to the plaza's center where the decorated liberty pole stood. He indicated the chiefs should sit, then joined their circle in the same cross-legged pose they favored. Orion awkwardly followed.

"Will you offer up the prayer to the Great Spirit, Numaga?"

"Yes."

The four Indians closed their eyes. Hank waited to be sure Orion was cooperating before he closed his own, then listened as Numaga prayed in the lilting Paiute language.

Once finished, Numaga slowly filled his pipe, tamping the tobacco with his forefinger.

The chief's pipe had always fascinated Hank. On one side of the end of the stem was an ornate pipe bowl, on the other, the head of a tomahawk. Hank had never figured out the logic of having a combination war axe and peace pipe. He glanced at Orion.

The secretary's gaze was glued to the tomahawk head.

Once the pipe was going, Numaga drew deeply, then slowly exhaled the smoke. After his one long puff, he passed the pipe to his right. Chief Maungwadaus took a deep breath, exhaled, then handed the pipe on.

It was passed around the circle the ceremonial five times. Then the chiefs chanted five songs and the time had come for them to speak their feelings.

"The white man," Numaga said quietly, "has brought trouble to our land, Mr. Secretary. He builds houses near our waterholes, near our villages and camps. He spreads strong liquors among us.

"Other Indian bands have brought war to the white man for some seasons now. Still, we four have kept our braves peaceful.

"But now things happen to make that impossible. The white man now destroys our land.

"No animals, no plants, no birds or fish were exterminated in this land by Indians. The Indian is kin to all living things.

"But the white man has no reverence for mother earth. He hunts our food for sport. His spotted buffalo make our land barren."

Hank caught Orion's quizzical glance. "The cattle," he murmured. "The herds of cattle that are being grazed on the plains."

"This is our country, Mr. Secretary," Numaga continued. "Our forefathers lived on this land from sea to sea. The Great Spirit created the plants and animals and my people. All lived in peace until the white man came. Now you take our land.

"You give it white names. First, you call this land where we sit part of Utah, call it Carson County. Now you call it Nevada Territory. You do not care that it is not your land to call.

"We must have our land. It is large. We will share. But the white man must share, as well. You must tell your people this, Mr. Secretary.

"There must be space for us to spread our blankets...space where the white man does not destroy the earth and its creatures. To the east are white man's cities. To the west is the ocean. We must have space between.

"This is what we want from you, Mr. Secretary. A treaty to tell the white man that the part of this land that was lived on by our forefathers is still our land...only our land. Then there will yet be peace."

Numaga gazed at Orion.

Orion looked at Hank.

"Chief Numaga," Hank offered quickly, "what you have asked is reasonable. Would you trust me to talk further with the secretary on your behalf? Would you trust me to help draw up a fair treaty that will assure you keep your land? Will you meet with us again tomorrow and discuss what Mr. Secretary feels is a fair treaty?"

Numaga looked back at Orion. "We do not trust many white men, Mr. Secretary. Too often they have promised one thing and done another. But Hank Lockhart is a good man. I trust him. If you listen to him speak for us, the tomahawks can be buried forever. We will meet tomorrow. We will hear what your treaty offers."

As one man, the chiefs rose.

Hank nodded to them. Orion followed suit.

The chiefs turned and walked to their ponies. Without a backward glance, they mounted and began their ride out of Carson City.

"Well, Hank? Think we can draw up something that'll satisfy them?"

"I'm sure we can, Orion. But do you think you'll be able to enforce our promises to them? Think you'll be able to make the settlers obey the terms of your treaty?"

"I," Orion declared, straightening his shoulders, "I am the Territorial Secretary of Nevada. Treaties with local Indian tribes fall under my jurisdiction. If I order settlers to stay out of certain areas of the territory, they will. My word is law."

Hank eyed Orion closely, trying to decide if the man was actually such a pompous jerk that he truly believed the settlers would listen to his laws. They wouldn't. Hank had no doubt they wouldn't.

So why was he taking part in this futile exercise? Numaga trusted him, and he was encouraging the chiefs to sign a treaty that was doomed to fail. Was he betraying their trust? Was he being completely self-ish... wanting only the magic White Cloud had promised him... wanting only that Billy might live?

No. That wasn't his entire purpose. Even if Erica had never appeared in his life, he'd have done what he could to help the Paiutes, have done what he could to help formulate a treaty that would be fair to them.

Only now that he knew what would happen to the Indians—now that he knew what would happen in the future—how the treaties would all be broken, how the Indians would be forced onto reservations, his efforts seemed so useless, of such temporary benefit.

Hank gazed along Carson Street, watching the chiefs riding away. They were such proud men. They still had hopes of preserving their land, their way of life.

Hank felt sadness for them. For their future. For his own future.

He was going to succeed. He and Orion would draw up an acceptable treaty. Yes, he was going to succeed. And his reward would be losing everything that mattered to him.

USING A THICK TOWEL as a pot holder, Erica pulled her latest batch of breakfast biscuits from the stove. She grinned down at them. For the first time, not a single one had burned.

She heard Billy opening the kitchen door and offered up another tiny prayer of thanks that he'd recovered so rapidly. She'd followed Mrs. McCully's advice to the letter and, after only a few days rest and care, Billy had bounced back to health.

His recovery had struck her as miraculous. But she never wanted to go through anything like what had happened again.

"You were awfully fast, Billy," she said, turning. Her breath caught. It wasn't Billy. It was Hank. Filling the doorway with his presence.

"Welcome home." She slid the tray onto the stove top and tossed the towel aside.

"How did the meeting go?" Her words sounded inane, as if she was Harriet Housewife, greeting her husband after a ho-hum day at the office.

She stood in a state of suspension, waiting for Hank to tell her what had happened in Carson City, waiting to learn what course her future would take.

He walked across the room, pulled something from his jacket pocket and held it out to her.

She stared at the small, brown leather pouch lying in his palm. It was decorated with elaborate white beadwork. A length of narrow rawhide tied its top tightly closed.

"From—from White Cloud?"

"Yes. It contains the magic, Erica. I rode back from Carson City with Numaga. We reached his camp late last night."

Erica continued to gaze at the fat little pouch, not quite able to believe the shaman had given them the magic, not feeling quite brave enough to take it from Hank's hand.

"You managed to do what White Cloud wanted, then," she murmured. "The Indians were pleased."

"Yes. I don't know how much actual help I was or how long the treaty will last but, at the moment, they're satisfied. And I gave White Cloud the credit she wanted."

Erica couldn't force her eyes from the leather pouch. "What is it, Hank? What's inside?"

"I don't know exactly. You're not to open it. You simply hang it around your neck once you're in the mine—once it's time to leave. When you get home, the pouch will be empty. The magic will have been used up."

"I simply hang it around my neck when it's time to leave," Erica repeated dully. "And..."

"And you wait outside the secondary tunnel. You wait until you see the shimmering blue light. Then you hold Billy's hand and walk into the light."

"I hold Billy's hand..."

"Yes."

"Only Billy's hand?" she whispered, praying Hank had changed his mind, yet certain her prayer wasn't going to be answered.

"Erica... Erica I thought about us the entire time I was away. Even during the meeting. Even when I was supposed to be concentrating on helping the chiefs, all I could think about was you... and whether or not I could...

"But I can't, Erica. I just can't."

Erica didn't take her eyes off Hank as he spoke, but his gaze didn't leave the floor.

"I've always thought I was a brave man," he added, as if to himself. "But I reckon, deep down, I'm a coward, afraid of the unknown—of being a failure in your world.

"Oh, dammit, Erica! I'll tell you the deep dark truth. It's not a fear of failure so much as a fear that I wouldn't be the man I am now...that I'd grow to hate myself because of that . . . and you and Billy would grow to hate me, as well."

Erica began to protest. Hank cut her off. "Traveling to the future wouldn't be like my coming west was, Erica. There'd be no heading home if I found I'd made a mistake."

Finally, his eyes met hers.

She nodded, clenching her fists at her sides, not certain she could speak and determined not to cry. She'd known he wouldn't change his mind. So why should the confirmation of that be making her heart ache so terribly.

"I—I understand, Hank," she managed to say. "And when . . . when will it be time for me to leave?"

"This afternoon."

"This afternoon? So soon? I didn't think . . . I assumed we'd have a little time. I only just learned how to bake biscuits properly . . ."

Hank stared down at his outstretched hand. "You'd better take this magic. I'll get you something to tie it to, something you can hang around your neck."

Erica reached for the pouch, feeling as if she was in a trance. *This afternoon.* In a few hours she'd be gone. She and Billy would be gone, but Hank would still be here.

No! That simply couldn't be how this ended. It wasn't right. If Hank couldn't bring himself to come with her, maybe . . .

An image of Billy formed in her mind's eye—an image of Billy feverish, his face red, breathing rapidly. She could almost hear his heartbreaking, wracking coughs, could almost feel his thin body trembling in her arms.

Billy couldn't stay here. And that meant she couldn't stay with Hank. She shoved the magic into her pocket, knowing out of sight wasn't going to mean out of mind.

"Where's Billy, Erica?"

"I...he just took something over to Johnnie McCully. He'll be back in a minute. Hank... Billy was sick while you were away. I didn't know what to do. Hank, he needs you. I—"

"Did you manage all right with him? He's better now?"

"Yes, but he needs—"

"Erica, what he needs is medicine I don't know anything about. He'll be fine in the future. He's young enough to learn how to live in your world. And the future is where you belong, Erica. You'll both be fine."

"And two out of three ain't bad," Erica whispered.

"What?"

"Nothing, Hank. It was just something silly that popped into my mind. Just words from an old Meatloaf song."

"A song about old meatloaf?"

Erica shook her head wearily.

"No. Meatloaf is a singer...a rock-and-roll singer...a... Forget it, Hank. It doesn't matter." Nothing matters, she reflected miserably.

"Well... well, I'll talk with Billy as soon as he gets back. I reckon he's going to be mighty upset for a while, Erica. I'm sorry you'll have to deal with that."

"It can't be helped, Hank. And I can handle it. It'll take time, but Billy and I have been getting along fine."

"Good...I'm awfully glad of that.

"After I've talked with him, Erica, I'll go to the bank. I don't have much savings but I can probably get a fair-sized loan. I'll take it in gold. Hopefully, what it's worth in your world will at least be enough to cover Billy's medical treatment."

"Hank, I don't want your savings! And I don't want you going into debt for me. Without all your help I'd be..."

What she'd be doing without all his help would be staying here. And that was the opposite of what she'd been insisting she wanted to do. And she knew it was impossible for Billy. So why was she wishing— It was so damned futile...so damned sad.

"Erica, stop being argumentative. You have to take whatever I can give you. Billy will be with you for a long time."

Hank met her gaze once more. Despite his matter-of-fact tone, he was clearly as close to crying as she.

She wanted to hug him, wanted to hug him and never let him go. But—

"Pa!" Billy raced through the doorway. Cheyenne hurtled in after the boy.

"Pa! You're home!"

Hank caught Billy up in his arms and swung him around.

Erica could see tears gleaming in Hank's eyes. She turned away and fumbled with the biscuits, burning a finger on the tray, biting back tears of pain. If she began crying she might never stop.

"I want to talk to you for a few minutes, son. Let's go into my office."

As she heard the office door close, Erica gave in and allowed her tears to begin falling.

Cheyenne brushed against her thigh. Sightlessly, she stroked his head, trying not to imagine the scene in the next room.

HANK CLOSED HIS OFFICE DOOR and crossed the room, breathing slowly and deeply, trying to calm himself. It was going to take a lot to get through this conversation with Billy, to get through the remainder of this day.

"Son, come and sit over here beside me."

Billy bounced across the room and scrambled onto the couch.

Hank wrapped one arm around Billy's boney shoulder. He was such a skinny little boy. And that, Hank reminded himself, steeling his will, was the reason his son had to leave him and go to the future.

"Billy, Miss James is going home—back to Boston."

Billy looked at his father curiously. "Why? I thought . . . you said she might be staying here."

"I said I wasn't sure, Billy. It turns out she won't be. And I want you to go to Boston with her."

"To Boston?"

"Yes. That'll be fine, won't it son? You like Miss James."

Billy nodded slowly. "But not just me," he said uncertainly. "You'll come, too."

"No, Billy. I've barely gotten back from a trip. I can't keep leaving my patients. They'll up and find themselves another physician."

Billy's grin said he was certain Hank was joshing. "I thought there wasn't another doctor for over a hundred miles."

"Well...a man can't be too cautious. But I want you to go, son—for a very important reason."

"What?"

"There are physicians in Boston who can make you better, Billy. So you won't have any more of your sick spells."

"I—I was sick while you were gone, Pa. Did Miss James tell on me?" Billy looked at Hank guiltily. "Is that why you want me to go? Are you mad at me? I didn't mean to be sick."

"No. No, I'm not the least bit mad at you. I know you didn't mean to be sick. So does Miss James. But the physicians in Boston will cure you—so you won't ever have any more spells."

"Pa...why don't you cure me? You're the best doctor in the world, aren't you?"

"Well, maybe not in quite all the world. I'm not a specialist, Billy. That's the kind of doctor you have to see. There are specialists in Boston."

"But how long do I have to go for? How soon can I come home?"

Hank cleared his throat, barely able to look at his son. "That's...that's the only problem. You see, it's very difficult to explain this, but Miss James is from the future. She lives in the future Boston."

Billy gave Hank a nervous looking smile. "Pa, what do you mean 'future'? I don't understand."

"Son, I don't entirely understand myself. But the important thing is you'll be well. You won't get sick anymore."

"And when I'm well I can come back. But not till then?"

"Billy...the thing is...even after you're well, you'll stay there. You'll stay with Miss James in the future. You won't be able to come back."

"Pa...I don't want to stay in the future! I don't want to go to Boston. I want to stay here with you. I can still be sick. It's all right."

"It's not all right! It's not all right at all! Billy, listen to me...the illness you have is very serious. Billy..."

Oh, damnation! Hank looked away. He couldn't cry in front of his son! He fumbled with his pipe, surreptitiously wiping his his eyes, finally turning back.

"Billy, you have to go to Boston. You have to be cured. If you stay here you're going to die of that sickness."

Tears began rolling down Billy's cheeks. "Pa! I don't care! I don't know anyone in Boston. I don't have any friends there. My friends are here, Pa. Johnnie's here and you're here. I don't want to go anywhere. Don't make me. Unless you come, too."

Billy buried his face against Hank's chest.

Hank hugged the boy tightly, his own tears escaping again, trickling down into his beard.

"I can't, Billy. I can't go with you. You're too young to understand, but Erica—Miss James—will explain it to you when you're older. You'll understand then."

"I won't! I won't understand! If I have to go, why won't you come, too?"

Hank swallowed hard. Why wouldn't he come, too? That was almost all he'd been thinking about from the moment White Cloud had told him it was a possibility.

His going to the future sounded like such a logical idea when Erica argued it...sounded so right when she talked about them all being together...seemed so right with Billy begging him to go.

But it was one thing for them to say he should go with them and another for him to ignore the internal demons that were constantly telling him about the risk he'd be taking, constantly warning him he'd be a failure in Erica's world. A failure to both Erica and his son.

Billy believed his father was the best doctor in the world. He was so proud of that. How would he feel about a father who couldn't even support himself? Hank could imagine, only too clearly, how Billy's love and respect would change if his father was suddenly as helpless and ignorant as a child.

Losing Billy to the future would be bad enough. But traveling with Erica and his son would be worse. If he did that, he'd lose Billy in an even more painful way. The boy's love would gradually turn to contempt. He'd grow to despise rather than idolize his father.

Yet how could Hank explain all that to Billy? Explain that he knew he could never succeed in the future when he was forcing his son to go there?

"Billy...Billy, I can't go with you because my life is here. I—everything I know is here."

"Everything I know is here too, Pa!" Billy wailed.

"Well...well it's that I'm so much older than you, son. It'll be easy for you to make new friends. And you'll have Miss James. She really wants you to go with her. She'll look after you."

"I want you to look after me! You look after me fine! Pa, don't you love me anymore?"

"Oh, Billy." The words choked in Hank's throat. Tears began streaming down his face once more. He hugged Billy more tightly. "Son, don't ever think I'm not coming because I didn't want to be with you. Don't ever think I don't love you."

He stroked Billy's quivering back, wishing his touch could take away the child's pain...and wondering if his own pain would ever subside.

ERICA SAT at the kitchen table, listening to the muffled sounds coming from Hank's office. Her heart ached for Billy. Her heart ached for all three of them. She felt emotionally drained—numb. She imagined the others did, as well. And this afternoon was still to come.

Hank had been talking with Billy for over an hour. Erica could hear the occasional whimper that had replaced the child's earlier sobbing.

Eventually, the sound of his crying ceased entirely, leaving only the deep murmur of Hank's voice interspersed with strained sounding words from Billy.

Finally, the office door opened. Hank and Billy stepped into the kitchen.

Erica held out her arms. Billy rushed to her, pressing his thin body desperately against hers.

She hugged him closely. "It'll be all right, Billy. You'll see. You'll be healthy. And you'll like the future. We'll be happy there."

"Do you...do you really want me to come with you, ma'am?"

"Yes. I really do. Very, very much."

"And they won't hurt me, will they? The special-ists?"

"No, they won't hurt you, Billy."

The boy glanced across the kitchen, his gaze fastening on his dog. "And can we take Cheyenne, too?"

"Take Cheyenne?" Erica stared at the wolf-dog, alarmed by the prospect.

Cheyenne licked his chops.

"Billy," Hank murmured. "I'd really like to keep Cheyenne here. That way I won't be alone."

Billy looked over at the dog and swallowed audibly. "But he'll miss me. Who'll play with him?"

"I'll take care of him, son."

"But I'll miss him, too! Pa, I won't have my friends. I won't have anyone to play with. Cheyenne and me are partners, Pa. Lucky partners. And he'd like the future."

"You'll like the future, Billy," Erica said softly. "But I don't think Cheyenne would. Boston isn't a very good place for a big dog. The city's awfully crowded, so dogs have to be kept on leashes. I don't think Cheyenne would like that at all.

"There's a dog in the apartment across the hall from mine, though. I'm sure you'll be able to play with him. His name is Franklin."

"That's a silly name for a dog," Billy muttered fiercely.

"Well, it was meant as a joke. His owner's name is Paul Roosevelt. So he named the dog Franklin...you know, Franklin D. Roosevelt...?"

There was no flicker of comprehension on either male face.

Of course there wasn't.

"Oh...oh, Franklin D. Roosevelt was the thirty-second president so..." Erica shrugged. The explanation was pointless. Why should Hank or Billy care who the thirty-second president would be?

At least, she reflected blackly, she wouldn't have to try much longer to keep facts from two different centuries separated in her mind.

"Anyway, Billy, Franklin's just a little guy. But he thinks he's the roughest dog in Boston. If we took Cheyenne with us, Franklin would probably challenge Cheyenne to a fight. Then Cheyenne would eat Franklin, and Paul Roosevelt would be awfully upset with us."

Billy bit his lip, obviously holding back fresh tears. "I won't have anyone," he murmured.

"You'll have me, Billy," Erica said gently, taking his hand. "You'll have me, and I'll have you. Why don't we go upstairs and decide what you want to take with you?"

HANK HELPED ERICA DOWN from the buggy. Billy clambered after her, sober-faced. Cheyenne whirled around the little boy in a demented four-footed dance step.

"I didn't realize Cheyenne would follow us all the way to Broken Hill," Erica said quietly.

"He always follows Billy. I should have closed him into the house."

They walked in silence to the mine's entrance. Erica looked from Hank to Billy, certain the three of them constituted the most sombre-looking trio in history.

"Buck? Buck Dursely?" Hank hollered into the mouth of the mine shaft. "It's Hank Lockhart!"

"'Lo Doc! Be right there!" Buck's muffled reply echoed back along the black tunnel to the entrance.

Erica glanced quickly at her long white dress, wondering once again if the outlines of her jeans and T-shirt beneath it were very noticeable. She tucked the camouflage blanket more securely around her red backpack.

Her gaze drifted to Hank, although she knew she shouldn't look at him. Every time she did, she felt like crying again. That was the last thing she wanted to do.

She intended to make as composed an exit as she could manage from this century. She had to—for Billy's sake. She was an adult. She mustn't do anything that would make the boy even more upset.

He was clearly trying his best to be brave, hugging the small case they'd filled with his toys and books. There'd been no point packing clothes that would look strange in 1989.

A lantern's light appeared in the darkness of the tunnel. Moments later, Buck Dursely stepped outside, covered in dirt, shading his eyes from the daylight.

"'Lo, Doc. 'Lo Billy. Come for another look, ma'am?" He treated Erica to his three-toothed grin.

"Yes. Yes, I have. I'm heading back to Boston, Mr. Dursely. I wondered if I, if we, could see that side tunnel again before I go. It was very interesting."

"'Course. 'Course you can. Here, Doc." Buck handed Hank the lantern. "I wouldn't mind a breath of fresh air. Why don't you go along in and I'll wait out here for you."

"Thanks, Buck . . . but we may be a while."

"Take as long as you want. I'll just sit with the sun on my face. Maybe catch a nap. Gettin' a mite tired of mining—of all that darkness. Fact is, I think I'll be givin' up on this old gal soon. Ain't near as promisin' as we first figured she was."

Hank shook his head. "Don't give up on Broken Hill, Buck. Like I told you, I've got a real good feeling about this mine. I think you're going to make your fortune out of it. In fact, I feel right certain about that. Just give it a little longer."

Buck grinned again. "You really believe that, Doc?"

"I really do."

"Well...I'll think on it, Doc. I'll think on it for a spell."

Hank pulled his gold watch from his vest pocket and glanced at the time. "We'd best get on with this," he murmured, turning to Erica and Billy. His voice broke slightly as he spoke.

Erica looked away. It was far too late for discussion, far too late for persuasion. Hank had made his choice. All that was left was to carry off this charade of emotional control for Billy's benefit.

The three of them headed into the tunnel, Cheyenne trailing behind them.

Inside the entrance, Billy kicked viciously at a loose rock. Cheyenne snuffled after it.

They trudged silently along until the lantern's light faintly captured the entrance to the side shaft a few yards ahead.

Erica forced her feet to keep moving, her gaze fastened on the opening, her heart pounding. She didn't want to go! Didn't want to leave Hank! Despite all the logic, this seemed like a terrible mistake.

She glanced at Billy, knowing she had no choice about leaving.

They stopped outside the secondary tunnel.

"Billy, I want to talk to Miss James in private for a minute. And then I'll want to talk to you, son. Don't go very far. Don't go out of sight of the lantern."

Billy gave his father a baleful, teary look and scuffed a few yards along the tunnel. He hunkered down against the wall, hugging Cheyenne and staring into the darkness.

"Where's White Cloud's pouch, Erica?" Hank asked quietly.

"In—in my pocket."

"And the gold is safe in your backpack?"

She nodded, not trusting her voice.

Hank held something out to her. "Here. This belonged to my mother. You can use it to hang the pouch around your neck. And it's something to remember me by for a while.

"Maybe...maybe when Billy's a man...when he marries...you'll give it to his wife. By then, you'll have forgotten all about me."

"Oh, Hank!" The words choked their way out. Tears suddenly blinded her. "Oh, Hank, I'll never forget you. I'll miss you for the rest of my life. Hank, can't you—" She couldn't continue. Her throat was a solid mass.

She took the chain he was holding, trying to see it through her tears. It was beautiful—a heavy gold chain interwoven with pearls. Its beauty made her feel even worse. She wouldn't have believed worse was possible.

"Erica, please don't cry." Hank put the lantern on the tunnel floor, took the backpack from her and put it down, as well.

"Give me the pouch, let me tie it to the chain for you."

Erica dug into her pocket for White Cloud's magic and thrust it at Hank.

Moments later she felt him behind her, his hands on the back of her neck, fastening the chain, setting her skin on fire with the mere brush of his fingers. They lingered for a moment, caressing her neck.

She begged time to stand still. She'd never know the delight of Hank's touch again if they went through with this. How could she live the rest of her life with only memories of him . . . with only memories of what she'd known and lost?

She pressed back against the security of Hank's body, unable to stop herself.

"I love you, Erica," he murmured, his breath warm against her ear. "I'll always love you."

"Oh, Hank!" His name rushed out in a sob. Erica turned and threw her arms around his neck. "Oh, Hank! I'll always love you, too! Why can't there be an always for us together? Why can't you hold me forever?"

"If only I could, Erica," he whispered, hugging her tightly. "If only I could."

Erica clung to Hank, engulfed by misery, certain her heart was going to break. What if she didn't let go of him? What if—

"Erica," Hank said, his voice thick, "Erica . . . the light—the moon shadow. It's begun to shimmer in the tunnel. You can see its glow now. Quickly. We only have a few minutes."

Gently but firmly, Hank removed Erica's arms from around his neck and turned her toward the opening.

Through her tears, she could see the shimmering blue light. It looked exactly as it had the first time... mere weeks ago... when she'd fallen back through time, when the moon shadow had carried her to Hank. But this time it would carry her home, would take her away from him forever.

"Billy," Hank called. "Come here, son."

Erica stood, frozen in place, while Hank knelt and spoke to Billy. He tucked his gold watch into the little boy's pocket, hugged him for a minute, then stood up.

Vaguely, Erica was aware of Hank helping her on with her backpack, aware of him placing Billy's hand in hers, aware of Billy's trembling, of his quiet tears.

"It's time to go," Hank murmured. "I love you both."

He gave Erica a tiny push.

She entered the tunnel, Billy's hand clutched tightly in hers, her entire body screaming that it didn't want to go. They started down the incline.

Erica numbly fingered the chain Hank had given her, pressing the magic pouch securely to her chest.

Each step was taking them farther away from Hank. The blue light eerily beckoned ahead of them.

They'd almost reached it. She couldn't stand this!

She stopped and looked back. Hank stood in the main tunnel, the lantern's light dimly illuminating his figure. He was holding Cheyenne by the scruff of his neck.

"Hank?" she pleaded. "Hank... are you certain...? Hank, please!"

He slowly shook his head. "I can't, Erica. I just can't. I'm sorry."

Eyes burning, throat aching, tears streaming down her face, Erica turned away from Hank, certain her heart would break before she reached the light.

Her feet felt like lead. It took all her effort to walk on. But she did.

The blue light was only a few feet in front of them now. Her blurred vision made its glow seem to shimmer even more intensely.

It was catching at the whiteness of her dress, highlighting the tiny flowers that dotted it, making them look like impossibly blue teardrops.

She glanced at Billy, knowing he needed reassurance. "One more step, love. Just one more step."

And then there was a sound behind them. Erica whirled around, jerking Billy with her, her hopes soaring wildly from the depths of despair to the heights of—

Cheyenne was dashing down the shaft after them— Only Cheyenne. Hank still stood motionless, a lone, forlorn shadow at the tunnel's entrance.

Cheyenne leapt through the air at Billy.

The shimmering light suddenly surged, encircling them, its blue brilliance blinding Erica.

CHAPTER FOURTEEN

"WELL, BILLY what do you think? Is it perfect yet?" Erica stepped away from their Christmas tree to take a full-length look.

Billy moved back, a red ornament in his hand, and stood beside her, eyeing the tree, mimicking her critical pose. His dark eyes were dancing.

Erica smiled at his quiet excitement. Everything about the Christmas season in Boston had enthralled him—from the store displays and houses decorated with lights to the holiday television specials.

And today, when snow had begun falling, blanketing the city in white, he'd insisted they go to the Common and save decorating the tree for later.

They'd stayed out for hours—while Boston had turned into a winter wonderland before their eyes.

And this evening, each time the radio announcer broke into the string of carols with a "news update" about sightings of reindeer pulling a sled across the sky, about Santa Claus being en route from the North Pole to New England, Billy stopped what he was doing to listen intently.

Erica was enjoying sharing Christmas with a child. And she was trying to make their celebration as old-fashioned as possible, with a real tree and a fire crackling in the fireplace.

The apartment was scented with a combination of pine and smoke, an aroma that was reminding her of her grandmother's house at Christmas.

Or perhaps it was seeing Christmas Eve through Billy's eyes that was recalling her childhood memories. He was so fascinated by everything, so full of energy to share in what was going on. And he was so healthy!

If only Hank could see his son. Erica fingered her gold chain—Hank's mother's gold chain—wishing Hank was with them, wishing he'd been able to take the risk.

She'd give anything to have him know how well Billy had responded to treatment.

Barely two weeks into his daily drug therapy, his doctor had told Erica there were definite signs of symptomatic improvement.

By the second month, the child's X rays had showed the infiltrates on his lungs were clearing.

And now he was almost completely cured. There'd still be drug therapy for another six months or so but, after the Christmas break, he'd be switching from the Children's Hospital classes to a regular school.

Erica was certain he'd take that transition in stride. He'd already made neighborhood friends who'd be his classmates. And the intensive tutoring he'd gotten at the hospital had filled in most of the gaps in his knowledge of history and current events. When it came to arithmetic and reading, he'd actually been ahead for his age.

Cheyenne interrupted Erica's thoughts with a contented sounding sigh.

She glanced over at him. He was lolling in front of the fireplace as if he owned the apartment, one yellow eye partially open, lazily watching his humans.

Or, more likely, he was watching their tree...waiting for his first opportunity to water it.

He was bad enough with the trees in the park. She'd have to make darned sure they kept him shut out of the living room when they weren't around.

"Aunt Erica, I think all the tree needs to be perfectly perfect is this red ball...right here." Billy stepped to the tree, hung the final ornament on a low branch, then grinned back at her.

"You're right, Billy. That makes it perfectly perfect. Except for the star that goes on top."

Erica rummaged through the boxes and tissue until she located the gold star. "Would you like the honor?" She handed Billy the treetop ornament and absently brushed a stray pine needle off her jeans.

"Come on. I'll boost you up." She bent down, offering him her knee as a step.

Billy scrambled up, just managing to reach to the top of the tree with the star.

"Voilà!" he exclaimed.

Erica laughed. "When on earth did you start speaking French?"

"It's my only word so far," he admitted, struggling to straighten the star.

Erica shifted his weight a little. He felt heavier than he'd been only days ago. He was gaining weight like crazy—shooting up in height, as well. He'd grown bigger and healthier before her eyes. And, with every slight physical change, he reminded her more of Hank.

Billy jumped down.

"Plug the lights in," Erica suggested. "Let's see the complete effect."

Billy squeezed past the branches to the outlet.

A moment later the tree twinkled to life, its tiny flickering lights a sparkling brilliance amidst the dark green.

"Wow!" Billy whispered. "Wow. I wish my pa could see this."

A rush of sadness swept Erica. She tried to ignore it. She'd become adept at focusing on how well things had worked out between her and Billy, rather than on how their lives might be if Hank had come with them.

Billy had fit into her life more easily than she'd ever hoped he would.

She'd told her parents the truth about Billy and Hank. She didn't imagine they actually believed her. She was certain they didn't think time travel was possible any more than she once had. But at least they'd humored her and pretended to believe.

No doubt they actually thought Billy's sudden appearance involved deep secrets they were better off not knowing about.

Erica's friends had politely bought her vague story about Billy being the son of a good friend who lived in Nevada and had accepted the boy as someone simply staying with her for a while.

Yes. Billy had slipped into her life and her heart as if he'd always belonged with her.

And even Cheyenne had successfully wormed his way into her affections. Once she'd realized he wasn't going to eat Franklin—that he thought even acknowledging a Jack Russell terrier was beneath a wolf's dignity—she'd relaxed a little.

And Cheyenne did have his pluses. Walking him was good exercise. And she hadn't been panhandled once in the entire five months.

But perhaps the best thing about having Billy and Cheyenne with her was they kept her busy, kept her mind from constantly dwelling on Hank.

Between Billy, Cheyenne and her job, she barely had a spare moment. Sometimes, she wondered what she'd done with her time before the trip to Nevada had changed her life so radically.

Hers was definitely a busier life now. In some ways it was fuller. But, in one way, her life was emptier than it had ever been.

She felt as if there was a hollow space where her heart used to be. There wasn't a single day—not a single waking hour—when the desire to be with Hank didn't surface, when she wasn't aware how much she missed him.

And at night, while she tried to fall asleep or when she dreamed, he was constantly on her mind.

"Aunt Erica?"

She turned her attention back to Billy.

"You don't think my pa'll come to Boston, do you, Aunt Erica? You don't think he'll surprise us 'cuz it's Christmas?"

"I—I know he'd like to Billy. I'm sure he wants to see you again more than anything in the world. But I don't think he'll be able to manage it."

A disappointed expression appeared on the boy's face. He turned back to the tree, leaving Erica feeling guilty. She knew she should say something more to him about why Hank couldn't come to see them. But she didn't know what to say.

She often reassured Billy that his father loved him, that Hank would have come with them if he possibly could have. But the child was too young to fully understand what had happened, too young to grasp the concept of time travel.

Lord! Erica still didn't have a good handle on it herself, although she'd read enough books and articles on the subject to fill a library. But she simply couldn't figure out whether Hank was actually alive, living in a different time continuum or whether he was long dead.

Whichever was the case, Billy was too young to realize a man born in 1827 couldn't be alive in 1989. And yet Billy had been born in 1853 . . . and here he was.

Erica shook her head. If she still didn't understand how people could travel through time, how two different centuries could exist at once, she certainly couldn't expect a child to.

She glanced across the room at the cabinet that held her videotapes. After Billy had gone to bed, after she'd put his presents beneath the tree, she'd play the tape of Hank that she'd shot to convince him she was from the future—the tape she'd brought back with her from the past.

She watched it now and then, whenever she couldn't manage to resist the temptation. And tonight was undoubtedly going to be one of those times.

Seeing Hank's image caused a bitter-sweet reaction, filled her with a mixture of happy memories and sadness. But the sadness, the pain of missing Hank, usually overwhelmed the happiness.

Perhaps tonight would be different. Perhaps she could convince herself they were sharing a bit of Christmas together.

But deluding herself into believing that would require a major effort. Looking at a video of Hank hardly compared to being with him, to feeling his arms securely surrounding her, to tasting his kisses, to spending a night of love in his bed.

Probably, she should stop watching that tape altogether. Her obsession with memories of Hank undoubtedly wasn't healthy. Maybe trying to forget him would be her New Year's resolution. She doubted it, though. She hadn't the least desire to try forgetting Hank.

If she could only stop thinking more and more constantly about being with him she'd be fine. But those thoughts were beginning to dominate her... so much so that she knew, if there was any chance she could go back in time again, if returning to his world was a possibility, she'd make plans to go.

Billy was well. Only a few more months and he'd be fully cured. She could take him back to Hank—healthy. And she would explain to her parents where she was going, not simply vanish from their lives.

Yes, if she and Hank could be together once more, she'd do anything to make it happen—even leave her world again.

But the thought was a futile one. Because there was no way she could time travel back to Mountainview. Blue moons came only once every three or four years.

And even if, three years from now, she missed Hank as desperately as she did now, going back would still be impossible.

She might be able to locate a Paiute tribal calendar and pinpoint the time of the next blue moon. But she'd never been clear how many days the blue moons' shadows were away from the full moons themselves.

And she had no idea whether they appeared in the same place each time.

So what would she do? Try to camp for a week inside the Broken Hill Mine, hoping against hope to see a shimmering blue light?

Someone would undoubtedly hustle her off to a funny farm in short order.

Or...what if, by some miracle, she did make it back...only to find Hank had left Mountainview...or had died...or had married?

The thoughts of Hank dying or loving another woman tore at Erica's heart. But there was no point thinking about what Hank would or wouldn't do. Because there wasn't any way she'd ever be able to return to his world, no way she could recapture the magic of their brief days together.

Trying to time travel again would be pure folly. She simply didn't know enough about the process, would be as liable to find herself in the fourth century or in 1930 as back in 1862.

Cheyenne stretched noisily in front of the fireplace, then rose and ambled from the living room to the hall, glancing expectantly at Erica on his way past.

"Come on, Billy. Let's take Cheyenne for his walk. By the time we get back, it'll be your bedtime. And, when you wake up, Santa will have been."

Billy followed her into the hall wearing a peculiar-looking grin, making her suspect nine-year-olds didn't actually believe in Santa Claus, making her wonder what his new-found friends had been telling him about the old fellow.

It didn't really matter, she decided while they were putting on their jackets and boots. Billy would enjoy tomorrow, would love the presents she'd bought.

And her parents would make a huge fuss over him at Christmas dinner. They spoiled him outrageously.

Erica suspected they'd decided he was the closest they were going to get to a grandchild. And they were undoubtedly right. After Hank, she couldn't imagine ever falling in love with another man.

She grabbed Cheyenne's leash as Billy unlocked the apartment door.

THE MURMURING FROM Billy's bedroom had ceased. Often, he talked into the darkness for a while after Erica had tucked him in and kissed him good-night. She knew he was talking to Hank.

She glanced under the tree, at the two presents Billy had proudly put there—one for her, one for Cheyenne. Then she wandered from the living room to check on the child.

Once settled, he slept soundly through the night, but his settling was often a very active process. Tonight, his blankets were half off the bed. She crossed the room and straightened them.

Beside Billy, on the pillow, lay his father's gold pocket watch. Erica held it for a moment, thinking of Hank.

She brushed back a stray lock of Billy's hair that had fallen over his eye, then put the watch safely onto the dresser and headed for her own room.

Her gifts for Billy were stacked on the shelf of her closet, hidden by a blanket. But she had no doubt Billy'd located her hiding place mere hours after she'd wrapped the presents and put them there. She smiled ruefully to herself. She'd certainly learned a lot about children in the past five months.

Erica opened the closet door. Her gaze fell on the white cotton dress Hank had bought for her. Her eyes grew misty, looking at it. She forced herself into action, reached the packages down and made two trips into the living room with them.

The stacks of brightly wrapped parcels beneath the tree transformed it into a perfect picture.

Erica went back to her bedroom and dug Billy's Santa stocking from the bottom of her blanket box, from beneath layers of sheets and towels, congratulating herself for thinking to use two hiding places, unable to detect any sign that Billy had discovered the stocking.

"Score one for the adult," she murmured, closing the lid.

She paused on her way out of the bedroom to shut the closet door. Her glance lingered on the white dress once more. She fingered it lovingly, knowing she was being silly. A long cotton dress in December? While she sat, all alone, watching a tape that would likely reduce her to tears?

She laid Billy's stocking down and took the dress from its hanger, running her palm down the pleated bodice. It was the most beautiful dress she owned. Whose business was it but her own if she wanted to wear it on Christmas Eve?

Erica pulled off her jeans and sweatshirt and put on the dress. She glanced in the mirror. The image of a woman from 1862 gazed back at her.

She turned away, muttering guiltily about having a long talk with herself, knowing she was going to have to make a few rules about dealing with memories of Hank Lockhart. Otherwise, she'd be in danger of losing touch with reality.

Yes, she'd have to do that soon...but not tonight.

Erica took the Santa stocking to Billy's room, hung it carefully on the inside door handle and pulled the door shut.

Back in the living room, she poked at the fire and added a log. Then she turned out the light and sat watching the flickering fire, stroking Cheyenne's head. She'd save the tape for a little later.

The drapes were pulled against winter's chill. The only source of light was the dancing fire. They might be sitting in a room that existed before the advent of electricity. They might be sitting—

Erica swore silently at the tapping of her apartment's door knocker.

She remained seated, tempted not to answer...not wanting her thoughts interrupted.

The knocker tapped again. No one had buzzed from the vestibule, so it had to be a neighbor at the door. And whoever it was probably knew they were home— had seen or heard them coming back from walking Cheyenne.

"Let's see who's out there, fellow." Erica headed into the hallway and switched on the light, Cheyenne at her heels. She glanced down at him, recalling that when she'd lived alone, someone unexpectedly coming to her door had always sent a silly little ripple of nervousness through her. Yes, Cheyenne did have his good points.

Erica glanced through the peephole.

Outside the door stood Santa Claus—decked out in complete attire from the tip of his red velvet hood to black boots. At least she imagined he was wearing black boots. She couldn't see all the way to his feet. A large, lumpy sack was flung across one shoulder.

Over his face, Santa wore a smiling, apple-cheeked, rubber mask complete with a flowing bushy, white beard.

"Who is it?" Erica called through the door.

"It's Paul, Erica . . . Paul Roosevelt."

Paul's words were muffled. Erica glanced down at Cheyenne. His tail was swishing back and forth like a bushy gray windshield wiper. Muffled or not, the dog clearly recognized their neighbor's voice.

"If you're really lucky, Cheyenne," Erica murmured, unlocking the door, "Franklin's sent you over a boney Christmas present."

Erica opened the door. "What are you dressed up for, Paul. Going to a Christmas Eve party?"

"If I'm invited."

Erica froze at the sound of Santa's voice. He wasn't Paul Roosevelt from across the hall. He was . . . he couldn't be!

Her glance darted down. The man was wearing black boots. But they weren't traditional Santa issue. They were cowboy boots!

Oh, please, she prayed silently, *please don't let this be a dream.*

Cheyenne whirled into his demented four-footed dance, bounding around Santa in feverish circles.

"I . . . Erica, I reckon I'd feel a mite better if you were as happy to see me as Cheyenne is."

"Oh, Hank!" Erica threw her arms around his neck, automatically pressing her lips to his face. "Oh, Hank, take that damned mask off! Let me look at you!"

Hank tossed the mask aside. The long white beard was replaced by a neatly trimmed dark one. He grinned down at Erica for a moment.

"Sounds like it's a good thing I came when I did, Erica. You've taken to cussing again."

He bent to kiss her, dropping his sack in the hallway, sweeping her into his arms, holding her so tightly, she was certain he was going to smother her to death. What a wonderful way to die!

Hank's kiss was warm and real and alive. It sent the most marvelous sensations she'd ever experienced racing through her. Hank was here. Alive. With her. But how...?

Rational thought slipped away, replaced by the overwhelming joy of Hank's nearness, of his arms around her, his lips on hers, his body pressing firmly against her.

Erica clung to him, unable to believe he was with her, afraid to release him in case he vanished in a puff of smoke.

A distant male voice drifted into her consciousness. "I'd say you're taking unfair advantage of Santa, Erica. That's a pretty brazen way to get extra presents."

Reluctantly, she stopped kissing Hank and glanced across the hall, her arms still possessively about his neck.

The real Paul Roosevelt, Franklin on a leash, was unlocking his apartment door, grinning at her.

"Hank, this is my neighbor, Paul. Paul, this is Hank Lockhart. He's a good friend," she added lamely.

Paul laughed. "I know. Hank introduced himself when I was on my way out with Franklin. I'm the one who let him into the building so he could surprise you—figured with a hundred presents for you and Billy in that pack, he was legit.

"I didn't expect to find the two of you still in the hall by the time I got back, though." Paul disappeared into his apartment with a knowing leer.

"Were...were you planning on asking me in, Erica? Or are we going to stand out here and amuse more of your neighbors?"

Erica untangled her arms from Hank's neck, slipped one securely around his waist and propelled him inside, barely giving him time to grab his sack from the floor.

She shoved the door closed behind them and hugged him again. "Oh, Hank, I don't know whether to kiss you or ask you how you got here."

"There's no rush to do everything at once, Erica. We have all the time we want. To appease your curiosity, I got here through a different kind of White Cloud's magic. But I was right about her not giving me a return passage. I'm here for good."

Erica knew she was grinning like an idiot. She didn't care. And, if she had, she knew there wasn't a danged thing she'd be able to do about it. Hank was here for good!

He was grinning back at her. "You look mighty pretty, Erica. I always did like that dress best. The blue of the flowers matches your eyes."

He drew Erica closer, enveloping her in an aura of love, his lips lightly kissing the top of her head.

"And Billy?" he finally whispered.

Erica pulled away a little so she could see Hank's face. "Billy's absolutely wonderful. He's cured! A few more months and he'll be one hundred percent. Come on."

Clutching Hank's hand, she led the way to Billy's room and opened the door. Light from the hall streamed in, dimly illuminating the sleeping child's face.

Hank walked quietly over and knelt beside the bed, gazing at his son. "He's grown so much, Erica. I can scarcely believe it."

"Do you want to wake him?"

"I—" Hank leaned forward and kissed Billy's cheek. "No. He'd be up all night if I did. Let him sleep till morning. I'll be an extra Christmas present for him."

"Hank," Erica whispered, "you're the best Christmas present possible—for both of us."

ERICA SNUGGLED against Hank's chest, pulling the blankets tightly around their nakedness. The apartment had grown cool during the night. She should turn the thermostat up before Billy woke. But that would mean getting out of bed....leaving Hank...

She scrunched even closer to him. He smiled at her, his features barely discernible in the faint light from her clock radio.

"I still can't believe you're here, Hank."

"That doesn't say much for my lovemaking, Erica. It's five o'clock in the morning. We've been in your bed for over six hours. If you're still not certain I'm here—"

Erica kissed away his teasing.

"You know what I mean, Hank. I can't belive you decided to come...can't believe that once you got to the twentieth century you coped on your own. You can't have had any money that was legal tender. How did you get to Boston without money?"

"Well, I recalled you talking about antique jewellery and pawn shops. So I bought a few expensive gewgaws before I left Mountainview, then sold them as soon as I got to 1989.''

''And then you figured out how to get yourself on a plane? You took taxis and went into stores to shop?''

''Well, I did feel like a stupid dunderhead a few times. But I remembered most of what you'd told me about this world, Erica. I managed.''

''It just seems so incredible that you found us. How did you even get my address?''

''I copied it from your driver's license before you left Mountainview. It wasn't very gentlemanly, but I looked through your backpack.''

''So you knew there was a chance you'd come after us! And you put Billy and me through all that torture? If I didn't love you so much I could hate you for that!''

''Well, I wasn't anywhere near certain I'd come, Erica. I wasn't even convinced it was a sane thing to contemplate. I'd asked White Cloud if there'd be a way of me getting here. So I knew it was possible. But, tarnation! I wasn't anywhere near certain I'd ever get up the courage.

''I just knew there was a chance I wouldn't be able to live without you and Billy. And, once you'd gone, it became clearer and clearer that I couldn't. That's when I decided I'd have to come after you.

''So I began spending every spare moment writing, working my stories over and over again. And I started to see that my writing was improving. The more I polished and edited, the better those stories sounded.

''Then I wrote some fresh material. And I liked it. I began thinking you might have been right. That it was possible I could succeed.''

"After a few months of writing every day, I got up the nerve to ask Sam to read my work again."

"And he said?"

"He said it was much better than it had been. He could see the improvement, too. He encouraged me to come here . . . told me if people in the twentieth century liked his writing as much as you said they did, that they'd like mine, too . . . told me I could make it as a writer.

"You know, I wish I could have done something for Sam, Erica. He did so much for me."

Erica grinned lazily at Hank. "You did do something for him. Or we did. I bought a collection of Sam's books after I got back. And it turns out that in 1889 he wrote a novel about time travel. It's called *A Connecticut Yankee in King Arthur's Court*. So we did help him. We gave him an idea. And he certainly did help us," she concluded, nuzzling Hank's shoulder contentedly. "He convinced you to follow Billy and me."

"Well . . . he didn't quite convince me. I was still mighty concerned about not succeeding here. And, even if I eventually started selling my work, I knew it would take a while. I couldn't figure out how I'd be able to earn a living in the meantime."

"Oh, Hank, I told you that didn't matter, that we could manage on what I earn. I'm just glad you decided I was right."

Hank shook his head. "I could never let a woman support me, Erica. So getting the gold was a right fortunate happenchance."

"Getting the gold?" Erica looked at Hank's face. A tiny smile was playing on his lips.

"Oh. Did I forget to mention the gold, Erica?"

"Probably not. Probably you told me about it in great detail but I wasn't listening to you. For heaven's sake, Hank! What gold?"

"The gold from the Broken Hill Mine. Buck Dursely hit the mother lode. He's got so much gold he doesn't know what to do with it."

"So he gave some to you!"

"Right. Remember me telling him not to give up, that I thought Broken Hill would make him a rich man."

Erica nodded excitedly.

"Well, Buck figured that—between Billy and me—we brought him his luck."

"Miners are a superstitious lot," Erica murmured, recalling Billy's story about Three-finger Jack. "And they're convinced they have to reward whoever brings them luck."

"Right. Well, Buck insisted that if it hadn't been for us, he'd have given up on Broken Hill. And the strike was so rich that he'd settle for nothing less than giving me every ounce of gold that was refined from the first wagonload of ore he shipped to the quartz mill."

"And how many ounces was it, Hank?"

"Well...it's a mite embarrassing. I felt plum guilty taking it, Erica. But Buck was so convinced that his luck might dry up if I didn't. And I knew he'd be getting tons of rich ore out of Broken Hill. And it meant I wouldn't have to worry about how I was going to support you."

"So, well I took it from Buck and brought it with me. What I could easily carry, that is. I gave a little to the McCullys."

"How many ounces did you bring, Hank?"

"I brought twenty...but not ounces, Erica. Pounds."

"Twenty pounds? Of pure gold? Hank, that's..." Erica multiplied rapidly in her head. "Hank, that's three hundred and twenty ounces! Do you know how many hundred dollars an ounce of gold is worth today?"

"Down to the last penny. First thing I did when I reached Boston was talk to a bank manager. Very helpful fellow. He looked after selling the gold, then opened an account for me in his bank.

"There's a lot of money sitting in that account, Erica. A whole lot—even considering how much things seem to cost in your world."

"Our world, Hank."

"Our world." He smiled. "So what do we do next in our world?"

"Well, tomorrow...today, rather, we try to live through Billy's excitement when he finds you're here. Then we're going to my parents' house for Christmas dinner. I reckon they can make room for you at the table."

"Good. The sooner I talk to your father the better."

"Why?"

"Well, in my world, I'd be asking your father for your hand, Erica. We'd be getting married. That's...that's still the way things work, isn't it?"

"Oh, Hank." Erica kissed his neck. "Yes. That's still the way things work. At least that's the way they work when a woman loves a man as much as I love you."

"Glad to hear it, Erica," Hank murmured, grinning at her sleepily. "Because I obviously love you enough to follow you anywhere."

"Oh, Hank! And I—"

"Aunt Erica?" Billy called loudly through the bedroom door. "Aunt Erica, are you awake yet? It's Christmas!"

Erica clutched the sheet up around her neck, glanced at the Santa suit on the floor beside the bed and then at Hank. "Our being in bed together isn't exactly seemly."

Hank grinned at her. "Don't be so danged old-fashioned, Erica."

"Aunt Erica? Aren't you going to get up? Santa's been!"

"I know, Billy," Erica called, smiling at Hank. "In fact, he's still here. Come on in and wish him Merry Christmas."

Harlequin Superromance®

COMING NEXT MONTH

Harlequin Superromance®

LET THE GOOD TIMES ROLL...

Add some Cajun spice to liven up your New Year's celebrations and join Superromance for a romantic tour of the rich Acadian marshlands and the legendary Louisiana bayous.

Starting in January 1990, we're launching CAJUN MELODIES, a three-book tribute to the fun-loving people who've enriched America by introducing us to crawfish étouffé and gumbo, zydeco music and the Saturday night party, the *fais-dodo*. And learn about loving, Cajun-style, as you meet the tall, dark, handsome men who win their ladies' hearts with a beautiful, haunting melody....

Book One: *Julianne's Song*, January 1990
Book Two: *Catherine's Song*, February 1990
Book Three: *Jessica's Song*, March 1990

Especially for you,
Christmas from
HARLEQUIN HISTORICALS

An enchanting collection of three Christmas
stories by some of your favorite authors captures
the spirit of the season in the 1800s

TUMBLEWEED CHRISTMAS by Kristin James

A "Bah, humbug" Texas rancher meets his match in his
new housekeeper, a woman determined to bring the spirit
of a Tumbleweed Christmas into his life—and love into
his heart.

A CINDERELLA CHRISTMAS by Lucy Elliot

The perfect granddaughter, sister and aunt, Mary Hillyer
seemed destined for spinsterhood until Jack Gates arrived
to discover a woman with dreams and passions that were
meant to be shared during a Cinderella Christmas.

HOME FOR CHRISTMAS
by Heather Graham Pozzessere

The magic of the season brings peace Home For
Christmas when a Yankee captain and a Southern heiress
fall in love during the Civil War.

Look for HARLEQUIN HISTORICALS CHRISTMAS
STORIES wherever Harlequin books are sold.

Harlequin Historicals

Step into a world of pulsing adventure, gripping emotion and lush sensuality with these evocative love stories penned by today's best-selling authors in the highest romantic tradition. Pursuing their passionate dreams against a backdrop of the past's most colorful and dramatic moments, our vibrant heroines and dashing heroes will make history come alive for you.

Watch for two new Harlequin Historicals each month, available wherever Harlequin books are sold. History was never so much fun—you won't want to miss a single moment!

Wonderful, luxurious gifts can be yours with proofs-of-purchase from any specially marked "Indulge A Little" Harlequin or Silhouette book with the Offer Certificate properly completed, plus a check or money order (do not send cash) to cover postage and handling payable to Harlequin/Silhouette "Indulge A Little, Give A Lot" Offer. We will send you the specified gift.

Mail-in-Offer

Item:	A. Collector's Doll	B. Soaps in a Basket	C. Potpourri Sachet	D. Scented Hangers
# of Proofs-of -Purchase	18	12	6	4
Postage & Handling	$3.25	$2.75	$2.25	$2.00
Check One				

OFFER CERTIFICATE

Name _____

Address _____ Apt. # _____

City _____ State _____ Zip _____

ONE PROOF OF PURCHASE

To collect your free gift by mail you must include the necessary number of proofs-of-purchase plus postage and handling with offer certificate.

HS-3

Harlequin®/Silhouette®

Mail this certificate, designated number of proofs-of-purchase and check or money order for postage and handling to:

INDULGE A LITTLE
P.O. Box 9055
Buffalo, N.Y. 14269-9055